I0537240

# MANHUNT

Book Two of the Peak Democracy Trilogy

G.D. Leon

G.D. Leon
Greenwich, CT

Book Layout ©2013 BookDesignTemplates.com

Manhunt / G.D. Leon -- 1st ed.
ISBN 978-0-9977637-2-0

*For my wife.*
*With her I'm brave. With her I have direction.*

*The tree of liberty must be refreshed from time to time with the blood of patriots & tyrants. It is it's natural manure.*

—Thomas Jefferson


*It's the people. We haven't gotten hold of the people yet. Every minute we let them organize themselves, we lose control.*

—Jude Dennings

# CHAPTER ONE

# Out of the Dark

*Dennings – Day 0 (April 21, Fairview, MT)*

From his office on the top floor of the 75-story building, Jude Dennings watched the early nightlife in Fairview, Montana. The building had the shape of a large sail and had been designed by a star architect. Twenty-five years ago, The Holding had left Seattle to benefit from a hundred-year tax deal with Montana. Within a decade Fairview had grown from a sleepy nest to a city with a quarter of a million residents.

The interactive screen layered over the large, floor-to-ceiling window enhanced the view with insights about the Joint Chiefs of Staff and the other generals and admirals who were in the city for renegotiations of company contracts. Each one was tagged with their name, rank, location and a dollar amount. Some had already used a few dollars for a coffee, but for most of them the amount was still zero. Dennings leaned back in his large chair, put his feet on the table and took a puff from his cigar. His tight Italian suit made his slender posture almost gangly.

*Funny, how they all flock like sheep at one bar.*

The screen showed increasing dollar amounts next to each name and rank. A smirk went over Dennings' face. He had made sure they each had enough distractions and unlimited funds on their Fairview company credit card.

Dennings got up and strolled over to his private rooms to freshen up. His office was large, high enough to play basketball in, and equipped with all kinds of amenities, from a large couch and bar on the second floor to a private one-bedroom apartment. He used the private apartment more than his own house. Still, there were none of his effects, except one picture of his hometown, Phoenix, on the wall.

He checked his watch once more; in one hour he would join the generals along with Vice President McNally. By that time their tongues should have loosened up. In the bathroom he took a shower, got dressed again and started shaving. In the mirror, he continued to watch the generals, who were getting their third bottle of bourbon.

That was when the lights went out and the emergency lights came on.

*Damn*, thought Dennings, wiping the shaving cream off his face.

The emergency light flickered and went out as well.

*Damn!*

Dennings felt his way out of the bathroom. His entire office was dark and the large window had lost the back-glow of the augmented reality overlay. Moonlight was the only thing helping him to orientate himself. He plodded to his desk and tried to activate his e-pad and his Comm-Dongle, without success. Dennings frowned and looked out of the window. The city was dark.

*The power supply should have seamlessly switched over to emergency power.* He shook his head and walked towards the heavy office doors. *I guess I'll have to fire some people tomorrow.*

The doors reached almost to the ceiling of the office. Opening them was a strenuous thing to do; it took a few seconds and all his strength to open one wing two inches. *Damn security doors. They're supposed to be failsafe.*

"We'll help you," said somebody from the other side through the open crack.

With a little jump, the door moved another few inches.

"Frank? Is that you?" asked Dennings.

"Yes," said the voice. A few more seconds and pushes and the door was open enough for a brawny guy with a cubical head to squeeze his massive body through. "Stay," he said to somebody outside.

"What happened?" Dennings puffed.

"I don't know. I was in the elevator and had to climb my way out. No connectivity on any devices." Frank put on a questioning expression as if he was expecting Dennings to have the answer.

"The entire city lost power," Dennings pointed to the window. "We have to get down to the lower floors to organize emergency procedures."

An explosion outside made them flinch. They hurried over to the window. A building was ablaze in an industrial park at the city border. While they were staring at the burning building, another explosion in another part of the city startled them.

"That was the power station," Frank frowned.

Dennings clenched his fists. "This is big."

#

*Dennings — Day 15 (May 6, Fairview, MT)*

Dennings was thirsty when he entered the Fairview Convention Center. The Center was located a little west of the city center so that its flat, shell-like shape matched the height of the surrounding buildings. The squad of company bodyguards that had accompanied him relaxed when they passed the soldiers at the entrance. Now protection was their job.

The past fifteen days had been gooey. The military had taken over after Vice President McNally declared martial law. Since then they had kept themselves occupied with two things: hoarding the resources they found in and around Fairview, and conducting lengthy meetings at the Convention Center.

Unlike his squad of bodyguards, Dennings didn't relax; he was late, and he hated to be late. He glanced at his watch. Lucky him, his chronograph was self-winding and had not been linked to the web. Only a few people knew the time; the military had switched to a sundial and used hourly alarms to keep everybody in synch. Without pausing, he marched towards the stairs, followed by Frank Clutsky and another bodyguard. The bodyguards kidded around with the soldiers hanging out in the lobby. They stopped when Dennings threw them a stare on the way up.

Upstairs, in contrast to the lobby, felt like a beehive. A mix of uniforms was running around, each man carrying small papers which they handed to higher-ranked officers. In the back, Dennings heard the noise of two-way radio communication. *They finally established communication*, he thought, fighting his way through the drones. Two guards stopped him in front of the entrance to a large conference room.

"Identification," said the lieutenant who stood next to the guards.

"And how do you want to verify it? Are the servers up and running again?" Dennings growled at the lieutenant.

"I have to ask, sir."

"I've been here every day for two weeks. You should use your brain more often if you want to get further than lieutenant."

The lieutenant ducked his head and added, "Sir?"

"What?"

"Please, your weapons, sir." The officer pointed to the body-guards.

Dennings sighed and shrugged. Frank took out his gun and handed it to the other bodyguard. "Stay put." Then he followed Dennings into the meeting room. The door closed behind them.

Dennings nodded to another guy standing right next to the entrance. "Bruce."

"Sir." Bruce was one of the few men in the room with a gun, as he was responsible for the security in the Convention Center. Before the blackout he was leading McNally's protection detail, but as he had been a colonel before, General Cox and McNally had agreed to have him secure the Convention Center.

The meeting room was more like a hall. The large table in the middle looked lost. At one end they had put the usual buffet, and a bunch of generals and admirals stood around it small-talking.

*Morons*, thought Dennings. *As if everything will turn on again any minute.*

Two generals approached him, both grinning.

"Ah, Dennings. We've established communication with other stations in the country," said one of them.

"Good news. It wasn't the Russians or the Chinese." The other one was still chewing. "Their mess is even worse. Get something to eat," he added, licking his fingers and pointing to a buffet on the other side of the room with his other hand.

"And how is that good news?" Dennings stared at the general.

Both generals retreated as if they had been beaten.

Dennings turned to Frank. "I want a direct link into that radio. Hell, I want my own radio."

Frank nodded sharply.

"And get me a bottle of water."

Frank nodded again and moved away.

Dennings glanced around. Vice President McNally was walking over to him. He was sweating, even though the temperatures weren't so hot yet. At least not as hot as they would be later in the day.

"Jude, you heard?"

"Yeah, it wasn't the Russians or the Chinese." Dennings smirked.

"No, there were riots in DC. They even raided the White House. Evans and Hernandez got killed."

"Adriana?" Dennings tried to remain cool. Not that he cared about the others, but *she* was still in DC.

"She told me. She was in the hospital when it happened—she took the White House back with a company. They're holding out."

Before Dennings could answer, another high-ranking officer approached them. "May I ask you to take a seat? The meeting is about to begin."

Dennings and McNally took a seat and, like every morning, Dennings poked McNally. "It's your meeting. With the President missing, you're in charge." And like every morning, McNally didn't move.

After a moment, General Cox, who had been sitting at the end of the table, stood up. "With the radio back, we have been able to establish an inventory of our forces. Unfortunately we could only install three radio stations—we need to save on the few diesel reserves and as long as we don't have supplies..." He glimpsed at Dennings. Cox was of small stature, which he tried to compensate for with arrogance and ambitiousness. Dennings had mocked him behind closed doors for being a wannabe Napoleon.

The generals and admirals around the table mumbled acknowledgment. Dennings didn't react, although he had a mixed urge to chuckle and shake his head. *How foolish to think they could prevent us from getting a radio station on our own with this argument, but one has to pick one's battles.* The two-way radio was Clutsky's to fight.

"So much for the good news," General Cox continued. "As our most important next steps, we need to restore our nuclear defense and regain our cyber forces. McNally, get us the codes from DC."

"Since when does a general give orders to the chief in command?" Dennings threw his stare at the general.

"I don't have to remind you that he declared martial law, do I?"

The general's snippy answer amused Dennings. "Well, it still ends up with him."

"You have no say at all here, son." Cox glowered at Dennings.

Dennings leaned back and glanced around. "I agree that we need to get our defenses back: nuclear, cyber, conventional, whatever. But more importantly, we have to regain order. We have to secure the supply of food, industrial goods, medical goods, etc."

Few generals nodded. They stopped when they got a scowl from Cox. Dennings noticed Frank appear again in the door, signalling him with a short nod. *He got the water.* "How many troops do you have under order right now?"

Nobody answered. Dennings looked around and frowned. "Please?"

One of the lower-ranked generals answered in a low voice. "One company here in Fairview, a battalion in the surroundings of Fairview. There are only sporadic replies from the bases on the East Coast and none from any of the fleets. However, we have around a quarter million across the major bases in the Midwest and the Pacific. They're still counting after the waves of desertion—" The lower-ranked general stopped when he noticed Cox's glare.

"I suggest we use twenty thousand to secure the food supply and the industry," said Dennings. "That leaves you with more than enough to establish your defenses. But we need a direct command structure. We can't have interference."

"No way a private person gets command over military." The face of the four-star general turned red.

Dennings narrowed his eyes. "Not a private person. You can assign one or two of your generals to report to McNally. We leave you alone with your military games and at the same time we ensure that we all survive."

Cox's face still looked as if he had not exhaled yet.

"In the end it's McNally's decision." Dennings smirked.

McNally swallowed. "We do it Jude's way," he said with a low voice.

Some generals sitting further away didn't understand, judging by the way they tilted their heads.

McNally got up and repeated, "We follow Dennings' plan."

#

*Niklas — Day 45 (June 5, Manzanilla, Mexico)*

It was a feast unlike any the small Mexican port of Manzanilla had ever seen. Beef from Argentina, kiwis, bananas—the town was overflowing with the best the continent had to offer. Niklas Soderstrom was stuffed. Two dollars for a steak was a steal. *The salad for three dollars is almost expensive compared to that*, he thought. All he missed was bottled water. The first few days he had gotten diarrhea from the tap water, but after a while he got used to it, with the help of an occasional glass of tequila at night.

His T-shirt felt sweaty. He pulled it away from his body to get air underneath it. When he was younger he had not minded the heat, but turning forty two years ago was like turning on a switch: joints started to hurt after running, heat exhausted him and for the first time in his life he had had the flu. It seemed the heat was getting worse every day. The only cold place was the cool house down at the harbor, but he had heard they would soon run out of diesel too.

He got up from his chair and ambled over to the window. The apartment—if you could call one room with a kitchenette right under the roof an apartment—was located on a hillside with a nice view of the port. The port was cluttered up with boats, and, further out, the large container ships that did not fit into the small port filled the sea. A few ships were creeping up and down along the coast, but most of them were anchored outside the harbor and unloading their goods. A sailor had told Niklas days ago that the US ports were not working. The machinery in the more modern ports was out of order and Manzanilla was the closest port to the US that was running. *No wonder*, Niklas had thought, *with these old cranes.*

He needed to be moving again, but he was waiting for optimal circumstances. Right now there was too much chaos. Only if he kept calm would he be able to survive. At least that was how he had survived so far. He had got a fake birth certificate in the name of Eduardo Hernández. With his dark hair and bronze skin he could get through as a Latin American, but the moment he opened his mouth his accent gave him away. *I need to move on, before they recover.*

A sound outside the door startled him. He held his breath and into the silence somebody knocked on the door.

"It's me, Manolo," said a male voice, and despite the door it sounded as if he was standing right next to Niklas.

Niklas opened the door and let the guy in. Manolo was smaller and more compact than him, with a sloppy crew cut. When he entered the room he put on his usual stern facial expression, but after the door closed he dropped it and embraced Niklas with a big smile.

"Anything to drink? I can offer warm beer?" Niklas chuckled.

"Why not? I don't care anymore."

Niklas went to the bathroom and got a beer out of the bath tub. Whenever he had a chance he filled it with ice from one of the freight ships, but that only happened every other day.

"I have good news, my friend," Manolo said after Niklas came back.

"Better than the steak you brought me?" Niklas rubbed his belly.

"I got you a passage to Lima, on a freight ship." Manolo grinned and patted Niklas' shoulders.

Niklas frowned. "Won't that be suspicious? I mean, me as the only passenger?"

Manolo tapped his finger on his temple and his grin grew wider. "They are shipping deported guys from the US further south."

"This is perfect." Niklas gave him a thumbs up. "You are a master of organization."

Manolo's grin got even broader and he took a gulp of beer. "I'll let you know when it leaves."

#

*Jenny — Day 46 (June 6, West of Flagstaff, AZ)*

Jenny was starving. For days she and Eduard had not eaten anything except for the wild berries and corn they had stolen from a field. They had been able to grab a few cobs before guards had detected them and chased them with guns for almost half a mile.

From her hiding place inside, Jenny watched the entrance of the barn, or at least what she could see of it in the dim moonlight. The barn was the size of a two-car garage with a small storage area right under the roof for drying straw. Eduard could only stand up in it towards the middle; the roof got too low towards the walls for him. They had covered their hiding place with straw and boards so they could watch the door downstairs through the gaps in the floor.

Jenny hoped Eduard would return soon with something to eat. Right now she would even eat a banana, and she hated bananas. The old quilted blankets they had found in the barn were itchy on her skin, but that was the smallest evil. They were still wearing the same clothes from the night the police had arrested them. Vermont springs were chilly, but now it was June and the hills west of Flagstaff were sticky hot during the day and cold at night. Her head was itching as well from her regrowing blonde hair, which they had cut in prison.

*I hope Eduard comes back before dawn.*

The zinging sound of bullets flying past them when they had tried to get food from the nearby fields still gave her nightmares. And in the nightmares there was always her dad.

"You left me behind," he said to her. "I came to rescue you and you left me behind!"

"You were dead. The radioactivity killed you," she screamed as prison guards dragged her away. "You were dead. I saw it." Sometimes Eduard was in the dream, being dragged away with her. Sometimes it was Eduard dragging her away.

There were creepy people lurking around. Actually, they hadn't seen any normal people since they had been let go right outside the 100-mile quarantine zone. The prison guards had left them and a dozen other inmates in the parking lot of a grocery store. It had been like a war zone—first the soldiers had jumped out of the armored personnel carrier and secured the environment, before the prisoners were rushed out of the vehicle and the convoy took off again. They had checked out the store for food, but it was as empty as if had been robbed or had sold out before a blizzard. Even the dumpsters behind the building had been emptied and the contents spread over the loading dock.

Jenny startled out of her thoughts. There was a rustling behind the barn. She ducked deeper into her hideout.

"Jen," whispered Eduard from the door.

She jumped up, put down the ladder and climbed down. "I'm so glad you're back. I hate it when you're gone. Next time I'm coming with you," she said into his hoodie while hugging him.

"We talked about this already. It's too dangerous."

Jenny pouted.

"But I got food," said Eduard quickly and her expression cleared up. He went outside and came back with a bag. Jenny cheered.

"There's only one issue." He showed her the contents of the bag. "The pizzas are frozen."

The revelation didn't cloud her mood. "I don't care. I'd eat anything, even if it had pineapple on it." She glanced over to the door and her eyes narrowed. "There's somebody," she whispered.

"That's ok." Eduard turned around. "Come in."

A boy, about ten years old, appeared in the door. He made a scrawny impression and his T-shirt was ripped apart underneath the armpit.

"This is Max. He showed me the freezer, but he couldn't open it, so I thought he might as well have some of the haul."

Max didn't move or say anything. He just stared at Jenny and she thought she picked up a sad expression in his eyes.

"Come in. Don't worry, we'll figure out a way to warm it up." Eduard waved the boy over to him. Max took one step forward and stopped again.

Jenny grabbed the bag out of Eduard's hands and climbed up to their hideout. "With a little luck they'll thaw by this afternoon. We'll have to wait."

The moment she turned around, Max took three steps forward and took Eduard's hand; they followed Jenny. Ten minutes later they were all sleeping.

#

*Eduard — Day 46 (June 6, West of Flagstaff, AZ)*

Jenny's shouting and cursing woke Eduard up.

"That little fucker! He'll be dead if I ever see him again."

He took a while to get his senses together. The sun wasn't high yet; he couldn't have slept long. Jenny was crawling around. "What's wrong?" Sunrays provided light through the gaps between the boards.

"He's gone and he took the pizza with him!" She threw a piece of wood against the wall.

Eduard jumped up and hit his head on a beam. A sharp pain pinched through his head. He ducked and closed his eyes. "What?" He shook his head and opened one eye again.

Jenny pointed to the corner where they had put the bags of stuff they had collected since they were released, including, until recently, the bag of pizzas. "That... kid stole our pizzas."

Eduard peeked out of their hideout. "There's the bag," he whispered. He crawled towards the bag, which was lying next to the opening for the ladder in the middle of the floor.

"Watch out. This could be a trap."

Eduard peeked around before he crawled further. Seconds later he came back with the bag. "There's still one pizza in it."

"There were ten in there." Anger boiled up in Jenny's eyes. She pressed her lips together and her cheek muscle worked her jaw. "He'll pay for that."

"Still, he left us one." Eduard opened the box. "It's still stiff, but I think we can eat it now."

"I don't want to eat it. I want the other nine."

Eduard ripped off the plastic and the aroma of dough got into his nose. His stomach reacted with a grumble.

Jenny almost jumped at the piece of pizza he gave her. For minutes he only heard chewing—heavy chewing, as the pizza was still more frozen than Eduard had expected. "We should keep half of it for later today."

She swallowed and pulled a face, but after a second she wiggled her head and lay down.

Eduard put the rest of the pizza away and lay down too. "It's funny how you forget about being hungry until you see or smell food again."

Jenny turned her head to him. "I never forget about being hungry. But on the positive side, I'm finally losing those pounds I gained in college." She grinned fiercely. "But I still hate that kid." The grin yielded to the pinched lips again.

"It might be worse," said Eduard after a moment of silence.

"Worse? What's worse than this?"

"We might need to find another hideout tonight. We don't know who he will tell." Eduard was looking at her with a worried look in his eyes and he could see her anger turning into desperation. The sun started to heat up the barn. Sweat ran down his back.

"I hate this. Should we go back to Flagstaff? Somebody must help us. They can't just throw us out again."

Eduard tried to caress her cheek, but she turned her face away. When she turned back she had narrowed her eyes. "What's wrong with the world? It's as if there's anarchy or a civil war."

He sat up. "I don't know. Towns are deserted when I roam for food, like ghost towns, but I can feel people watching me. And there's no electricity—nowhere. Remember at the beginning we heard the diesel generators? That's gone now."

"Could this be caused by the same thing that meant they didn't recognize us in the prison? Why else would they hand us the wrong effects when they let us go? Even our driver's licenses are wrong: Don Quixote and Sancho Panza?" For the first time in days, she smirked a little.

He copied her smirk. "For the last time, you're Donna Quiroz and I'm Sebastian Best."

Her face turned serious again. "I have a theory. But it's crazy."

"What do you think?"

"Niklas."

He tilted his head and frowned. "What about him?"

"Remember the first meeting? That plan he had with his data centers—the one to change the data? Could that have caused this?"

Eduard shrugged. "I don't think so. I mean, that wouldn't cause power outages, would it?"

Jenny pressed her lips together. "Maybe he executed that 'in-surance policy' he gave you the codes to." She yawned. "What was it again?"

"22.65qq.205.ff11.scramble," said Eduard without delay. *It's strange how you remember certain things.*

"I wonder what he's doing." She gazed at the wooden planks as if they were a movie screen.

Eduard lay back down. It was costing him quite a bit to stay awake. "I hope your mom is doing well."

He raised his eyes when she didn't reply. Her lips were pinched again.

"I'm sorry... I didn't want to..." he stammered. *Why did this all have to happen? Why couldn't we just stay out of the Resistance and live a happy life?* Eduard clenched his jaw.

Without looking at him, Jenny replied, "Can't we go home? It might take a while, but instead of meandering around here, wait-ing for somebody to help us, we might as well go home by foot."

Eduard mumbled with his eyes closed, "Yeah, let's do that."

#

*Eduard — Day 46 (June 6, North of Flagstaff, AZ)*

Eduard woke up again in the afternoon, feeling more re-freshed than he had earlier in the morning. The wet T-shirt was sticking to his chest and the straw was stinging him through it. He glanced around. "Jenny?" he whispered.

"I'm here." Her voice came from right outside their hideout.

He crawled out.

Jenny sat with her back against a beam.

"Did you have nightmares again?"

She shook her head. "As far as I remember, they threw us out somewhere west of Flagstaff." She had cleared an area of straw and pointed to one of the stones she had arranged. "Over there," she flicked her head to the other side of the barn, "is Vermont."

Eduard came closer and got down on one knee. "That'll take us a million years!"

"I still hope that somewhere, someday it will get better and we will find a motorized way to travel. Maybe this is only local."

He shook his head. "I'm not so sure about that. Have you seen any planes in the sky?"

Her shoulders slumped. "Still, we need to go home. I want to go home."

Eduard stood up. "We should leave as soon as the sun isn't so strong. I guess we can only walk for four to five hours a day, between four-ish and nine-ish. During the day it's too hot, and it's too dangerous at night. As soon as we're back on the plains, we might be able to achieve more. And we should avoid large cities, like Flagstaff. Better go around north."

Jenny moved over to Eduard and hugged him. There, in his arms, she cried. "I'm so sorry I got us into this situation," she sobbed.

He rubbed her arm. "It's ok. This is not your fault and at least this way we're together. Whatever it is, imagine if it had hit while we were separated at college."

It helped. She stopped crying and after a while she added, "I'm glad we're together. I don't know what I would do without you." She took a breath. "Where do we start?"

"Let's eat the rest of the pizza before we leave. North of us, somewhere here, is the Grand Canyon, and further south is the desert. We should walk east towards New Mexico and then turn north towards Colorado. I hope we'll find more food there."

Jenny shuddered with the word food and snuggled back into his arms.

While they sat there just holding each other, the 'why?' gnawed its way back into Eduard's thoughts. *Why couldn't they just have a happy life?* He was angry, but he couldn't tell with whom. *Why?* He chewed the inside of his cheeks until he tasted blood.

#

### Niklas — Day 55 (June 15, Manzanilla, Mexico)

It wasn't hard to get into the harbor: controls had become lax with the number of cargo vessels, and the extended hours of operation had resulted in twelve-hour shifts for harbor security. They just stood next to the open wire-mesh gate watching the people going in and out. Behind the run-down guardhouse they had put up tents for the guards to sleep in. The reddish dawn gave the scenery a fiery look.

Still, Niklas passed the guards with raised hackles. When he was fifty feet away one guard shouted, "Hey!" Niklas winced, but so did the surrounding workers. The next thing he heard was gunshots. He ran without turning around and so did the others. The stampede slowed when they turned behind the first containers and some of them looked back. Niklas didn't. He stopped when he reached the mole where his freighter, the *Southern Cross*, was docked. Two guys were still running, but most of the harbor workers had hidden and were waiting out whatever would happen next. The situation calmed down, but Niklas' hackles didn't.

"Pst," said a voice out of a dark corner next to him.

"Are we clear, Manolo?"

A hand waved him to come closer into the dark. "Yes, my friend."

They embraced each other.

"The ship is full of deported people," said Manolo. "If my country was only as disciplined and efficient in everything as it is in deporting the backflow—"

Niklas pricked his ears up and put his finger on his lips. He peeked around the corner.

"Nothing," he said, looking into Manolo's questioning eyes. "Thanks for all your help."

"I will miss you, my friend," said Manolo.

"You are sure you don't want to join me?" Niklas put his hand on Manolo's shoulder. "You might be better off down here."

"All my life I dreamed of getting this far. I can't give up now."

Niklas relaxed and took his hand away. "Just do me a favor. Follow the coast, East or West. I know they say that there are less controls in the middle, but don't go through Phoenix."

"I know. The contamination."

"And supplies: water, food, etc. You won't get them up there right now."

Manolo pointed to the freighter across the mole. "There, the sign."

Niklas turned his head. At the abaft of the ship he could see a small light that was dancing like a firefly. Manolo took out a flashlight and switched it on and off. The light on the freighter copied the signal.

"Come." Manolo rushed over and Niklas followed him. At the gangway he stopped and so did Niklas. They embraced again.

"Good luck, my friend."

"Good luck." Niklas walked across the gangway. He only hesitated for a second when he noticed the way the sailor eyeballed him. The grim look on the sailor's face gave Niklas the creeps.

*I have to watch out*, thought Niklas. *I might need to spend more money to be safe*. "Where can I find the captain?"

The sailor flicked his head without losing his grim expression.

#

*Dennings — Day 60 (June 20, Fairview, MT)*

From the window of his new office, Dennings watched Bruce Warner turn the corner out of the alley between the buildings. Frank Clutsky looked up at him and nodded sharply. Dennings turned towards the large desk in the middle of the room. It had taken the crew three days to get it from his office on the 75th floor to the second floor.

Now there was no room around the desk and the six people he had called for a meeting had to squeeze in. The picture of Dennings' hometown, Phoenix, hung on the wall—he had got that from his old office too. Next to his new office he had turned two more rooms into a small apartment, a living room and a bedroom. All three rooms together were smaller than his old one-bedroom apartment on the 75th floor.

"McNally," he snapped.

"Yes."

"We need you to sign these papers." Dennings pointed to the documents on the table.

McNally gazed at the papers.

"Now," snarled Dennings.

The others around the table looked up. McNally hesitated and signed sloppily. He shook his wrist afterwards as if it hurt. Clutsky entered the room and took a seat.

"Let's get started. Frank."

"Supplies are in your bunker," replied Clutsky, ignoring everybody else.

"We should have kept food and water here." McNally swallowed. "I'm fed up of waiting for a meeting with the military every time I'm thirsty."

Dennings waited until the murmur at the table faded away. "Until we have regained control of the food supplies, we have to manage our resources. Let them waste their supplies. The way they're doing it, they'll be knocking on our door within weeks."

Now the other meeting participants were chuckling, except McNally.

"Where is this bunker anyways?" McNally tried to make it sound by-the-way.

Dennings peered out of the window again. "Frank, continue."

"Radio is up and running, but we are waiting for the military to give us the frequencies we can use."

"What frequencies?" McNally continued to poke around.

"They don't want us to interfere with their command structure," said Frank.

"And they want to control us." Dennings chuckled.

"What are we going to do about this, Jude?" McNally leaned back.

Dennings stopped chuckling and turned his head a bit. "Well, McNally, I guess we have to play by their rules—for now, at least." He could feel McNally opening his mouth and closing it again.

"Next steps?" Dennings asked without waiting for McNally's reaction.

"We finish our game plan. First crops and water, later the beef." Frank rolled out a map. Dennings turned around.

"I got it from a local high school." Frank grinned. "The largest farms are automated, hence useless with the outage. Here," Frank pointed to another part of the map, "are older farms—not as productive as the new ones, but their trucks are still manual. They're probably even still producing."

"Water?"

"Still working on it."

Dennings hemmed. "Good work. Let's do it. McNally, this needs your signature." He threw McNally another paper.

"What about the people? Shouldn't we inform the people?" McNally looked around, seeking help from the others.

Dennings sighed. "Frank?"

"The military is taking care of security. They have put a re-peating communication on air to say that we are in a state of emergency and that they will do everything to restore law and order." Frank chuckled. "There were riots across the country and they put them all down. Our friend Cox is a hawk."

"We'd better have food before we communicate," snorted Dennings.

McNally wanted to say something but shut his mouth again.

"Frank, you're with me." Dennings strode out, followed by Frank. On the stairs, Dennings turned to him. "He's right. How do we prevent the military from spying on us? Are there any other frequencies?"

Frank shook his head. "All other frequencies are full of background noise from civilians."

"Perfect cover—use code words."

"There's one more thing." Frank stopped walking, forcing Dennings to stop. "It's the nuclear power plant at Indian Point: the core melted down, worse than Palo Verde after the terrorist attack, and nobody was there to close the holes. The cloud is moving south. Washington will be uninhabitable within one week. Same with Oconee and Harrisburg. The entire Atlantic Seaboard—"

"Arrange to get Adriana out. Trade whatever you need." Dennings frowned.

"No need. I already arranged the necessary. She will be here in 48 hours."

"Through Bruce?"

Frank nodded.

"Good." Dennings continued down the stairs, Frank right behind him.

#

*Dennings — Day 64 (June 24, Fairview, MT)*

Adriana arrived four days later. Dennings was happier to see her than he was ready to admit. She was limping and she looked tired when she got out of the old truck. The multi-cam trousers were too big on her. Still, her eyes were fierce and rebellious. Behind her a captain and his company, or rather what was left of it, jumped out of the truck. With his red hair and those ears the captain seemed like a younger version of Prince Harry. The name tag was dangling from his uniform; Dennings could read 'Stark' from a distance.

"Welcome to the new capital of the..." Dennings opened his arms and shrugged, "well, whatever this is." He grinned.

Adriana did not grin, but her eyes narrowed. Dennings' grin turned into a smile and he turned to Clutsky. "She's my deputy. Whatever she orders comes from me."

Clutsky nodded slowly.

"At least she's the FLOTUS." Dennings grinned again and entered the building.

Adriana walked alongside him. "More like the FLO-whatever-is-left."

Frank followed at a distance with Adriana's company; further back the other bodyguards covered their backs.

"I have information."

Dennings shook his head. "Wait."

Without saying another word, they went upstairs to Dennings' rooms right behind his office. She remained in the doorway.

He gazed at her until she opened her mouth. "If you want me to sleep here, we need to clarify a few things."

"I don't, but these are the only rooms where we can discuss things."

"So you throw me to the next one. Who is it? Frank? McNally?" She got that rebellious look again.

"I should never have asked you to get into this." He blew out air through his nose. "But that's changed, as has everything." He walked over to his bar and poured a whiskey. "I ran out of bourbon, and unfortunately we have no rocks. Have you talked to

McNally yet? He's still Vice President and you're still Secretary of National Intelligence."

Adriana's eyes were wide open when he turned around.

"What?" He followed her eyes to the water bottles in the bottom of the bar. "Water?"

Her body tensed as if she wanted to lunge at the water. Dennings chuckled and threw her a bottle. After she had emptied it, he approached her with the whiskey. She took the glass and took a gulp.

"So, how was DC? I heard you did great things."

Adriana drank up her whiskey. "I don't want to talk about that."

Dennings refilled it and she continued without being asked again.

"We were one company and we took the White House back room by room and held it against everybody: criminals, raids and hungry people. It was not pleasant and it got worse when the first ones suffering from radiation sickness showed up." Her gaze went out to a point far away. "For the first time I killed somebody with my own hands." After that she stared back at the water. "Can I have more?"

"Sure." Dennings got her another bottle. "One thing: these are my emergency reserves. Our reserves." He looked deep into her eyes. "We supply ourselves from the military."

"You surprise me." She emptied the glass and held it up again. "So few reserves..."

He refilled. "The rest is in the bunker."

"Bunker?" She raised one of her eyebrows.

"Frank got an old bunker in the..." Dennings rushed past her to the door of his office and peeked out. "In the Bitterroot Mountains," he continued when he got back to her. "But this has to be the last time the location is mentioned."

She tilted her head. "Who else knows?"

"Frank's guys. Only talk to Frank. The rest are pawns."

"So where's my room if not here?" Adriana emptied the second glass.

"What's the information?"

"I know what this is." She looked around the room.

"This?" Dennings frowned and tilted his head.

"I know what caused this, who caused this..." she raised her arms, "this chaos. Can I have another one?"

Mechanically he refilled the glass. She visibly enjoyed it. After another gulp she moved away from him and walked up and down. "We captured a fat guy trying to get south. At first there was nothing special. I let the boys play with him a little, they needed the outlet, until he spat out the whole story."

Dennings noticed the effect the whiskey was having on his body. He still didn't speak a word.

"Fatty was working in the Vermont engineering office with a guy—Niklas something. He thinks... he thought this Niklas guy caused this."

"Doesn't ring a bell. Niklas, you said? Hmm. How?"

"He said Niklas had a bot that caused the outage of the data centers simultaneously. Allegedly, he tried to stop it."

"Did you believe him?" Dennings squinted. *He can't have done this alone.*

"It would explain why everything crashed." Adriana shrugged, emptied her whiskey and held out her glass to get more.

Dennings was too deep in thought to notice. "It would. Who else knows?"

"Three of the squad picked it up, but two of them didn't make it. Only Captain Stark knows. Fatty got killed when he tried to escape, but we got a description of this Niklas out of him before that." Adriana wrestled a paper out of her pocket and gave it to Dennings.

He chuckled. "That description could fit 20% of the male population. Well, it's better than nothing." His face turned firm again when he moved over to the window. "Let's get this description to Clutsky and have his contact discreetly look for him, but the rest needs to stay between us."

He turned around when he didn't hear a reply from Adriana and smiled; she had fallen asleep on the couch. He left and closed the door behind him.

#

### Niklas — Day 65 (June 25, On the ocean between Mexico and Peru)

After ten days at sea, Niklas dared to go into the mess hall for the first time. Even though Manolo had reassured him he would be safe, Niklas just didn't want to risk anything with the other passengers. So far he had had sailors bring him food and he only went on deck at night.

It was late afternoon and a mixed crowed was sitting around the six tables, three on each side of the room. The right side was empty, except for two sailors, while the left side was cramped with passengers of all shapes and colors.

They eyeballed Niklas when he entered the room. He pretended not to notice as he passed the table. He did notice, though, that there were clear hierarchies: the men sat at the center of the tables, playing cards, while the women and kids sat or stood around them. That is, except for one young woman with unusual frizzy black hair; she was sitting in the middle, shouting "Truco!" with a big, triumphant beam on her face. And she was the only one not checking out Niklas.

He sat down at a table on the right side, triggering one of the sailors to jump up and stride towards him.

"You can't sit here," he said in an overly loud and unfriendly tone. "There." He pointed to the left side.

*German?* Niklas tried to guess where his accent was from, and he was still considering how to react.

The sailor bent down to Niklas and added in a low voice, "I'm sorry, sir, but..." He flicked his head over to the other passengers.

Niklas nodded and left. The other passengers followed his movements with their eyes—again, everybody except the girl with the frizzy hair. She wasn't beautiful in a strict sense; her nose was rather long, even for her oval face, and the way she had her hair bound back showed her forehead and made her face even longer. But all this was forgotten when she beamed, when the corners of her mouth turned from pointing down to up. He guessed she was in her early twenties. Niklas had almost passed her table when she eyeballed him with the corners of her eyes.

Back on deck, he wasn't sure what to do next when the radio room caught his attention. Usually it was locked, but now the door was open and the radio operator was standing next to the door, smoking. Niklas ambled over and the guy straightened. A chair was placed in front of an old two-way radio and static noise was coming out of the speaker. Two computer screens on the other side of the room were pitch dark. *They must be at least twenty years old—before everything switched to virtual machines*, Niklas thought.

"Not working?" asked Niklas in his best Spanish.

The operator squinted and wrinkled his nose.

"Can I try to make them run again? I know my way around computers."

The operator still didn't reply, but when Niklas took out two twenty-dollar bills, he let Niklas in without another word.

A green blinking cursor appeared in the upper left corner of the left screen when Niklas turned it on.

"See?" said the operator and grinned.

Niklas just loured at him until the guy shrugged and turned away. Niklas closed the door, rushed back and feverishly typed '22.65qq.205.ff11.', and two lines later he added 'scramble'. A series of numbers and letters appeared on the screen; most looked like gibberish, but some were in plain language, such as 'moon data center' or 'access confirmed'. As expected, the satellite system was corrupt. Good job he had made sure that a point-to-point connection with a dish antenna would still be possible. *Pretty chaos, I created*. He chuckled. *But they brought it on themselves*. The chuckle turned into a grim grin.

A sound outside startled Niklas. Quickly he severed the connection and switched the computer off and on again. The green blinking cursor appeared again, right on time. The door opened a few inches, and to Niklas' surprise the slim body of the girl with the frizzy hair squeezed through.

"Hurry, the captain is coming and he looks really mad," she said in English, with only a hint of a Hispanic accent.

He got up and they left the radio room. They managed to rush around the corner before the captain saw them and then they ran down the stairs to a lower deck, where they stopped. He wasn't sure who giggled first, but in the end they were both laughing.

They stopped when the tumult upstairs got louder, and hid between two lifeboats. The captain yelled at the operator. Niklas understood only half of it, but it sounded bad. The sun started to set and they watched the coast in the distance slowly turning red. Eventually the row subsided.

"That will cost me extra bribes, I guess." Niklas raised his eyebrows. "Thank you for warning me."

"Welcome. Hope it was worth whatever you were doing."

Niklas shrugged. "What's worth anything these days?" His closeness to the girl made the hairs on his arms stand up.

"Friendship." She stretched out her hand. "I'm Marcella."

Niklas grabbed it. "Eduardo."

She raised her eyebrows and scanned his face with a cheeky smile. *She knows* flashed through his mind.

"Well then, Eduardo, I'd clink glasses with you if I had something to drink."

"I could get us something."

"I might get back to you on that." She looked back out to the coast. The sky now showed every color from red far into violet. She yawned.

"Too much partying yesterday?" he asked. "I hear there are parties all night long."

"There are, but I stay away from them." Her face was firm when she turned back to him. "I haven't really slept in days. They tried to rape me four times in the past ten days." She shook her head in disgust.

"You should tell the captain." Anger boiled up in Niklas.

"Twice it was the crew." Marcella bristled and rolled her eyes. "But I'm faster than them and I always have a way out."

Niklas pressed his lips together. Marcella peeked out from between the lifeboats. "I think we can leave. They're gone."

"You can stay in my cabin if you want," said Niklas quickly before she was able to get up.

She examined him with her head tilted. "Get me that drink first and then we'll talk."

"Fine, come."

They got out of their hideout and Niklas led her to his cabin two levels beneath deck. She followed but made sure she was at least six feet behind him. When they arrived at the cabin, he unlocked the door and entered. She remained in the doorway, inspecting the inside of the cabin. Her eyes wandered from the bunk bed on the right, over to the small desk in front of the porthole, to the small locker on the left. For the blink of an eye her gaze rested on the door to the bathroom. Niklas opened the locker and took out a half-full bottle of tequila.

"I have no glasses, though."

Marcella shrugged, peeked left and right and stepped into the cabin. The cheekiness had gone from her face when she looked at him. "Fine, but under two conditions."

"Shoot." For the first time Niklas noticed that she had amber eyes.

"First, I want to know your real name."

His throat went dry and he swallowed. "Niklas." And he added quickly, "But no more questions than that."

She nodded, still standing right by the door. Even though the cabin was not large, it felt as if she was standing miles away.

"The second?" He asked with a tone of awe.

"I will sleep six hours." She briefly smiled as if she wanted to give her request some silliness. "Alone, with the doors locked. Any other time, the door remains unlocked."

Niklas took a breath and wanted to say something, but he changed his mind. "Fine."

He opened the bottle, took a gulp and held it towards her as if she was a small bird he was trying to lure in. She peeked left and right outside the cabin again and closed the door behind her, but she didn't lock it. Slowly she took two steps, grabbed the bottle and took a gulp as well. While she walked over to the porthole to take a look out, he cleared the upper bed.

"You're fine with the top bunk? Do we need to get your stuff?"

Marcella yawned. "Not necessary. I have my bag well hidden. We can get it tomorrow." She took another gulp and put the bottle on the table. "Now I have to try the bed." She raised her eyebrows.

Niklas nodded and left the room. A clicking sound told him that she had locked the door. He hadn't asked what she was doing here and she hadn't asked about him, but he knew that she knew he was on the run.

# CHAPTER TWO

# Putsch

*Jenny – Day 80 (July 10, South-east of Flagstaff, AZ)*

D ark clouds were building mountains on the horizon. Eduard watched them with a troubled expression on his face. "We should leave this trench."

The trench was about eight feet wide and had started at about five feet deep, but was now seven feet deep. It seemed to be natural, created by water draining after a flood, with uneven, porous walls of clayey soil. For weeks they had been wandering through this dust desert. Reddish soil with small bushes changed to yellow soil with no bushes, or dry grass with large bushes, but no water anywhere. Multiple times they got lost or walked in circles, until Jenny suggested they follow the trench to not get lost again.

Jenny protested against his suggestion to leave the ditch, but she realized how useless that would be at the moment. His mind was somewhere else. "Hey! Are you listening?" She poked him.

"Sure," Eduard replied without letting go of the dark clouds.

"No, you weren't. Just like you weren't listening when I told you we should go north-east. We would already be further by now." She clenched her teeth.

Despite her snapping, it still took Eduard an instant to look at her. "Sorry, ok? I was just thinking—"

"I heard you, but I don't think we should leave our cover. Soon it'll get dark and this gives us perfect protection."

"But the rain—I don't want to be in here when that thunderstorm gets closer. We'll be trapped if there's a flash flood." *Do I have to explain everything?* Eduard pinched his lips. "And you're right, it will be dark soon. We should get out now."

"Fine." Jenny pouted. "But let's go forward to find a spot to climb out, not backward."

Eduard still didn't seem convinced, but then he shrugged and they continued walking. Just minutes later she regretted her words. The rim got steeper and higher with every yard. It was still daylight, but the sun had already started hiding behind the wall of the ditch. She looked over at Eduard; by the way he had slowed his pace, she could tell that he was thinking the same. "Let's go back, Edu."

"I told you so," he growled at her.

Jenny tilted her head. "There's no need to be angry with me," she snapped back.

He pressed his lips together as if he needed to suppress answering. They turned around and ten minutes later they were back where they had been before. The walls were still high, but Eduard could reach the rim if he stretched.

He stopped and held his finger in front of his lips. "Do you hear that noise?"

Jenny closed her eyes to hear better. It was a gurgling sound like in an apartment building when somebody is having a shower. She opened her eyes wide. "Water. Run!"

She turned back to the deeper part of the trench, but Eduard grabbed her arm. "We have to get out." He leaned with his back against the wall and folded his hands into a foothold. She stepped onto it and tried to hold onto something on the rim, but there was nothing but sand and dry clay. The gurgling got louder and was now accompanied by the rustling noise of a fast mountain creek.

"Step on my shoulder," he said.

She managed to get her upper body out. Eduard pushed her legs up and then she was out. She flipped around and looked back into the trench, still lying on her stomach. Eduard hastened to the other end of the trench for a run-up. He jumped and pushed himself off the wall with one leg, but he only got his arms out. Jenny tried to grab them, but he slid down again. The noise was getting louder by the second. In the distance she could make out something moving fast. "Hurry! The water..."

Eduard ran and jumped again and this time she could grab him. He tried to get grip beneath his feet, but the clay broke off. She could now see the wall of water gushing towards them.

"Eduard!"

He tried harder, but he only lost grip. Seconds before the water reached them Jenny grabbed Eduard's arms tightly, but she had no chance. The torrent carried him away as if he was a leaf.

"Eduard!"

She jumped up and ran along the trench, trying to make him out, but he had been dragged underwater. After two hundred feet she slowed until she tripped over a stone and fell. She didn't bother to get up. "Eduard," she sobbed and wrapped her arms around herself. Seconds later the water lowered and after half a minute the ditch was empty again, except for a few small puddles.

Jenny stood up again and walked along the trench, sobbing the entire time.

#

*Jenny — Day 81 (July 11, South-east of Flagstaff, AZ)*

She must have searched for hours. A thin slice of light on the horizon announced the dawn.

*Finally.* Jenny pressed her lips together. *I must return to where it happened, search again in daylight. Maybe I missed him.*

That's when she saw the shapes of three men pulling a fourth from the trench.

*Edu!*

She run towards them, not even thinking it could be dangerous. Getting closer, she realized that they had a child with them, and it was the child who alerted the others to her presence. One of them turned around and grabbed something out of his pocket.

*A knife*, thought Jenny. *Or a gun—no, a knife, the way he's holding it.*

Jenny slowed down. The man was tall and slender and the way he took that defensive position it looked as if he had been drilled.

"Is that Eduard?" she asked loudly when she was about thirty feet away. *Stupid, how would they know? Damn, now I've given his real name away.*

The boy poked the man. *Max* flashed through Jenny's mind. *That rat*. Her body tensed up.

"Come closer, but show me your hands," said the man.

Now that Jenny was close enough, she could tell that the man with the knife was African American, while the two others looked Caucasian. And the man they were pulling out of the trench was definitely Eduard. She faltered over, suppressing the urge of her feet to run to him.

"Good," said the man.

"Is he...?" Jenny swallowed hard.

"He's alive, but injured. We need to take him to the camp." The man lowered his knife and stepped out of the way. Jenny rushed over and kneeled beside Eduard. He looked dreadful: several abrasions and bruises covered his arms and legs, and the left side of his face was covered with dried blood.

"Edu," she whispered. He didn't react.

"We have to go." The man glanced left and right as if he was expecting more people to come. "You can come with us, but it's a long march." Then he turned to one of the other men. "Tank, you carry him first. We'll switch afterwards." He turned back to Jenny. "I'm CJ, this is Tank and that's Jason."

CJ seemed friendly, although most of the time he put on an impenetrable facial expression. Jenny guessed him to be in his late thirties.

The others lifted their hands quickly in a reserved way to say hi. Tank was even taller than the others, but also bulkier. He lifted Eduard up as if he was a bag of empty plastic bottles.

"And you already met Max," added CJ.

Jenny nodded. Max stealing their pizza felt like a long time ago. "I'm Jenny and this is my boyfriend, Eduard." Jenny looked at Eduard's body sagging over Tank's shoulders.

"Well, I guessed that," said CJ and gave her a friendly grin for a second before his face turned opaque again. "Let's move."

They hiked along the trench, further down towards where the water had gone. From what Jenny had learned from Eduard over the past days, she knew they were going south. *Not towards Phoenix or into the contamination zone*, she hoped.

Finally, after hours they reached a forest and Jenny guessed from the others' faces that it wouldn't be much longer. During the entire hike, Jenny had not taken her eyes off Eduard, except for once, when Max had taken her hand. She had looked down and Max had smiled shyly at her.

#

*Jenny — Day 81 (July 11, Donna's Farm, Apache-Sitgreaves National Forest, AZ)*

Eduard opened his eyes when Tank set him down at the outskirts of the forest. Jenny was glad to get out of the sun. Her shirt felt soaked with sweat. Tank was sweating as well; only CJ and Max seemed to be impervious to the heat.

Jenny caressed Eduard's hair. "We are safe. CJ says we'll be there soon."

He closed his eyes again. Jenny wanted to keep talking, but Eduard only answered with random moaning. A rustling sound made Jenny look up into the woods. The forest was an endless-seeming, rather loose collection of gigantic, half-naked trees; they had no branches on the lower parts so you could walk beneath them, while the needles on the upper parts provided a pleasant sunroof without making the forest too dark and menacing.

Eduard moaned again and Jenny turned back to him. She wanted to continue talking, but a moment later Tank picked him up again. Eduard's head dangled as if he was unconscious. Jenny bit her lips.

They continued to hike and the surroundings changed the deeper they got into the forest. Dense barriers of bushes beneath the trees and creeks forced them to walk on a zigzag course. While they were walking a little uphill, Jenny noticed how soft the ground was. The mix of moss and needles from the gigantic pines around them was like a carpet. They reached a little creek and followed it upstream. The creek opened onto a view through the needle-roof and revealed that they were heading towards a mountain range.

The gurgling sound of the creek had a calming effect and it swallowed other sounds. That was probably why she didn't hear the voices and children shrieking until they had reached a small clearing at the foot of a mountain, with two old farmhouses and a few cabins and stables around them. The clearing was surrounded on three sides by woods, and the steep, reddish stone of the mountain on the fourth side presented welcome variety for the eye. Two pipes led out of the mountain, one to the main house and the other one feeding a trough with water. Kids were playing around. As soon as they spotted the group appear, they came running and CJ and Jason kidded with them for a moment before CJ turned to Tank. "Take him to the infirmary." To Jenny he added, "Go with him. We'll catch up later."

Jenny followed Tank to a building at the edge of the clearing. While the other buildings seemed to have been rebuilt or at least taken care of, the cabin they were heading to seemed as if it had been abandoned and had started being used again only recently. Jenny saw the faded and flaking colors from afar and when they got closer she noticed the rust-rotten wood beneath the handrail. Inside, unoccupied beds stood along both side walls. It seemed to be one large room, and only after a moment did she see the doors that opened onto a back room.

Tank put Eduard down on one of the beds and disappeared through the front door again. Jenny stood lost in the room, alternately looking at Eduard and at the back room from where she heard a squeaking noise. When after two minutes nobody had appeared, she went to the back room and found an elderly man dozing in a rocking chair. Beads of sweat gave his bald head a polished look. Where gravity got too strong, the beads of sweat joined and ran down the furrows of his face.

Jenny stomped towards him, and he almost jumped up when he noticed her.

"Hello, sorry I didn't hear you. Who are you?"

"My boyfriend is hurt. He's in the main room." Jenny flicked her head towards the other room.

"Oh, I'm coming."

He got up slowly and inched to the door. It took him far too long to get over to Eduard. *Hurry!* Jenny felt her pulse racing as if it could compensate for his slowness.

"Let's see what we have here. How did this happen?" he asked when he finally reached the bed. "What's his name and what's yours? I'm Dave."

Jenny told him the entire story, but got the feeling she lost him halfway. He bent over Eduard twice and grunted. Then he examined his eyes and pricked his feet. A slight twitch went through Eduard's legs. Dave grunted again.

"He'll be alright. A concussion maybe, but it's hard to tell with these instruments." He looked around. "And being dragged around didn't help."

Jenny was relieved, somehow.

"He needs rest." He must have noticed that she appeared a bit lost. "You can go over to the main house. Ask for Donna—she's my sister." He smiled mildly. "It's the building in the middle," he added when she didn't move.

She smiled back, glanced at Eduard and left.

#

*Eduard — Day 82 (July 12, Donna's Farm, Apache-Sitgreaves National Forest, AZ)*

*Jenny!* dashed through Eduard's mind when he woke up again. He felt his heartbeat in his throat. *Where's Jenny?* The sun shone bright through the windows. He felt better; at least that's what he thought until he tried to sit up. It almost felt as if every bone and every joint was yelling "Don't move!" After the pain receded he tried it again, by first turning to the side and then sitting up.

Now he could see better. He was alone in a room. Through a door on the far side of the room he heard somebody humming. It was quiet outside. Judging from the shadows, it was probably the calm right after noon when the temperature was hitting 100. A day ago they had been stumbling through a lunar-like landscape, or rather a reddish Martian landscape. Hard to believe. Was it yesterday? How long had he been passed out?

"You should take it slowly," said a rusty voice from across the room.

Eduard looked up. An old man had entered the room. Children's laughter sounded through the door.

"Where is Jenny?" Eduard pulled a grimace.

The man chuckled, but it sounded more like a rattle. "She was already here twice today. I guess she will be back soon."

"She's here?" gasped Eduard and closed his eyes. He took a deep breath before opening them again. A slow smile appeared on his face.

The man shambled over to Eduard. "My name is Dave. I run the infirmary and in that capacity I have to tell you that you should rest, at least for another day." The last words were eaten by a heavy cough.

Eduard lay down slowly. Dave supported him as far as he could and examined him, poking his legs, arms and rips. Eduard flinched twice and Dave grunted, satisfied.

"Nothing's broken, just a concussion. You were lucky," Dave added, before he turned around and shuffled out the door in the back.

Shortly thereafter the main door opened and Jenny peeked in. As soon as she realized that Eduard was awake she ran to the bed and hugged him.

Pain streaked through Eduard's body, but he didn't care. "I'm glad you're here."

"I'm glad you're all right. My heart froze when I saw you being dragged away by the water." Jenny hugged him tighter. He groaned inwardly.

"Sorry," said Jenny and helped him lie down again.

Eduard smiled. "Don't be. I needed that hug—it's just that I can feel every bone in my body."

Jenny caressed his cheek.

"I dreamed of you, that you were in here, and you said that you snuck in just to see me."

Jenny chortled. "That wasn't a dream. I was in here three times. They kicked me out twice. I just couldn't sleep."

Eduard smiled again and squeezed her hand, but his smile dropped with the pain flashing through his arm. He bit on his teeth. "Who are they? I mean, they're nice, but what is this place?"

She shrugged. "I'm not sure. Donna and Dave are siblings—they own this place. They've been living here for two years or more. All the others are like us, people trying to get along in this... this... gosh, it feels like the aftermath of a war. It's like in the movies."

"It does." Eduard cleared his throat. "Can you do me a favor? Is there any water?"

"I'll get you some." Jenny jumped up and Eduard groaned again silently. "I'm sorry, honey," said Jenny and disappeared through the door to the other room. A minute later she was back with a glass of water.

Eduard drank eagerly. "Thank you," he said after he had emptied the glass, and he added after a moment, "How many people are there?"

"About forty or fifty. They come and go. The core who stay longer are about twenty. The rest are looking to get somewhere, most of them to the Gulf in the south or to California." Jenny peeked around and added in a low voice, "I think they're some kind of religious group. One room in the main building is full of religious things: crosses, prayer rugs, a menorah and other things I didn't recognize."

Eduard shrugged. "Dave was nice. Maybe there's a reasonable explanation for that. Did you notice anything else?"

"You're probably right. They are really nice. We had deer for dinner. I can't remember the last time I had deer." Jenny licked her lips.

"And you're telling me this so casually. I'm starving."

Jenny chuckled. "I saw Dave going over to the main house. He should be back any minute with lunch. They made fresh bread this morning."

Eduard swallowed hard and, as if it had been given an order, his stomach rumbled.

"Oh, before I forget, Max is one of them. You remember, the boy who stole the pizza?" Jenny giggled.

"Seriously? That's funny."

"Yeah, he did it for them. Nick, Donna's partner, already apologized for it."

Eduard frowned. "But that was almost a hundred miles away. We've been walking weeks since then."

A door went in the back and there was Dave's humming again.

"They have small groups going around to search for food. One of them picked you up, actually. They've just started to grow food and they have to do quite a lot of hikes to keep everybody nourished."

Eduard listened only half-heartedly. His nose had picked up the smell of fresh bread and it had made his blood sugar drop to the point that he had become nauseous. A moment later Dave appeared in the door with a tray.

"Who wants to have bread?"

Jenny held her hand up. Eduard raised his hand only halfway and grimaced in pain.

"Good job that I brought enough." Dave put the tray next to Eduard on the nightstand and turned to Jenny. "You'll have to help him, probably. He shouldn't move too much, at least for today." He patted her shoulder and left slowly.

Minutes later they were devouring the meal.

Dave came back a little later. "Already done? I wish I had more. But it will be dinnertime soon anyways."

"Can I ask you something?" Eduard pressed his lips together.

"Sure. Judging by your face, it's probably not 'what's for dinner?'"

"Jenny told me that people are travelling south or west, but is there anybody travelling east?"

"Hmm, where do you want to go?"

"Vermont. Back home," said Jenny.

"I'm afraid that will be difficult." Dave shook his head slowly.

Eduard threw Jenny a look.

She shrugged. "We know that it'll take us months, but it's ok."

Dave intensified his head shaking. "There have been incidents. You'd better ask my sister. She knows all the details. But tomorrow—today you still need to rest." Without awaiting an answer, he turned around and left again, shambling.

#

*Eduard — Day 83 (July 13, Donna's Farm, Apache-Sitgreaves National Forest, AZ)*

The next day, Eduard was able to get up. It didn't hurt too much if he moved slowly. Jenny took him over to the main house. It was a beautiful day and kids were playing on the grass between the buildings. Eduard counted seven buildings and in the back they were building an eighth. "Where's Max?"

"Max is always out with CJ. He has hardly left his side since CJ found him," said Jenny and squeezed his hand.

A little pain flashed through Eduard's arm, but he resisted cringing. "He found him? Where?"

"I don't know, but I heard he was still a toddler."

They were strolling through unevenly mowed grass, and bees were flying around looking for flowers. The grass tickled Eduard's ankles.

Jenny pointed to the back of the main building. "Let's go through the kitchen. I helped out there yesterday." She smiled. "It's my favorite place."

Eduard smiled as well. The peace in this place felt unreal compared to what they had been through in the last half a year.

"You know what's strange?" continued Jenny with an unburdened voice Eduard had not heard in years. "Remember that Max didn't speak a word when we first met him? I still haven't heard a word from him at all."

"Do you think he's mute?"

They reached the building and walked around it to the back.

"No clue." Jenny shrugged and opened the door to the kitchen.

The kitchen was busy; six people were whirling around as if they were the arms of a whisk. It didn't seem that there was a clear head chef. There were no commands given and the division of work seemed to be clear without saying.

"Everybody, this is Eduard, my fiancé," Jenny shouted into the noise. The kitchen crew looked up, waved, welcomed them and continued with whatever their business was.

Eduard's heart jumped and he had a hard time suppressing a grin. "Fiancé?" he asked when they were walking through the door to what appeared to be a dining room with an enormous table.

"That way we can stay in the married cabin. Otherwise we would have been separated—Donna's rules."

Eduard nodded. *I guess they've had their share of bad experiences with all the people coming through here.*

At the other end of the table three people were eating and the same procedure repeated itself; Jenny introduced Eduard, they looked up, waved and continued to eat. The next room was a kind of living room, with two sofas and a broad variety of different chairs, like in an antique furniture store. A large fireplace behind the sofas gave it the look of a mountain lodge. In a corner Eduard spotted a bookshelf with well-used books and next to it an opening in the wall led to another room from which he heard a murmuring sound.

"That's that religious room I told you about." Jenny pointed to the room the sound was coming from.

Eduard stepped closer and peeked around the corner. Two men were kneeling on prayer rugs, resting their foreheads on the floor.

"That's our sanctuary," said a female voice behind them. They turned around and looked into the face of a tall, wiry woman in flap trousers. Her hair and her shirt were covered with sawdust and her hazel eyes gave her a warm and welcoming appearance. "I thought I saw you limping over. I'm Donna. Welcome to our farm."

She had a strong handshake that made Eduard flinch.

"Let's sit down. I'm sure you have lots of questions." Donna went to a sofa and they followed her.

Eduard flicked his head over to the room with the murmuring. "What is that?"

"It was our library, but when people started showing up they would use it to pray. First we established a kind of a chapel, but we rebranded it as a sanctuary the more people from different religions came. That way everybody has a retreat. Do you believe in God?"

Eduard and Jenny wiggled their heads half-heartedly.

"I do believe in a higher power, but I am agnostic about whether we call it God, Allah, Zeus or Thor, and I'm pretty sure it doesn't care for me." She paused. "Dave told me you were on your way home. Where is home?" Donna tilted her head.

"Vermont." Eduard felt silly telling her.

"We are aware it's far," Jenny threw in hastily. "It might take us a year or two."

Donna exhaled through her teeth. "I'm sorry, darling, but there's a problem." She hemmed and fidgeted on the sofa. "There have been incidents at the remaining three nuclear power plants. They should have switched them off years ago, like all the others—damn lobbyists. They all knew the risk after Palo Verde. Apparently they couldn't shut them down—they were ablaze for weeks until the army was able to pour enough cement on them to cover them."

Eduard listened with growing unease. Jenny's fingernails clawed into his arms.

Donna's face took on a pitiful expression. "The radioactive fallout is covering the entire Northeastern Seaboard, down to the Carolinas. Right now the Appalachian Mountains are serving as a kind of a natural border for the winds. We pray every day it doesn't come through."

Jenny and Eduard remained with hanging shoulders and wide-open eyes. Donna lowered her eyes as if she couldn't bear their expressions.

"Mom," whispered Jenny and sobbed. "Mom."

Eduard put his arm around her shoulders. "I'm so sorry, honey."

Jenny couldn't reply. He felt her muscles tense and release again with a shiver. Her tears were dropping onto the floor. Only after a few minutes did she calm down.

"How do you know?" Eduard raised his eyebrows.

Donna looked up again and shrugged. "People passing through, hearsay. We have people in our graveyard who died of radiation poisoning."

Jenny was still quiet on the sofa and the mention of radiation poisoning made her shiver.

"How did you come to be here?" Eduard tried to distract Jenny's thoughts.

Donna didn't answer right away, looking at them as if she was trying to screen her own thoughts. "About three years ago I was pushed out—out of my job and soon after out of society. They cut all my loans and my savings were gone."

"We know how that works," added Jenny, still snivelling. "We heard stories like that in the Burlington cell—"

Eduard's alarmed gaze interrupted her. At that moment, two men came out of the sanctuary, nodded towards Donna and Jenny and left.

"So, you were part of the Resistance." They must have looked dismayed, because Donna started to laugh heartily. "Don't worry. I took part in two meetings myself, but it seemed more like a self-help group than something worth participating in."

Eduard and Jenny relaxed.

"Anyway, my brother and I got this farm from my uncle and we refurbished everything. Good job we made it self-sustaining."

He pricked up his ears. "Is that what's happened? A complete power outage?"

Donna shook her head and started to fidget again. "This smells like a problem with the computers, but I don't understand what's happened. I was the CIO of The Holding, until I refused to sign an illegal deal. My successor gladly did, that... no, moron is the wrong word. He was just naïve and scared."

Eduard noticed Jenny opening her eyes wide when she heard the words 'CIO of The Holding'. *I hope Donna doesn't recognize us.*

"Anyway, what I wanted to say is, I have some knowledge about this and it smells so much like it's computer related. Maybe a virus or a cyber-attack." Donna examined her hands as if the answer was to be found there.

Jenny opened her mouth. Eduard squeezed her hand and pain flashed through his arm. She closed her mouth again. She looked at him and he slightly shook his head. *Don't...* He formed the word with his lips and his mind finished the sentence. *...tell her about your dad. We have no clue how they'll react. They might throw us out.* When he turned back at Donna he realized that she was looking up again and observing them. Her eyes were narrowed and she had her head tilted. Then her eyes opened wide and she blushed. "I'm sorry, I didn't realize," she stammered. "I didn't mean to... You are..."

Jenny bit her lips. "It's ok. They kept me out of the news—all focus went to his new wife. The past years have been difficult. But my dad came to Palo Verde to save us. He died there of radiation..." Jenny started to cry again and couldn't finish the sentence.

"I'm sorry. I knew him as someone who put family first and I was always sure he was forced to do what he did, including after the arson attack in Burlington." Donna paused and glanced out of the window. "Did you...?"

"No, we didn't," said Eduard with a firm voice. "We had nothing to do with the attack."

"I'm glad to hear that." Donna was visibly relieved.

"But we—" Jenny was again interrupted by Eduard squeezing her hand. She ignored him and started again. "But we might know what happened."

Donna tilted her head again.

"It's just a theory. There was this other guy in the cell who informed us about a back-door entry he had created."

Donna signalled her to hold off and strode over to the sanctuary. She glanced into the room and came back. "It's ok."

Jenny told Donna the entire story, from the data centers to the scrambling routine and the promise Niklas had made her father to protect them.

Donna looked out of the window during the story and after Jenny had finished she turned around and said in a low voice, "That story is actually the most probable explanation so far. I'll need to check some things." She turned back to the window.

Eduard glanced over at Jenny and she nodded after a moment.

"There's more." He waited a moment for Donna to turn around, but she remained looking absently out. "On the last day we saw Niklas, he taught me a series of numbers and letters. He called it his 'insurance policy'."

From the side he saw Donna curling her lips. "Write it down." She turned and wrestled a small notebook out of the side pocket of her trousers.

Eduard took it and wrote down the numbers and letters he had memorized. On the other side of the page she had already put seemingly random numbers. When he finished, he gave it back to Donna.

She curled her lips again. Then she narrowed her eyes at Jenny and Eduard. "I need you two to keep this to yourself. Tell nobody anything about this—not about who you are or about your theory. If this information gets into the wrong hands, you might as well hand them the world on a platter. They will do anything to get the last bit of information out of you and execute you the moment they have it." She came closer them. "Do you understand me?"

They both swallowed hard.

#

*Niklas — Day 90 (July 20, Outside Lima, Peru)*

Niklas could see Lima though the porthole, but the ship was not allowed to enter the harbor. "Quarantine," they had said.

During the day they stayed in the cabin and at night they watched the city's sparse lights from deck. It was the first time in weeks they had seen lights on the coast. The mood had flipped from friendly to nervous when the ship was put under quarantine, and Niklas had had to start bribing the chief mate in addition to the usual bribes to the captain.

The waiting drove Niklas crazy. Marcella made fun of his restlessness. Six weeks they had been on the ship and there was no sign that it would end soon. In those past six weeks she had started to allow him in the cabin while she was sleeping and now she was fine with keeping the door locked. She realized that the danger from outside was bigger than he could ever be.

One day Niklas overheard two sailors talking. While talking was still difficult for him, Marcella's Spanish lessons had helped him to understand a lot. He had almost rounded a corner when he heard them, but he stopped before they could see him.

"This quarantine sucks," said one of them.

"I hope they find what they're looking for."

"Looking for?"

"You haven't heard? You should stop trying to hit on the girls down there."

The other sailor grunted.

"They're searching each ship, one by one. Tomorrow they'll finally check the *Southern Cross*. I'll be glad when they do. We're running out of food, even for the crew."

Niklas' heart stopped beating for a moment. At least that's how it felt. That night he didn't sleep for one minute. Were they looking for him? Why here? Nobody knew that he was on this ship. *Except maybe*... He shook his head. No, if they had restored the data there wouldn't be such chaos anymore. From time to time Marcella looked at him with sorrowful eyes; he saw it out of the corners of his eyes, but he pretended to sleep.

He got up before dawn and marched up and down the deck. The Andes made the sun rise later and provided Niklas with a wonderful rainbow across the sky. This calmed him down as well.

"Do you have money?"

He turned around. He had not noticed Marcella had come on deck as well. She was wearing one of his T-shirts. "I can get us off the ship if that makes you feel better."

Niklas raised his eyebrows. "How?"

She smirked and threw her hair back. "How do you think I got so close to the US in the first place?"

"I do have money, but I don't think it will work, not in this chaos."

"It will." She strolled over to him and looked over to Lima.

The sky right above the peaks of the Andes was now bright yellow. The sun would rise soon.

"Have you noticed how the entire crew is collecting cash for small favors and services, or... oh yeah, how some of the crew spend the same cash again for a night with one of the female passengers? They're all hoping to get a little wealth out of this and live a nice life as soon as it's over. Trust me." She laughed, turned to him and stopped when she noticed his frown. "What?"

"There they are." Niklas pointed to a small vessel approaching the ship. "Let's go down."

Back in the cabin, he cleared the small locker and moved his bags into the bathroom. When he came back out of the bathroom he gave her one thousand dollars in cash. She took two hundred and gave the rest back. "We might need it for the captain."

Niklas shook his head. "I have the second half of the passage for the captain in a safe place: two thousand dollars."

"Not that captain—the one from the vessel of the coast-guard." She winked and put half the money into a pocket of her shorts and kept the rest in her hand.

He rubbed his face. "So what's your plan?"

"When they come, you hide, listen and learn." She smirked.

He wanted to reply, but a sound outside the cabin interrupted him. Niklas looked around for somewhere to hide and squeezed into the locker. He was barely in when somebody hammered on the door. "Coastguard inspection. Open up."

Through the air slit Niklas saw Marcella amble over to the door and open it, still with the money in her hand so the guy out-side could see it. "*Si, señor.* Why don't you call your captain down here?" he heard her say in her Argentinian Spanish. She had taught him the difference during her Spanish lessons. The guy's answer was less understandable, but it seemed to work; he left and she closed the door again. When she turned towards the locker he could see that somehow the money had exchanged owner.

Five minutes later the captain of the coastguard vessel was at the door. Before she opened it again, she made sure the money in the front pocket of her shorts was visible. Then she pressed her fingers against her eyes for a couple of seconds and opened the door.

"You wanted to see me?" asked the captain.

"You need to help us, *señor*. We are desperate. My uncle and I just want to go home, but we got caught up on this ship."

"I'm sorry, the ship is under quarantine. I can't help you." He entered the room. The conversation was in Spanish, but Niklas could just about grasp the context without understanding each word. Marcella moved over to the desk. The captain stooped down and picked something up from the floor.

*The money.*

"Where is your uncle?"

"On deck. Hiding. They want to kill him. He's the only reason I'm safe here." Marcella collapsed on the chair next to the desk.

"Not much of a help, hiding."

Marcella started sobbing. "We still owe the captain half of the passage. The only reason we're safe is because they don't know where the money is."

"I understand, but I can't allow civil passengers on my vessel." He turned around and walked towards the door, just to turn around again and nod.

Marcella smiled gratefully and wiped a tear out of her eye. She stood up and closed the door behind the captain. For a moment she paused and breathed heavily before coming over to the locker and letting Niklas out. She hurried into the bathroom to collect the bags. When she came back out again, he had put all his cash and bartering goods on the desk. Of the original fifty-four thousand he had only fifty left, but he hadn't had to use the tiny gold bars or the watches yet. Her eyes went wide looking at it all.

"Any idea where to hide this?" Niklas puffed. "So far I've just kept it in an old sock in my bag, but now that we're leaving the ship I'd rather split it between the two of us."

Marcella didn't answer. She held herself on the doorframe. When she found her voice again she asked, "How did you get so much money? And the watches?"

Niklas shrugged. "I'm always prepared."

"It's illegal in the US to own that much cash." Marcella raised one eyebrow. "You didn't care."

He didn't reply.

"Well, I can take a quarter of it in my pants."

A voice outside the cabin made them startle. "Departure in ten."

A hectic rush caught them. Marcella started pushing money into her pants. Niklas turned away. "I might get the same in my pants and I guess we could put more in our shoes."

"Don't forget we need a certain amount for the captain," said Marcella and added after a moment, "You can turn around again."

Out of the corner of his eyes he just saw her buttoning up. He pushed the rest of the money into a side pocket of his bag and mixed the watches in with the dirty clothes.

She pointed to the watch he was wearing. "If that's your favorite I'd suggest exchanging it."

Niklas nodded and switched his watch with one he had just put away.

Five minutes later they were climbing with their bags down the ladder to the coastguard vessel alongside the freight ship. As soon as they arrived on the vessel the captain of the freight ship appeared at the railing above them, fiercely gesticulating. They did not understand what he was saying to the captain of the coastguard, but they could imagine it was not nice. Two armed guards stepped in and the freight ship captain shut up, but his eyes spoke volumes.

Minutes later they were on their way towards Lima and the coastguard captain approached them. "He wanted his half of the passage."

Niklas looked up. Marcella didn't.

"I convinced him to let it go if he wanted to have a chance to unload his freight here in Lima." The coastguard captain looked over to the freight ship. "The *Southern Cross*—I've checked that ship a dozen times in my career, every time with a different captain. How much was it actually?" He studied Niklas again. "These are tough times." The captain's mouth mimicked a smile, but his eyes made it clear that there was no room for negotiation.

"Two thousand dollars," said Niklas.

The captain didn't move for a while. Then he nodded and Niklas got up and took the money out of his bag.

After the captain was done counting, he gave half of the money to his first officer. "They have families too," the captain added, answering Niklas' questioning look.

Lima came slowly closer. Niklas started to be able to differentiate between houses.

"You have a nice watch." The captain looked at Niklas' wrist. "Can I take a look?"

Niklas gave the captain his watch. After inspecting it carefully, he looked up again. "Please have your papers ready for Customs."

Marcella glanced over to Niklas and turned to the captain. "Would you mind leaving us at the local harbor? We might get a better bus connection from there."

The captain looked towards the harbor.

"We are grateful for what you've done for us," added Marcella. "*Tio* Eduardo, why don't you give your watch to the captain, as a thank you for helping us?"

The captain was still looking in the direction of Lima. After a while he said to his first officer, "It's been a long time since we inspected the fishermen in the old harbor—too long."

"Aye," replied the first officer and made the helmsman change course.

The captain let the watch slide into his pocket. Thirty minutes later Niklas and Marcella disembarked from the vessel in the old harbor of Lima and disappeared into the crowd at the fish market.

#

*Dennings — Day 90 (July 20, Fairview, MT)*

"So far we control about five farms in the surroundings of Fairview. Two of them will harvest soon. They could provide more crops than ten of us could eat." Clutsky smirked at Dennings and Adriana. "Another ten are spread across the country and we get more by the day, but we don't have enough old tractors to do all the fieldwork."

They were lounging on the couch in Dennings' living room as it was the room with the bar.

Adriana frowned. "How do we control them?"

"The local ones are under our direct control." Clutsky added a scornful tone to his smirk.

"Well, I know that."

Adriana's snippy answer made Dennings sneer. He took a sip from his whiskey and leaned back on the couch. Since Adriana had come back to Fairview, the three had had daily update meetings.

Clutsky sneered at Adriana again, which made her glare at him. Dennings sighed. "Stop it, both of you."

"Obviously I mean the ones spread over the country."

"Our part of the military controls them." Clutsky got up to get a beer. After a gulp he made a face. "How long until they fix the damn electricity? Can't be that difficult to hot-wire it."

"Imbecile." Adriana had turned her head so only Dennings could hear it, but her voice wasn't low enough.

Clutsky turned around and this time he gave her a stare. "What did you say?"

"I said stop it!" Dennings leaned forward. "Get used to the warm beer for the moment. Pray that they'll have it fixed before it gets cold again. Otherwise I'd be glad to have a warm beer."

Adriana continued to poke. "And how do you know they won't follow the military's orders in the end? I guess we don't really control them."

Clutsky shrugged. "We don't, but..." He glanced at Dennings and chuckled after he received a nod, "Bruce does."

"Bruce?" Adriana looked from Frank to Dennings and back.

Frank grinned. "Our secret weapon."

"Bruce is our mole." Dennings leaned back. "He's Secret Service, but he was a colonel before and he's got influence and loyal followers. You would be surprised how divided our military is." He snorted. "They were so stupid to split the bases instead of giving us troops in each base. Anything else?"

"Yeah, I can't believe you didn't tell me that." Adriana moved her chin forward, looking alternately at Dennings and Frank, but more at Frank. His grin made her even more furious.

Dennings jumped in before she could lunge at Frank. "Frank is the only one talking to Bruce. The fewer people know of this, the better. Having said that, I agree with you. There should be no secrets among us, but we also need to contain the information we share."

Now Adriana's fierce eyes were aimed at Dennings. "You don't trust me?"

"I do trust you." He squinted. "But your Captain Stark shares things with the military."

Her nostrils flared and she clenched her fist. "He shares exactly what I want him to share. That way he gets me the information I need."

"And why did *we* not know about this?" Dennings tilted his head, but his lips formed a sneer. "Let's move on. Any thoughts about distribution?" He looked at Adriana.

She pouted but her fists relaxed. "We will transport everything to the military bases and distribute it from there."

"Why don't we distribute it directly from the farms?" snarled Frank. "That's the most efficient way and—"

"I wouldn't do that," interrupted Adriana. "Or do you and this Bruce guy have enough forces to defend the farms? I guess not. We will end up with millions camping around the farms. Hungry people are like locusts." She turned back to Dennings. "It should go to the bases and then further from there. Food is control."

Frank wanted to reply, but Dennings pre-empted him. "I agree with Adriana. How do we distribute it further?"

"We'll combine it with registering people—that would solve one of your problems as well." Adriana threw a defiant look at Frank. "Everybody has to provide his name and fingerprints and then we mark them with something they can't get rid of for a day."

Dennings grunted and stood up. "Fine. Let's do that." He glanced at his watch. "I have to go. The usual feast in the control room."

Clutsky stood up as well.

"One more thing," said Adriana. " We talked about the food in the military bases, but do we ration the food here?" She looked up at Dennings. "We have enough now, but we might very well have to feed civilians."

"What civilians? There's nobody around. This is Montana." Clutsky chuckled.

Adriana got up, avoided glancing at Clutsky and turned to Dennings. "I've seen what hunger does to people and I've seen what people do when they're hungry, and word travels fast." She raised her eyebrows.

Dennings pinched his lips together and frowned. Then he blew air through his nose. "Ration food for everybody, but don't keep it too tight." He smirked. "I don't want riots—just enough to avoid those decadent parties."

Adriana smiled and sat down.

Dennings headed for to the door, Clutsky right behind him, but before he left he turned back to her and added, "Make sure the bunker is always full."

#

*Dennings — Day 95 (July 25, Fairview, MT)*

The generals had uttered their displeasure before about everything, but when they announced the food rationing, Dennings got to feel their anger. It was as if the city was holding its breath, and Dennings instantly knew it had gotten out of hand when Clutsky came storming into his rooms holding a gun. He jumped out of bed and Adriana covered herself up with the blanket.

"What the—!" she shrieked.

"They're coming." Clutsky shouted. "You have to leave. Now!"

Adriana jumped up, not caring about her nudity. Clutsky didn't either. He stormed out again. Dennings and Adriana pulled on their clothes and ran out of the room as well.

"Frank!" shouted Dennings.

Clutsky turned around.

"Take Adriana out the back. I'll go to the front." Dennings made a face that wouldn't allow any discussions.

Adriana wanted to protest, but Frank grabbed her arm and they ran.

#

*Adriana — Day 95 (July 25, Fairview, MT)*

Adriana followed Clutsky through a maze of corridors and stairs. Company guards covered their backs and some of them ran with them. Without light, it was like dashing over a dance floor when the strobe light is on. She had to watch out not to trip over dead bodies in military and company guard uniforms. Flashbacks from the White House mixed with glimpses of now.

Something fell against her legs and pulled them from under her. She fell hard. The cement floor hit her shoulder and her eyes went black for a second. Somebody grabbed her and lifted her up.

"Get up." Clutsky's face appeared blurred in front of her eyes, a square box of bones and muscle. His expression had lost any affection or emotion.

The taste of blood brought Adriana back. She stood up and continued to run. There was no time to be scared; it was just like in DC, but without her own gun. *Where the hell is Captain Stark?*

Two minutes later they pushed a door open and they were out. First the bright daylight dazzled her, but after a moment she was able to see things clearly. They were in the grey backyard of office building, but it wasn't the main building. They must have run to another building underground. Far away she heard gun-shots, but before she could look any further Clutsky dragged her over to one of the Jeeps waiting at the end of the alley.

The moment they reached the Jeep they were surrounded by soldiers. Looking into a dozen gun barrels on all sides, Clutsky gave in. He dropped his gun to the ground and put his hands above his head. Adriana was reluctant to follow until one of the guns poked her hard in the back and she fell forward. Clutsky's shoulders dropped.

"Got ya," said a voice from around the corner.

Clutsky's body tensed up again. "You asshole." After that curse, he grunted and relaxed again.

A man in a suit appeared with a broad smirk. Adriana had seen him once with Frank in the alley. *This is Bruce? I imagined him taller.* The man made a sign and the soldiers stormed into the building, followed by several dozen other soldiers. He came closer.

"You didn't think we would leave you alone, did you, Frank?"

"Nope, but I didn't think you'd be that fast." Clutsky picked up his gun again. "Jude went to the front."

The man chewed hard on his chewing gum. "You two have to retreat to the bunker. It's safer there now." He opened the door of the Jeep and they slipped inside. Behind the back seat, they could see the body of Vice President McNally.

"He was not as lucky as you guys. They literally executed him," said Bruce before he closed the door.

#

*Adriana — Day 96 (July 26, Bitterroot Mountains, MT)*

It took one day to get to the bunker—eight hours in a truck, mostly across unpaved roads, and another four hours by foot at night. The hike was exhausting and towards the end Adriana almost tripped twice. She wondered if they had to carry all the food that way as well.

When they arrived in the early hours of the morning, she was surprised that it was not actually a bunker but five mountain cabins arranged around a chapel. It was busy; people were running around carrying bags and boxes from somewhere to somewhere else. Adriana couldn't make out any patterns. Clutsky brought her to a cabin that was nicely furnished—a little rustic, but at least it had a bed and a fireplace.

"Wait here," he said and turned around.

"Wait. Where are you going? I saw radio antennas—do they know something about Jude?" Adriana tried to grab the door, but he was faster. A clicking sound indicated that he had locked it.

"Let me out! Immediately!" Adriana banged against the door but her fists felt weak.

When she stopped for a moment, Clutsky said from outside, in a surprisingly friendly voice, "I'll check what's up with Jude. You have a rest. We will have to make important decisions later."

Adriana didn't reply. With pressed-together lips, she heard Clutsky stomping away. After the sound disappeared, she let her shoulders drop and scanned the room, but there was nothing in the cabin that could have helped her to break the lock. For a second she thought about breaking a window, but Clutsky would for sure use that against her with Jude.

*I hope he's ok.*

Looking at the bed, she noticed how tired she was and lay down. Seconds later she was asleep.

#

*Adriana — Day 96 (July 26, Bitterroot Mountains, MT)*

After she woke up, Adriana had an hour to feed her grudge to the point where she was furious when Clutsky came back to the cabin.

"Never ever lock me in again," she hissed through her teeth. "What fucking game are you playing?"

"Standard procedure until you're briefed on the security details." Clutsky didn't even bother to shrug.

"Fuck you."

Clutsky didn't show any emotion. "Here are new clothes." He threw a pair of multi-cam trousers and a khaki jacket on the bed.

Only now did Adriana notice the boots he held in his other hand. He put them down at the door.

"I'll wait outside."

"Leave the door open."

Without another word he went outside, but he left the door half open. Two minutes later Adriana came outside as well. The surroundings were deserted. Adriana wondered where all the people had gone. Only stomped-down grass between the cabins remained from the soldiers who had been running around that morning. The chapel seemed as if had not been in use for years— the windows were smashed and the bell in the tower was missing.

Clutsky took a long drag from his cigarette and flicked away the snipe. "Come. They got Dennings."

"Where? We need to free him," she called out. The boots were too big for her and she had a hard time following him. *Damn it, Frank, I didn't fight in DC to be treated like a doll.*

At the chapel, Clutsky scanned the surroundings with a hint of worry in his eyes. "Let's go inside."

Before he entered the chapel, he looked up as if he was expecting to be watched from above. Adriana followed him. The corners under the roof were full of spiderwebs. Decayed pews stood in front of a faded altar. Two guards were waiting inside. Clutsky opened a trapdoor behind the altar and signalled Adriana to go down. It was dark and moist in the crypt. Before she could wonder why a chapel had a crypt, Clutsky and the guards came down as well. They had flashlights that gave at least a little light. With the four of them in the crypt, there was not a lot of space left and the air felt even damper.

"What—" started Adriana.

"Shh," Frank hissed back. They all remained silent for another minute. Then Clutsky nodded to a guard and opened another trapdoor Adriana had not even noticed before. All four descended and as soon as the trapdoor closed one of the guards opened a door and they entered a steel construction lit up with electric light.

"It's a bunker." Adriana tried to raise her eyebrows, but the light dazzled her.

Frank grinned. "Welcome to Sapphire City. Come."

Adriana followed Clutsky through a maze of corridors until they reached a large room with outdated computers and radio stations. The noise level was high; stomping boots mixed with the sporadic sound of static noise from the radios and the beeping of computers.

*Computers?* She frowned at Frank and pointed at the computers. "How?"

He grunted. "Useless. Twenty years old and we can't get any connection with anything."

"I might be able to get something out of them. Let me try."

Clutsky shook his head. "Dennings."

She pressed her lips together. "What's the situation?"

"They're still fighting." Clutsky rolled out a map on the table in the middle of the room. "Bruce holds the position at The Holding's HQ and a few streets behind the building. The boulevard in front of the building is a natural line of defense. The traitors have the Convention Center, but they are surrounded." He squinted and clenched his fists. "We have the backstreets here and here." Clutsky pointed to the back of the Convention Center, than he bent over the table, supporting his weight with his palms, and kept staring at the map.

"We have to get him." She set her jaw.

"Too risky. We've already decided how to move forward. We'll starve them out," he replied, still bent over the table.

"That's not your call." Adriana bent over as well and narrowed her eyes.

Clutsky scowled at her. "It's Bruce's call. He's in charge there." After a moment his eyes went back to the map.

She straightened up again and crossed her arms in front of her chest. "What if they order reinforcements?"

"They did." He smirked without looking up this time. "But the nearest base is ours. They ordered a Trojan horse."

"Jude will be killed in this. Don't you see it?" Adriana tilted her head. "Or do you want that?" She bent over again and fixed him with her eyes. "Is that what you want?"

Clutsky straightened up and put his shoulders back. His fists were clenched.

Before he could answer, she added, "I'll take ten men and get him. And I want Captain Stark."

"That's suicide, but if you insist." He pointed at one of the men in the room. "Get me Bruce."

#

*Dennings — Day 96 (July 26, Fairview, MT)*

Dennings noticed that there was only sparse gunfire after he woke up again. *They're rearranging.* He wasn't sure how long he had slept. They were keeping him in a room in the Convention Center. Daylight came in through a small window right under the ceiling. Instinctively he looked at his wrist and remembered that they had taken his watch. He sighed. At night he hadn't been able to recognize what room they had put him in; now he could see that it was filled with cleaning supplies.

He went through the racks. *I could spill soap and call them in, get the guard's gun and run. But what if there are two guards?* He shook his head. They couldn't spare more than one man to guard a prisoner.

A sound outside the door startled him. The door opened and two armed men came in, followed by that jerk of a four-star general.

"I see you slept well."

Dennings clenched his jaw when he saw the general was wearing his watch. "General Cox, it isn't going as planned, is it? Let me guess, you want me to convince them to give up."

The general snorted. "Not necessary. Reinforcements are on the way. In less than two days we'll accept your surrender."

"Well, then this is just a courtesy visit. I apologize that I don't have anything to offer, but you could have brought wine."

"Vice President McNally got killed. We are still investigating, but in light of the fact that none of the civil leaders are available, we took over control."

"So it's a putsch. Pretty convenient it hit McNally, but you got one thing wrong. Adriana is still a member of the cabinet."

"She's missing too, probably captured by the rebels."

Dennings kept his poker face, but it cost him a little to suppress the feeling of relief. "So you're the good guys. Why don't you let me go then?" The discussion felt like verbal chess and he was starting to enjoy it.

"I know that you have your bunker somewhere. I'll get you something to eat, as soon as you reveal its position." The general smoothed his bushy eyebrows. "I wouldn't want to waste resources to find it."

"Good luck with your search, General." Dennings smirked.

The general turned around and left without another word. After the door had been closed, Dennings heard him barking at the guards.

"No food, no water, no contact, even if he shouts, cries or curses."

#

*Dennings — Day 97 (July 27, Fairview, MT)*

*Stupid. So damn stupid*, Dennings thought. The setting sun covered the room with a red glow. *We are at the bottom and fighting each other like apes. So stupid.*

Dennings could still hear the casual gunfire outside. In the meantime he had tried the trick with the soap, but the guard had obeyed the general's orders. From time to time he heard the commands and updates from the guard's radio. The entire putsch seemed to have turned into a trench war and they were surrounded.

He had also searched the room for anything else he could use for an escape, but there was nothing. He wished he had paid more attention during chemistry in college. With all these chemicals around, there was surely a way to create an acid solution, or just anything that would help. He had even climbed up to the window and almost killed himself when the tower of boxes collapsed.

Now Dennings was sitting in a corner and watching the setting sun paint shadow pictures on the wall. *We need to do better, but for that we need a leader and zero tolerance.* Cox had crossed the line with this putsch, but where would they end up? *Separate territories, if we don't beat them? Dictatorship if they win? How could we ever trust in the institutions again?*

Slowly one thought crystallized out of the maze: if he remained part of this, there would be no leeway anymore. Zero tolerance, even if it meant temporarily suspending some liberties.

*For the greater good.* Suddenly out of all the things he had always striven for—corporate titles, wealth, power—only power remained. *Power to restore peace and civilization; all the power.*

A gurgling sound outside made him hide behind a rack. Soldiers stormed the room: four, five, six. The first ones slipped on the soap and crashed to the ground. The next ones were smarter and jumped over the slippery area. Then Adriana appeared in the door.

"I'm here," he said and came out from behind the rack. "Glad you made it."

Adriana showed a hint of a smile before she moved back to the door. "We need to keep moving." She peeked left and right before she went back into the hallway and the others followed her. Dennings grabbed the dead guard's gun. It was covered in blood, but he didn't care.

"That way," said Dennings. "There's a secret passage—"

"Barricaded," interrupted Adriana. "We came in through the sewer system. We lost five men getting in, and getting out won't be easier."

Dennings wrinkled his nose. "That's gonna be—"

Adriana held up her fist and they took cover to the left and right of the hallway. Voices came closer.

*That jerk of a general* flashed through Dennings' mind as Adriana peeked around the corner. Then she signalled the number four with her fingers and indicated that they should move backwards. They hid in a room across the hall from the storeroom where Dennings had been held. The steps came closer and at some point they started to run. "Find him!" bellowed the general. Boots were stomping outside the door as if there was a stampede. One minute later it was silent again.

"So much for leaving quietly," whispered Adriana. "Any ideas?"

"We could wait until nightfall and sneak out," said one of the soldiers.

Dennings shook his head. "They're awaiting reinforcements. I don't want to be here when they arrive."

"The reinforcements will be on our side, but I agree with Jude. They don't know we're here and there's a chance they'll kill us in the heat of the action."

The soldier who was listening at the door signalled them to be quiet, but it was a false alarm.

"How was the secret passage barricaded?" asked Dennings, whispering.

"I don't know. We just couldn't open it from the other side."

"Let's check it out." This time Dennings went to the door and peeked out. The hallway was empty and they moved out, but when they passed the storeroom they were startled by voices again. The soldiers took cover. Dennings remained upright, looked at Adriana and smirked. She copied his smirk and went over to the storeroom to get the radio from the dead guard.

To get to the secret passage, they had to go two levels down to where the building services were located. The central hub for the photovoltaic power supply was located on that floor as well. *They haven't figured out how to get that up and running again,* Dennings thought. *They lied—they haven't even tried.*

Then they heard shots from one level up and Adriana ordered, "Move, move."

They ran, trying to find the right way in the light of their flashlights. Dennings was the only one without a flashlight and he almost tripped twice. "It's right behind the next corner."

Muzzle fire flashed out in front of them and the sound of gunfire. The soldier next to Dennings went down immediately. Before Dennings could duck he was hit hard in his shoulder and yanked off his feet. Voices were shouting and gunfire sounds came from everywhere. He recognized Adriana's voice. He was grabbed by his clothes and dragged back around the corner and then cold darkness surrounded him.

#

*Dennings — Day 98 (July 28, Fairview, MT)*

The first thing Dennings noticed when he woke up was the pain in his shoulder. The second thing was Adriana, who was sitting next to the stretcher he was lying on, sleeping. The third thing was the neon light on the ceiling and a cool draft from the air conditioning. They were still at the Convention Center and neon light meant power.

Dennings tried to sit up, but the pain made him nauseous. From outside the room he could hear groaning and whimpering;

it seemed they had got him a separate room in the sick bay, or whatever rooms they were using for that purpose.

Bruce entered the room. He had switched his black suit for a military uniform. Dennings eyeballed him up and down.

"I swore to never wear a uniform again, but I guess things change." Not only had his clothes changed, his presence and his behavior were military again. Even the way he walked was more like stomping compared to his nimble movements from before.

"I wouldn't take it too hard—the black suit was a uniform too."

Bruce grinned and flicked his head towards Adriana. "She did a hell of a job to get you out. I gave her my best men, but to be honest I wouldn't have bet a dime on her."

Dennings turned his head. "She's a tough cookie." He chuckled. "She and Clutsky are like cat and dog."

Bruce raised his left eyebrow. "That could be the beginning of a wonderful friendship."

"So, how does it look?"

"We have the city. The generals gave in and three-quarters of the positions are under our control again. By the way, here's your watch."

"There's blood on it."

"Sorry about that. He didn't give it up willingly."

Dennings nodded. "What's next?"

"Get the rest of the country back."

Dennings nodded again. "We need to clean up the mess. There's only one man who knows how. We have to find this Niklas guy and I know exactly how: we put out a nice bounty."

"Sounds like a Clutsky job," said Adriana. "Let him run with that vague description from DC."

Dennings and Bruce turned their heads.

"How long have you been awake?" asked Dennings.

"Long enough," she said. "Had a strange dream, though. I was sitting in the Salzburg bakery in DC, having a raspberry Linzer cookie. I love them; the bakery uses real confiture."

"Used to." Dennings tried to move his shoulder, but he stopped immediately and grimaced.

Adriana sat up in her chair and frowned. "You'd better not move too much."

Dennings didn't react. When the pain ebbed away he breathed again. "I'd just be glad to have a cold beer."

"I can offer you that." Bruce smirked.

"I noticed." Dennings pointed to the neon light on the ceiling. "How did you do it?"

Bruce grinned. "It was actually easier than I thought—we just had to plug in a cable. They had figured it out already, but they didn't want to tell you. Our dear friends wanted to starve you of power."

"We will also need Clutsky to play policeman. We can't have these hidden agendas and traitors when we want to build up this country again. We need to clean out the stable." Dennings looked at the other two for confirmation.

Both nodded and Bruce asked, "Shall I tell him?"

Dennings shook his head. "We need to discuss the next steps together. Tell him to come down."

# CHAPTER THREE

# Insurance Policy

*Niklas —Day 101 (July 31, Lima, Peru)*

Niklas peeked out of the window. There was no movement on the lawn in front of the deserted Argentinean embassy in Lima. The wall and the dense mix of trees and large bushes around the property made it difficult to see to the street. From time to time you could hear a car, but they hadn't seen an open gas station yet. There must be alternative distribution systems, at least for some people.

*I hope they start to recover soon. But not before we reach a safe place—further south. We might need them to recuperate a little to not get stuck.* Competing thoughts chased one another.

"Do you see anything?" Marcella touched his shoulder and, like every time, it electrified him. Any thought of the chaos was wiped away.

He shook his head. "Let's go downstairs."

"Agreed." She glanced once more out of the window. "You know what's funny? It was here that I swore to myself never to go back to Argentina. And here I am again on Argentinean soil."

Niklas didn't know what to say and she didn't seem to expect an answer. He grabbed the bag of food they had acquired today and went into the basement.

The embassy had been marauded multiple times it seemed and the less they had found the more they had destroyed. There wasn't a single pane of glass left intact, much less a bed or other furniture. They had even slashed the mattresses in the guest rooms.

Down in the basement, they followed a narrow corridor and at the end of it entered the janitor's room through a secret door behind the boiler. Marcella had shown him this room after they had spent two days hiding on the street. "An employee of the embassy hid me down here for half a year," she had explained; it was the only room that had not been raided. It had been used as storage for what one would call the 'good stuff' and as an office for shady activities. The cabinets along the walls were filled with cigarettes from Cuba, single malt whiskey and wine from the Bordeaux region. A door opened onto a second room with computer equipment: old screens, desktop computers and a scanner. The only thing that looked modern was an oversized printer in the corner. During the day they had power from the solar panel on the roof, but Niklas was not able to connect to anything; that had been the first thing he had tried.

They had laid a mattress on the floor of the storage room: a queen size that fit right between an enormous desk in the middle of the room and an old safe in the wall. The drawers of the desk were stuffed with papers, some as much as twenty years old.

"That has always been like that," Marcella said.

When they were inside, they moved a desk in front of the door. They only spent the nights down here because the air got damp over time, and most of the time they had to feel their way as the solar panels only provided light during the day. When they ate or when they needed something from the cabinets, they lit a candle for a few minutes.

Tonight they left the candle lit a little longer, just to be able to see each other while they chatted.

"I was glad we could elude that checkpoint downtown," Niklas said as he poured a glass of Bordeaux for each of them.

The scenery was somewhat romantic; the candle gave the room a warm light and Niklas had the feeling Marcella's amber eyes were sparkling.

Marcella leaned back. "I agree. I'm not so sure if they would have believed you're Eduardo Hernández. You need a new identity, and a passport." She sat up again. "That's it: a new passport."

"Aren't you too old to believe in fairytales?" He grinned, but she ignored him. She jumped up and opened the lowest drawer of the enormous desk. He followed her with his eyes when she kneeled down to feel the bottom of the drawer from beneath.

"Ha!" She shrieked and jumped up with a shred of paper in her hand. "Give me the candle," she said, staring at the paper.

Niklas gave her the candle and she put it on the floor without taking her eyes off the paper. He got closer to her and moved the mattress out of the reach of the candle; if it caught fire, it could very well kill them. Without noticing anything, Marcella went over to the safe and started to turn the combination lock. Five seconds later he heard a clicking sound and she opened the safe door. He picked up the candle and took a closer look. His first glance fell on the packets of money on the upper shelf.

Marcella grabbed the money and grinned at him. "This should help us to get further."

Behind the money there was an instant camera, glue and something like a large stapler. Marcella crouched down and stretched her arm inside to grab a small box further in the back.

"This, my dear, is your fairytale." She opened the box and it contained Argentinean template passports.

Niklas opened his eyes wide, grabbed one out of the box and flipped through the pages. It seemed real: it had a punched out passport number in the upper part and the words 'República Argentina' reflected the candlelight.

Marcella got up to get her bag; she got her passport out and held it next to the template. They looked the same. "The templates are real. I never had problems with mine in any checks."

"Yours is fake as well?" Niklas marvelled at her.

She chuckled. "Not fake, just not official. Ultimately, the ambassador signed it. The guys in the embassy made some side money with passports. Or do you think Pastorutti is my real name?"

Niklas blew out air through his nose. "This is really a miracle, but how do we get the biometric data on it, and the laminate?" He ran his fingers over the laminate and the engravings on the picture page in her passport.

Marcella pointed to the other room. "They do everything with that equipment in there. I watched them do it. Let's try tomorrow."

Niklas nodded and closed the safe again.

#

*Niklas — Day 102 (August 1, Lima, Peru)*

The next morning, after they had spent half an hour upstairs to freshen up the air in their hideout, they returned back down.

"So, what name do you want?" asked Marcella when she switched on the computer.

Niklas shrugged. "I don't know. It can't be too Spanish, otherwise I'll give myself away the moment I open my mouth."

The screen came on with an input mask for the data.

"I suggest keeping it as close as possible to reality: your real birthday and a first name similar to what you're used to. We could try to get through as family—you could be my uncle. How about Nicolas Pastorutti?"

"Sounds great," he replied and she typed it in.

One hour later, after they had also scanned his fingerprints and his signature and taken a picture, they had a perfect passport. Niklas flipped through the pages and hugged Marcella in a rush of glee, but unlike their hugs before, they only let go after a half a minute.

"Now we just need to emboss it and tatter it a little." Marcella said and went back to what they cynically called their 'living room'.

Niklas remained for a moment in the other room, trying to sort out what had just happened.

#

*Eduard — Day 105 (August 4, Donna's Farm, Apache-*
*Sitgreaves National Forest, AZ)*

Eduard adapted to life in the community in no time—a lot faster than Jenny. There were rules and he didn't mind following them, but Jenny had more difficulties, especially with the numerous rules they had to follow without any say.

"I watched them. While we aren't allowed to be out at night, some go to the main building every other night," she asserted several times, usually followed by, "They don't tell us everything."

She wouldn't let it go until he let her convince him to try to find out what really was going on. He agreed to sneak out one night, but he still wasn't sure about it. They were already at the door when he stopped.

Jenny pulled Eduard out of the cabin they were staying in, making sure none of the other couples woke up, and into the shadow of the small porch. "Don't be such a baby. They won't catch us," she whispered while observing the area between the cabins. The moonlight was bright, but the shadow of the moving clouds made the scenery fluid.

"We shouldn't be out here. Despite the fact that it's against the rules, it's also dangerous. There might be a black bear around, or a mountain lion."

"Now." Jenny took off.

Eduard blew air through his nose and followed her. When they arrived in the shadow of the main building he could see her biting down a smile. *She enjoys this.* "And now how do you want to get in?" he asked, whispering.

"Easy."

Without another word, she sneaked along the wall towards the kitchen door. There was noise coming out of the kitchen and Jenny put a finger in front of her lips. Eduard frowned.

She turned towards him and whispered in his ear, "Just wait for it."

He didn't lose the frown and she suppressed a giggle. Eduard watched the scenery; with the moving clouds it was hard to detect any other movement in the area. Slowly he felt his body heat evaporating in the cold of the night. He had always imagined Arizona to be hot and was surprised by how cold it could get at night. The thought made him even more uncomfortable than he already was; no way did he want to risk the shelter they had found.

The kitchen door flew open and he almost jumped. Marvin, one of the kitchen guys, stomped out and lit a cigarette before he was even five feet away. Jenny again put a finger in front of her lips, but Eduard doubted that the guy would hear anything but his own trudging. Jenny squeezed his hand and they hastened in. The kitchen was empty; on the stove two large pots were boiling.

"They make their own corned beef—they caught a cow yesterday. That's why we had beef stew for dinner." Jenny wrinkled her nose. "Seeing a cow being slaughtered is another thing I didn't want to witness. You can be glad you work outside."

Eduard peeked into the pots.

"Come." Jenny sneaked through the dining room. Eduard followed her. She opened the door to the living room and they peeked around the corner; the room was empty, as far as they could see in the pale moonlight. They crossed the room and took cover behind one of the sofas.

"What's this all about?" whispered Eduard.

Jenny giggled. "Isn't it fun? Don't tell me you aren't bored. We help in the kitchen, help to get food, help with the cleaning. I feel as I've become a housekeeper."

"That's not funny—" he said, a little too loud.

"Shh... you don't want them to catch us, do you? Seriously, something is wrong here. We're working like donkeys, but they only organize. They call it a 'community' but we don't have a say in the rules, nor do we get any information or updates about what happens outside." Jenny looked at him and despite the very low light he could see her firm expression.

"That could have a simple explanation," he whispered and put his finger in front of his lips.

Jenny shook her head and continued in a normal voice, despite having just warned him to be quiet. "But rules should be rules and they should be the same for everybody. Unmarried people aren't allowed to live together, but Donna lives with her partner."

"They might be married."

"Right, then why doesn't she call him her husband? I tell you, something's wrong—"

Footsteps in the room startled her. Heavy steps, as if out of nowhere; multiple people. Candlelight lit up the room a little too much for Eduard's taste. Jenny and Eduard cringed together behind the sofa they were hiding. Two men left through the front door. Eduard recognized one of them by his posture: CJ. *Jenny is wrong*. He's involved.

The other footsteps went towards the stairs and disappeared upstairs. They heard them walking around for another ten minutes and then it was quiet again. A little later, Jenny crawled out from behind the sofa.

"What are you doing?" whispered Eduard.

She turned her head. "Checking where they came from. There must be a hidden room. I always thought the house seemed larger from outside."

Eduard peeked out from his hideout. Jenny was creeping over to the stairs, making sure to stay out of the moonlight. Eduard whispered, "Come back. We'll be caught and they'll kick us out." It came out far too loud and he swore silently and followed her. She stopped beneath the stairs.

"They must have come out of here," she whispered. "There's no other way. To the right is the dining room and there's nothing in the corner to the left. It's here, I tell you—"

A sound upstairs made her freeze. A door opened. Steps. Somebody was coming down the stairs. Jenny and Eduard pressed against the wall beneath the stairs. The door to the dining room flew open. More people. Candlelight blinded Eduard for a moment.

"I expected you weeks ago," he heard Donna saying with a voice that sounded 20 Fahrenheit below zero.

#

Eduard — Day 105 (August 4, Donna's Farm, Apache-
Sitgreaves National Forest, AZ)

"What should we do with them?" asked Nick. After they had dimmed the candlelight, Eduard counted five people surrounding them. He recognized Donna and her partner Nick. The others were guys he had hardly seen so far, and when he had seen them they had seemed to be patrolling the area. Now Eduard and Jenny were sitting on the sofa and Donna was walking up and down in front of them.

"Tell me, what should I do with you?" she asked without look-ing at them.

Eduard put his arm around Jenny and in the light of the candle he could see her rebellious glare he knew too well. Her shivering body was telling a different story. *She's scared as well.* Eduard took a breath. "I'm sorry, we didn't want—"

"Something's wrong here and we wanted to find out what it was." Jenny clenched her fists. "And we were right."

"Oh, were you? Go on, enlighten me." Donna threw a side glance at Nick.

Jenny stood up and put her hands on her hips.

"Sit down."

Donna's sharp command made Jenny sit down again, but her body was still upright and she held her chin high. "This is not a community. The elites get to make all the decisions and the serfs do the work. In a democracy, everybody should get a vote."

"You are right. And you are wrong." Donna's voice lost its sharpness but not a bit of its clarity. "This is a community. We all work for everybody. Food is shared evenly and we all get a bed and a roof."

"How about sharing information evenly?" Jenny narrowed her eyes, but Eduard wasn't sure if it was because of her mood or because Donna's expression was hard to grasp in the low light.

"You are wrong assuming that this is a democracy. Dave and I own this place and we rebuilt it, put all the nice amenities in as well as all the necessary enhancements to be self-sufficient. So why should I give people that are just passing through the voting rights for something they won't have to live with a year from now? They get a bed, a roof and food in exchange for hard work."

"We're not passing through," Eduard heard himself saying.

"No, you're stranded here, but that doesn't mean that you'll stay. I don't know if you might decide tomorrow to go west or south and, to be honest, I don't think you know either."

Jenny opened her mouth to say something, but Donna didn't give her time.

"Now, before you say anything else, go to bed. You have to get up again in two hours. Make up your mind and let me know what you want. Then we'll talk."

Without any more words, Jenny and Eduard were let out into the cool night. The moon was now glowing yellowish-red through the clouds—like a hunter's moon.

#

Dennings — Day 187 (October 25, Fairview, MT)

"In a hundred years, they will call you the founding father." Adriana was kneading Dennings' shoulders through the thick pullover. He flinched briefly when she hit the spot where the gunshot wound had been. They were sitting in his old office, back on the top floor of the building. Thanks to the regained solar power the city was mostly up and running again—at least, whatever could be circumvented without data. His groaning was interrupted by a chuckle.

"What?"

He turned around. "As long as they don't call me Big Brother."

She smirked and shrugged. "Well, if it serves the purpose. We can be proud of what we've achieved so far."

Adriana continued kneading his shoulders. He pressed his lips together and narrowed his eyes, focusing on the wideness of Montana in front of him. Soon there would be the first snow.

Adriana must have noticed his muscles tensing up again. "We really have achieved a lot, haven't we? We've got a good deal of the food supplies back: enough for us, the troops and twenty million civilians. Some industries work again—we can't build cars yet but we can repair the ones we have. We even got production in the oil sands in Canada back. That's not too bad for half a year."

Dennings grunted and stood up, still looking out of the window. "It's the people. We haven't gotten hold of the people yet. Every minute we let them organize themselves, we lose control."

Adriana didn't reply.

"Get me Clutsky." He turned around and rubbed his hands. "I need to know the stats."

She nodded and went over to the radio they had brought up to the room. He followed. The moment he stepped out of the sunlight that came through the window he started shivering.

Minutes later Frank's voice sounded out of the radio, interrupted by static noise and the occasional chatter from neighboring frequencies.

"We've got the food supply areas covered. Bruce has troops stationed in the large farms in Iowa, Indiana, Illinois, Wisconsin, Minnesota and all the other crappy states. His boys are also covering the industry we've been able to recover."

Dennings stretched his neck before he replied. "I didn't ask about Bruce. He has things under control. What about your job?"

Voices from the background came through again when Clutsky didn't reply right away.

"We've cleared everything around Bruce in a hundred-mile radius. That pretty much covers Montana, Wyoming and parts of North and South Dakota."

Static noise swallowed a couple of words.

Clutsky's voice came through again. "But it's like fighting mushrooms—the second you turn around these hobby warlords pop out of nowhere again. I hear there's a big one on the other side of the Mississippi. They control almost the entire state of Kentucky."

"Stop whining. I gave you a free hand to get these bastards. You might wanna get out of that cozy bunker and get your hands dirty."

"I'm in Wisconsin right now, making sure we got enough meat for the winter. I can only do as much as I can. Bruce gets all the good reservists and replacements and I just get the crap. I can't even break them in; one-third desert after a week." Clutsky put on a sharper tone.

Dennings took a deep breath. "We need to change the strategy. It doesn't seem to be working."

"Frank, can't we use these warlords?" asked Adriana into the microphone, still standing next to Dennings.

Again, Frank went radio silent for a moment.

"How's that?" asked Dennings into the silence.

She tilted her head and said into the microphone, "Assign them areas that are strategically unimportant and let them reign under our control. Let them be small kings."

Clutsky cleared his throat. "That won't work. They'll start fights with others, and the bigger they get the more they'll oppose us."

Adriana wanted to reply, but Dennings waved her off. "We need to apply a carrot-and-stick tactic. Remember how we got the CIOs of The Holding's companies under control?"

"Yes, but the stick won't work. These guys don't have anything to lose."

"*Au contraire*, my friend." Dennings smirked into Adriana's questioning face. "We assign them territories that are larger than what they have now and supply them with things they don't have: that's the carrot. And then we get rid of the Kentucky warlord: that's the stick. Just make sure the other warlords know about it."

Clutsky inhaled audibly. "It has to be bloody and loud. I might need to ask for some of Bruce's gadgets."

"Do what you need to do. Make sure they all understand the message. Dennings out." He fixated on Adriana. "We need to leave here. This week. Check with Bruce which base in the south could take us in."

"How many?"

"We'll leave two companies behind to secure the city. That way we only have to heat one or two of the smaller buildings. I'm so looking forward to sunshine and nice weather."

#

### Jenny — Day 230 (December 7, Donna's Farm, Apache-Sitgreaves National Forest, AZ)

It had taken Jenny and Eduard one day to decide what they wanted: to stay and help to build a new home, at least for the next years. Donna had been willing to accept the 'next couple of years' as not passing through. "How do we know where we all will be in the coming years?" she had said.

Things changed. They were called to meetings, participated in discussions and were included in decisions. It was as if they were now part of the pack. Every other day somebody had news or had heard something, and Jenny wondered where they got it from—after all, there were not that many new people every week.

Winter had been harsh. Cabin fever and food rationing had put additional pressure on the mood until a nice, sunny day in early December when Donna told Jenny and Eduard to stay in the main house while the others were about to leave for their cabins.

"I think it's time to show you something."

They waited until everybody had left, except for Nick who was lurking around in the corner.

"Come." Donna pushed a cabinet to the side beneath the stairs. The cabinet glided smoothly as if it was on rails and a hidden door appeared behind it.

Jenny opened her eyes wide. "I knew there was a door!" She turned to Eduard, but he only shrugged.

Donna opened the door and they all went through the door into a small chamber, just large enough for the four of them. The candlelight gave the scenery a Gothic flair. The door closed silently. Donna opened a door on the other side and Jenny's surprise grew even bigger when bright light glared her.

"You have power here?"

"Only downstairs."

As Jenny's eyes got used to the light she saw a wide staircase going down into a basement. The stairs were cement, but the walls and the ceiling was raw stone. Donna blew the candle out and put it on the first step, next to a lighter that was already lying there.

"But—"

"Later."

Silently, they went downstairs.

"Seventy steps," whispered Eduard when they arrived at the bottom of the stairs.

From there a corridor led twenty feet further and then it turned left. From time to time water was dripping out of the stone from the ceiling or the wall onto stains that must have been there for years.

"This is heading towards the mountain, westwards," whispered Eduard again. "Every twelve feet there's a light. So far we've passed eighty-five lights—we are in the mountain now."

Donna was ahead of them, but Jenny could see her smiling from the side.

Shortly afterwards they stood in front of another door. *This is more like a thick cement block on hinges than a door.* Jenny frowned again. *This is an old bunker!*

Nick swung the door open and the scene changed. They were still in a corridor, but in here the walls were nicely painted and the floor was made from polished cement. Doors were distributed evenly on each side; the word 'Apache' was written on each door, followed by a number. Jenny peeked into the rooms as they passed; most of them were quarters with bunk beds. Towards the end they turned into quarters with single beds and desks. They turned left and Jenny's ears picked up static noise in front of them. Once more they turned left and entered a large hall with all sorts of desks. A large US flag hung on the wall and beneath it three people were sitting in front of machines that appeared ancient to Jenny's eyes. The noise came from these machines.

Eduard had been as silent as Jenny, but now he found his voice again. "What is this place?" He tilted his head.

Donna turned to them. "This is the reason we are only involving some people. When I bought this place twenty years ago to go hunting once in a while, I didn't know about this. I found it by accident when I was digging a trench in the back of the house after a flood. Later I did some research and, apparently, this was an old nuclear shelter for celebrities and high-ranking military. Eighty years ago they had them all across the country before they shut down the majority of them."

Jenny was still gazing around and only listening half-heartedly. She took two steps in the direction of the noise. Maybe she could understand something.

"Don't worry, you'll get enough time to listen. We will need you to cover some shifts, but first let me show you around," said Donna and walked across the hall.

Jenny and Eduard followed her, having a hard time trying not to gaze at every single detail. They entered another corridor and the noise level changed again. *Air conditioning*. When they passed another room, Jenny was surprised to see a server farm in it.

"They still work?" she asked, surprised.

"Without interruption. I severed the connection to the web when all this started because I thought it was a virus or something, but you guys brought me another explanation. Come."

Donna unlocked the door to another room with three workstations and a large screen on the wall. The room was empty and it didn't seem like anybody but Donna came here. She sat down at one of the stations and connected to the screen. A series of pictures from webcams appeared, showing the light cones of a few streetlights which allowed for just a glimpse of deserted streets—except for one, which showed a street full of soldiers where the streetlights were all working. Jenny and Eduard gazed at each other.

Donna stood up and joined the pair. "That's Fairview, Montana, The Holding's headquarters."

"It's not countrywide?" Jenny was the first to find her voice again. "So I was wrong with my theory."

"No, you were perfectly right. What you see here is the miracle of solar power."

In the shine of the screen, Jenny could see Donna smiling at them.

"So this is how you manage to have power here as well? Solar cells?" asked Eduard without taking his eyes off the screen.

"No, this facility was equipped with a small nuclear reactor shortly before it was abandoned: submarine size, designed to work sixty years without refuelling. I guess we'll have power for the next forty years or so. When they left it, they capped the chain reaction but left all the fuel inside. CJ was reactor officer on a submarine and he brought it back to life."

Jenny turned to her. "But why—"

"Why we don't move all the people down here in the winter and have a nice life? Because of them." Donna pointed to the Fairview soldiers on the screen. "They are doing everything they can to regain power. The same people who were responsible for this chaos. I don't trust them. Back in September, they had a battle for power. We could follow it on the radio and, guess what? The Holding won. And you shouldn't trust them either, especially the two of you."

Jenny let her shoulders drop. "You're right, I don't."

"We have to protect this. The fewer people who know the better."

"Thank you for your trust."

"You deserve it. It was your 'insurance policy' that gave us access to the cameras and the data."

"Data? I thought that was all scrambled?" Now Eduard turned around as well.

"It was, but your insurance policy was a log file to unscramble everything, hidden in the moon data center. The policy number was a simple IP address which I could access via satellite. So far we've unscrambled bits and pieces."

"What do the moon crew say about it?"

"Nothing, they probably suffocated months ago." Donna crossed her arms in front of her chest and shrugged. "I'll spare you the pictures."

Jenny looked down and bit on her lips.

Meanwhile Eduard stepped closer to the screen. "What does all this mean?"

"That's what's bugged me since I started getting access. I don't know." Suddenly Donna appeared small and fragile. "My guess is as good as yours. We will see more people starving over the next couple of years as food production will not pick up as quickly as needed, but food distribution will be the bigger problem. People will gather in communities like this or wander around and raid communities like ours."

*There is no way out. How can we survive this?* Jenny's thoughts were galloping. *She can't protect us.*

Donna stared absently at the screen. "Then there's The Holding. They will try to get their hands on the food and the industry.

They will need more forces to control it, but they can only afford to feed so many soldiers. The rest of the weapons will end up with warlords. However, they won't be able to supply them with enough food, so they will allow them to procure their own food—again, more raids... We will soon start seeing raids around here as well."

Jenny looked up. Something on the screen had caught Donna's attention and she enlarged one of the webcam views. There was movement right outside one of the streetlight cones. Two men were fighting—no, three men, more. One man with a backpack got pushed into the light and five men surrounded him. One of the others tried to wrest the backpack from him. The guy tried to defend himself, but before he could do anything they stabbed him in the back. Jenny gasped and took Eduard's hand. He squeezed it. One of the attackers opened the backpack and rummaged around in it, only to throw it away and kick the body of the dead guy.

"That's what will happen," said Donna into the silence. "Be prepared to spend some time down here." She switched to another picture that showed a picture of a landscape from far above, like the satellite pictures they knew from before the blackout.

"I found a satellite that provides pictures of Arizona. I guess they used it to detect immigrants." Donna zoomed in until a ridge came up. "We are here." She pointed to the screen and pressed a button on the keyboard; the color of the picture changed. "Normal and thermal—that's our surveillance of the area. We need somebody down here around the clock. You can start tonight."

#

*Jenny — Day 271 (January 17, Donna's Farm, Apache-*
*Sitgreaves National Forest, AZ)*

Jenny was glad that she and Eduard were allowed to do their shifts together; it meant spending 24 hours in the computer room and the quarters downstairs before they could go up again. Twenty-four hours was a long time, but at least they got sleep and the chance to have sex.

It had been a while—years actually—since her dad had left the family. She had always wondered why Eduard had not left her in that time. She had been obnoxious and she felt sorry about it. At least now she had time to make it up. Also, Eduard seemed less angry with the world.

The days they did not spend underground, they were either out on food procurement trips or helping around the farm. There was always something to do, only this time Jenny and Eduard were leading the efforts and they had passing-through people working for them.

It felt good, until one food procurement trip ran into a warlord.

# CHAPTER FOUR

# Rooster Searches

*Jenny – Day 272 (January 18,*
*East of Apache-Sitgreaves National Forest, AZ)*

A branch almost hit her, but at the last second she saw it coming in the moonlight and ducked. The next one hit her face. Jenny stumbled, but Eduard caught her. Pain flashed through her ankle.

"Come on. Faster." CJ was ten feet ahead, a little further uphill, glancing back at them.

It was hard to tell where they were. The foggy night swallowed a lot. Jenny only knew that they were in a different part of the forest with lower trees and more thickets.

Jenny got back on her feet. She and Eduard had a hard time catching up with CJ, but not as hard a time as Jason.

"I think we got rid of them," said Jason with something between a wheeze and a gasp. He stopped and peeked back over his shoulder.

CJ paused for a second. "No, we have to get further away."

He turned around again and rushed further ahead. Jenny and Eduard followed, hearing Jason swearing behind them. Jenny's ankle hurt with every step on the uneven ground. She pressed her lips together and continued. Only a little further up and they would reach the crest.

"Shh..." CJ signalled them to duck.

Jenny and Eduard got down on their knees. The ground felt moist and wet. Behind them Jason breathed like a horse. Jenny couldn't see CJ anymore. He must have lain down—yes, there at the crest. She wanted to whisper something to Eduard, but she was interrupted by voices right behind the crest.

"These were all the runners you were able to catch today?" asked a male voice.

*How did they get ahead of us? Or are these different ones?* flashed through Jenny's mind, closely followed by *Hope they haven't found Tank and Max.*

Another guy said something Jenny couldn't understand. She only wished Jason would breathe more quietly. From far away she heard dogs barking. CJ raised his head a little, watching the guys talking behind the crest.

"I bet there's a burrow somewhere out here. There are too many catches to be a coincidence."

The voices disappeared but CJ signalled them to stay down. Jenny started to shiver and Eduard put his coat around her shoulders. She looked gratefully at him and whispered, "I just hope Tank and Max made it to the meeting point."

It had cooled down a lot. She could see her breath when she exhaled. After a while CJ got up and they sneaked along the crest, away from where the voices had disappeared to, always ready to duck down again.

Half an hour later they reached the meeting point and Jenny was glad to see Tank and Max had made it as well. She could even see a hint of relief on CJ's face.

"Let's go. We have to keep moving, down to the creek. We have to lose our scent."

Ducking, they hastened towards the creek. Jenny was out of breath when they neared it twenty minutes later.

CJ stopped. "We'll go down first, then we'll cross. I hope you don't mind getting wet feet. Tank, you'll have to carry Max."

They continued to rush along the creek for another half hour until CJ abruptly turned and walked into it. The others followed. The water only reached to their knees, but it was ice cold. Jenny was shivering before they reached the other side.

CJ was already out of the water when he told the others to stay. "Tank, you're with me. We'll be back in five minutes."

Tank climbed out of the water and they disappeared into the bushes next to the creek. A little more than five minutes later they returned, backwards, and they didn't turn around until they were back with the others in the creek.

Jenny thought her feet would fall off and the cold of the water crept up her legs.

"That should throw them off for a while. Now, let's go. The faster we go, the sooner we'll be out again." CJ started wading upstream.

Jenny bit on her teeth and followed, hurrying to get to CJ.

"Who are they?" she asked.

"Shh..." he hissed over his shoulder.

Jenny nodded, still trying to keep up.

"I don't know. Warlords. We've seen it before, but this is different. It's as if they were looking for something or someone. Now all: quiet and move."

Jenny let herself fall back until she joined Eduard.

It seemed to her they were wading forever. Most of the time the water only reached their ankles, but at some points it was even above their knees. Still, CJ wouldn't allow them to climb out—not until right before a series small falls.

Hours later they reached the farm and everybody but CJ and Tank reported to the infirmary. Jenny was more than happy when they were assigned a shift downstairs the day after. At least it was warm there.

#

*Eduard — Day 305 (February 20, Donna's Farm, Apache-Sitgreaves National Forest, AZ)*

Donna stared at the screen with a stony expression on her face. The camera showed multiple troops moving around right outside the first perimeter she had set as the threshold for system alerts. Eduard tried to guess what she was thinking.

"They've never been this close. That's less than ten miles away," said Nick, who stood next to her. Donna didn't react.

Jenny poked Eduard and whispered, "They're combing through the woods, but what are they looking for?"

"She's right." Donna frowned. Eduard had the impression that this was what she had been pondering. She turned to Nick. "You are sure our food scouts didn't leave any tracks?"

"CJ assured me that they're only using the creek to get in and out of the perimeter, and they're only going south—no more searches in the north. He knows what he's doing."

Jenny stood up and got closer to the screen. Donna watched her and tilted her head. "You're asking the right question, Jenny. If they were looking for us, they could be much more efficient. Their movements are far too small-meshed to be searching for a group of people. They are looking for one single man." She pressed her lips together and blew air through her nose. "Nevertheless, they'll reach the farm in a week. We need to prepare."

Eduard was watching Jenny and saw how her shoulders had dropped with every word Donna said. With Donna's last words she turned around. "What can we do? There must be dozens of men."

Donna tried to maintain her posture, but Eduard noticed that her shoulders were not as high as they usually were.

"Have CJ sidle behind their lines and capture one of them. We need to know who they're looking for," said Donna to Nick.

He nodded and left. Donna frowned back at the screen and Jenny and Eduard looked at her. After a while she said to herself, "We need to warn the people. Whoever wants to leave should leave now." She added to Jenny and Eduard, "You and everybody else who knows about this place will hide down here. Nick and I will deal with them."

Eduard glared at the screen. *These assholes destroy everything.*

#

*Jenny — Day 320 (March 7, Donna's Farm, Apache-Sitgreaves National Forest, AZ)*

Jenny felt her pulse in her throat. Her eyes flicked between the screen and the paper in front of them, unsure which was worse. Everybody in the room was deathly silent. Tank and Jason sat on chairs, both with their arms crossed in front of their chests. Two couples had not been able to bear the pictures and had left the room.

The paper had been crumpled and ripped on two sides. It contained five names and pretty accurate descriptions: her dad, her mom, Eduard, herself and somebody else. Jenny had guessed that it was Niklas, although his description did not fit him well.

She swallowed empty. *This is all because of me!* The flames were still blazing high, but she could see that the fire had already passed its zenith. Even though her view was blurred with her tears, she could still see the dead bodies in front of each of the farm's buildings, or rather what remained of them. She counted twelve bodies. Donna was right outside the main building and Nick lay next to her. They had been the first to go down, but they didn't stop with them. CJ was away getting food with Max, but Jenny wasn't sure if he had been able to help or if he was dead by now as well.

She couldn't tell who they were from the satellite camera. Some were moving like CJ did, nimble and precise. Others just ran and shot around. Ultimately, they had made sure that there were no witnesses; they had dragged everybody out of the buildings and shot them one by one. Two women, who had refused to leave, had been raped repeatedly before they shot them. "They won't shoot a pregnant woman," Jenny could still hear one of them saying.

Eduard was holding Jenny tightly and pressing his head against hers.

She closed her eyes. *What shall we do now? What can we do against such animals?*

#

*Dennings — Day 335 (March 22, Holloman Air Force Base, NM)*

Dennings leaned back and smirked. Sweat was running down his back and he could feel the moist patches under his arms. He had welcomed the warmth of the New Mexico Air Force Base back in November, but now with the March heat he was longing to get back to Montana. A month after he had arrived he had switched his suit for a uniform. There was no chance of keeping nice and clean without air conditioning. But more than the heat, he hated the dust.

A map was lying on the table in front of him and soldiers and corporals were moving toy flags, tanks and buildings around. As soon as the toys were placed, the military staff moved into the background again. Dennings stood up. Adriana, Frank and Bruce were sitting on the other side of the table and it was as if you could smell the testosterone wafting through the room.

"So, no more fights among warlords anymore?" Dennings squinted. Sweat ran into his eyes and gave him a burning sensation.

Clutsky shook his head. "You were right. Getting rid of that Kentucky warlord was a message they understood."

Dennings held the paper with the description of Niklas in his hand and gazed over the map; a bold red line along the Appalachian Mountains separated the eastern part of the country from the rest. He looked at Clutsky. "You're sure he's not hiding there?" Dennings pointed to the Eastern Seaboard.

Clutsky sighed. "No, I'm not, but I am sure if he was hiding there he would be dead by now. I sent in ten teams. Only two men came back and they survived barely long enough to tell us anything at all."

Dennings nodded.

"But the rest of the country is clear. The warlords searched every single acre from here to the Canadian border. They thought that they had a lead on the mother in the north-east, but they couldn't confirm. Other than that, none of them are in the country anymore."

Dennings stopped nodding and leaned forward again. "We need to search again."

"Again?" Clutsky rubbed his neck. "I'm not sure if those idiots will do it again if we just ask. They'd rather come back after a while and lie to me."

"Then how do you know they haven't lied to you already?" threw in Adriana, causing Dennings to smirk again while Clutsky threw her an evil eye.

"He doesn't," said Dennings calmly, "but he also doesn't have to. We just need to increase the bounty. Make them an offer they can't refuse."

Clutsky shrugged. "Like what?"

"A tank." Bruce leaned back as well, carefully looking at Dennings.

"Are you crazy? I'll have them on my back afterwards!" Clutsky jumped up.

"Calm down. We don't have to give it to them, or we'll just give them old crap. It needs too much gas for them anyways. It will be useless." Bruce was still looking at Dennings.

"Fine. Just get me results." Dennings stood up and studied the map from above.

Adriana watched his expression and tilted her head. "What if they actually left the country?"

"Then we need to expand the search. What do we know about the situation abroad?"

Bruce glanced at one of the corporals; the corporal stepped forward and handed him a briefcase. Bruce opened it and got some papers out. "We've been trying to connect with outposts, but we didn't get further than filtering the information out of the background noise of the radio." He looked at the papers. "Russia, China and Europe are as chaotic as we are, but unlike here it seems that those countries are completely under the control of warlords."

"You mean they have access to the nuclear weapons?" Adriana opened her eyes wide.

"Potentially, but they have neither the knowledge nor the capabilities to launch one—not yet. And I doubt it would find its target. However, we have to consider it as a potential future threat."

Dennings didn't lose his cool demeanor, but the thought of the contamination in his hometown, Phoenix, gave him an instant headache. "Bruce, you need to keep an eye on that."

Bruce glanced again at the corporal and only seconds later he got handed another piece of paper.

"Now, in Latin America the situation is a little different. The old aristocratic upper class always had their methods of keeping control—it seems they just re-established the death squadrons. It's a little chaotic in the Chaco around Paraguay, but overall they are holding up."

"Good, let's see what we can bribe them with. Bruce, why don't you offer them gold?"

Bruce nodded. Dennings got up and walked out, shadowed by Adriana.

#

*Niklas — Day 360 (April 16, Cuzco, Peru)*

Niklas could feel his pulse in his temples. He turned around; Marcella was right behind him. The duffle bag weighed heavy on his back and the thin air made him pant. The dust and sweet smell of garbage didn't make it better.

"Hurry. And stay out of the streetlight," said Ezequiel with a shouting whispering voice.

He stood at the corner and waved at them, alternately looking at them and peeking around the corner. Despite the dim light, Niklas recognized the that they were at the corner to a larger square.

"It's not far and then you're safe," Ezequiel added when they reached him.

Niklas needed a moment to get his breathing under control. "Where are we going? I can't run anymore. The air..." The urge to breathe cut him off. *This is how it must feel when you suffocate.* The stone wall of the house he was leaning on emitted the warmth it had absorbed during the day.

"Palacio de la Justicia. I tell you, there is no safer place in Cuzco than the court. Half of the rooms are empty and I know the janitor." Ezequiel smirked.

Marcella, still panting, hadn't been able to utter a word yet, but she had to smile at Ezequiel's comment.

Niklas raised his eyebrows.

"The safest place... for fugitives... is the court." Marcella slowly recovered.

Ezequiel peeked around the corner again. "Let's go."

They ducked and ran across the street. For a moment they dived into the orange of the streetlights. Behind them Niklas heard barking. *They have dogs—I didn't see dogs when the soldiers spotted us.* He shook his head. *No, those are dogs fighting each other.* They reached the back of a large white building with brownish blocks on the corners. The windows on the first floor were secured with cast-iron grids. Ezequiel took a pebble from the ground and threw it. It clicked when it hit a window on the second floor. He repeated the action, and just as he was getting ready to throw a third stone the window opened.

"Wait," hissed a voice in Spanish from above and a minute later a heavy door opened ten feet away from them. They rushed in and Niklas and Marcella hurriedly followed Ezequiel and the other guy through a dark and damp corridor to the basement, until they reached a room with two cots and a bunk bed. A single lightbulb and the orange streetlight entering through a small window under the ceiling transformed the room into a gloomy dungeon. Across from the wall with the window, a door opened into another room, but Niklas couldn't see where it led.

"You can stay here for a couple of days. Thursday night I will bring you to the train and ship you off to Bolivia, but it's gonna be a rough ride."

Niklas was still breathing heavily, but the other guy caught his attention; he switched between looking at them and gazing down the corridor. His right foot pointed towards the corridor as if he wanted to run away. In his hand he held a red plastic bag which dangled next to his leg. Every time the guy turned his head back from the corridor to face the group, his eyes went first to Marcella. After the third time he noticed Niklas frowning and lowered his eyes before he turned back to the corridor.

"Stay away from the window—Plaza de Armas is right outside there. Tomasz will bring you food and water at night." Ezequiel turned to the other guy and pointed to the plastic bag.

"Tomasz."

Tomasz startled and looked at Ezequiel, who was still pointing to the plastic bag.

"*Perdon.*" Tomasz handed the bag to Niklas. "*Pan, queso y agua.*"

Niklas scanned the content of the bag; it had bread, cheese and water, but it didn't seem as if it was fresh from the grocery store. He took Ezequiel to the side. "You're sure we're safe here? I don't like the way he looks at Marcella."

"It's the best place right now and he knows that if something happens to you he will be held responsible."

Niklas pressed his lips together as they turned back to the others.

Tomasz went over to Ezequiel and said something, almost whispering. Ezequiel took a bundle of money out of his pocket and gave some to Tomasz.

"Let me pay for that," said Niklas and grabbed for his pocket.

Ezequiel quickly turned towards him, covering Tomasz' view of Niklas. "Never," he squinted at Niklas, "never show him that you have anything of value—not him, not anybody."

Niklas' eyes widened. Ezequiel's face turned normal again. He hugged Niklas and Marcella. "*Surete*—good luck."

The two men left. The door closed with a metallic *dang* and they heard it being locked from the outside. Marcella looked at Niklas and in the orange light he could see her smirking sarcastically.

"Bunk bed, upper level. For the first time I'm really glad that you have those sleeping bags."

"I hope there's a bathroom behind that door." Niklas pointed to the other door.

Marcella marched towards it. "Let's find out." She opened the door and switched on the light, just to switch it off again. She turned around and closed the door.

"No?" Niklas raised his eyebrows.

A shudder went through her body. "Yes, but..." She closed her mouth again and took a breath. "I might go in there, just because I have to, but no way am I taking a shower or even washing myself in there."

#

*Jenny — Day 363 (April 19, East of Apache-Sitgreaves National Forest, AZ)*

Jenny could barely breathe with the weight of CJ's body on top of her. "Eduard!" she wanted to shout, but only a whimper came out through CJ's hand covering her mouth.

"Shh," he hissed.

Her eyes remained on Eduard's body. She could see his face through the bushes. The moonlight gave the scenery a hideous touch. This food-finding expedition had let them to the most eastern corner of the forest and they hadn't realized how close they were to a warlord's camp.

*Move! Show me that you're alive!* she begged silently.

His eyes remained closed.

"Bring that one to the base. Let's see what we can get out of him," said one of the guys standing next to Eduard. He had a bulky shape and his bald head stood out from the others.

"Is this one of them?" asked another one, smaller, with a high voice.

"No." The bulky guy spat on the ground. "I don't know. Who can tell? They all look alike."

Max must have taken cover somewhere behind them, out of Jenny's sight. A rustle next to them startled her and if it had not been for CJ's weight she would have jumped. Three men joined the group in front of them.

"Nobody else? I heard multiple voices: one woman and one guy." The bulky guy spat again. "This will cost you dinner. He knows they're never alone. They flock, and if we only bring back one there will be no dinner for the three of you."

"Why us?" protested one of the three other guys. He was the smallest of them and had a bushy beard.

"I found this one. Somebody must take the blame."

The bearded guy didn't reply. The two men behind him ducked a little with their arms and legs slightly angled, like cats awaiting a fight. It would have seemed as if time had frozen if it wasn't for the breath vaporizing in front of their mouths.

Jenny blinked. *Did Eduard just move? He moved!* Again, he slightly moved his arm.

"Good," said the bulky guy looking down at Eduard. "That way we don't have to carry him."

As if this was a signal, the bearded guy grabbed something from his waist. A gun.

*Don't shoot him!* flashed through Jenny's mind.

He had the gun only half raised when the movement lost its power. He fell to his knees and forward onto his face, accompanied by a sound that started with something like "Aaaarrrgh" and ended in a blubber.

With the bearded guy out of their line of sight, they saw the knife in the hand of the one behind him.

"Now you deserve dinner." The bulky guy chuckled. "Get him up. He'll be awake soon."

They put a jute bag over Eduard's head and lifted him up. His head was dangling when they moved away.

#

*Eduard — Day 363 (April 19, Camp east of Apache-Sitgreaves National Forest, AZ)*

It had been a long time since Eduard had sat in a car, or rather a motorized vehicle. His head was throbbing and the ties around his wrists cut into his flesh. He tried to distract himself from the pain. Judging by the noise and how cold it was, he figured that he had to be in something like an open truck, half covered by some tarp. He could see contours and silhouettes through the jute bag. It was hard to recognize anything, but he could hear the tarp flapping in the headwind. There were people around him. Nobody was talking, but he could see the glow of cigarettes from time to time: two of them. Was Jenny somewhere in here with them? He tried to whisper her name, but as soon as he did he got hit on the head with something hard.

When he came round again he tasted blood in his mouth. He was being carried on somebody's back. He turned his head left and right; he could see more now as the outside was lit up by spotlights. Multiple mobile lamps lit up something that looked like a car park. People were hastening around without actually running—all in some kind of uniform, but all of them different. In the back he thought he made out tents.

Then they entered a house. He was thrown to the floor and left alone again. He could hear the door being locked. Was he really alone? *Somebody is here, somebody else.* "Who are you?" Eduard tried to sit up.

"A friend," said a soft and clear voice to his left—a man—but the way he said it did not sound nice at all.

Eduard turned his head. "If you're a friend then get this off."

A chair moved and steps came closer. The cover was removed from his head and Eduard had to cough first before he looked up at the guy. His eyes needed a moment to adapt to the bright light. In the meantime, the man had sat back on his chair and crossed his legs.

He wore a full dress uniform that was well kept. It even had creases. Still, it was far too big for his stature; only his head seemed to be in proportion to the uniform. Another guy was standing at the door, tall and hulking. His bulging lips, on which he was chewing, made his appearance coarser. In one of the corners of the room they had bread and water on a table, but the bread looked old and the water had a brownish shimmer.

The floor felt cold through Eduard's jeans. "Remove the shackles."

"Na na. I made the first step—now let's talk." The man folded his hands as if he wanted to pray.

Eduard clenched his jaw. "Want do you want? I have nothing." *I need to know if they have Jenny.*

"Let's start with the simple questions first. Where are you staying?"

"Nowhere. I've been wandering around. I tried to get back home to Vermont but others have told me that it's contaminated. Now I'm trying to go west."

The man raised his eyebrows. "Really? Then where are your bags?"

"I have none. All I have is what I wear."

"Hmm." The guy stood up and walked over to the window. "Where did you stay last?" he asked, looking out. The bright light of spotlights created a corona around his head.

Eduard's thoughts were dashing. *How do I make believe?* His head jerked back almost unnoticeably. "I haven't stayed anywhere for a long time. I was just wandering around, sleeping in sheds or huts." *I have to give him something.*

The guy hemmed again, still looking out of the window.

"Can you remove the shackles now?" asked Eduard.

He chuckled. "Well, it depends." His bulging lips formed something like a sneer.

"On what?" Eduard felt his heartbeat in his throat.

The guy sighed. "On when you stop lying to me."

"I didn't lie," Eduard yelled.

The guy turned around. Any friendliness had gone from his eyes. "Your clothes are well maintained—nice shoes, by the way. You are well fed, you must have shaved in the last couple of days and you've had enough to drink."

Eduard glared at him. "And how would you know that?"

"If you were hungry or thirsty your eyes would barely see anything else than that table over there." The guy sat down again.
"Now, why don't we try this again? Where are you staying?"

"Nowhere."

"I see I won't get any further. How about I answer a question
from you and then you answer one of mine? Do you have any
questions for me?"

Eduard bit on his lips, evading eye contact.

"Not one? I would have thought you'd have dozens of questions, like who am I, what is this place or have we got the girl as
well?"

Eduard felt his heart freeze. *They have Jenny and Max. Do
they? Are they still alive?* He tried to jump up, but his bonds made
him fall again. The cement floor scratched his cheek.

The guy laughed with his clear voice. "Don't worry. She's fine.
She's in the infirmary: sprained her ankle but she will be fine.
Now, where are you staying?"

Eduard sat up again. His cheek started to feel moist and he
tried to wipe it off on his shoulder. *I have to start answering
something. They have Jenny.* He fixated on the floor in front of
him and mumbled something even he had a hard time understanding.

"Where?"

"At a farm somewhere by a mountain. East of Phoenix. Somebody burned it down."

"Ahh, the farm. Funny, we have a patrol there every week and
they haven't picked up anything."

Eduard waited a second, putting every word on a balance. "I
know, every Wednesday afternoon between three and five in the

afternoon. They're always picking on each other like an old couple. Sometimes they just shoot around for fun."

"Hmm, that is pretty dumb indeed." The guy stood up and got a chair from the table and placed it in front of him. "Sit. The floor must be cold."

As if the guy at the door had received an order, he came over, picked Eduard up and sat him on the chair.

"Thank you for answering my question. Now, do you have any?"

"Who are you?"

The hulking guy was still standing right behind Eduard, which made his hackles rise. He could almost feel him with the back of his head.

"We are the law enforcement company out here. This whole thing shook up everything and they were looking for volunteers to make sure there's still law and order out here. See, we even have badges." He showed Eduard a badge of the Coconino County Police. "I admit, they are still a little mixed up, but we don't complain."

"And you're their boss?"

"Na na na, now it's my turn with a question. Who are you?"

"E...rich, Erich Bloomington."

"Well then E...rich." The guy stood up. "Thank you for the nice chat." He walked towards the door. Eduard followed him with his eyes as far as he could. When he reached the door, he turned around. "Let me talk to the others over at the infirmary. Maybe your girl is in more of a sharing mood."

Eduard wanted to jump up, but the hulking guy's hand landed on his shoulder and pressed him down. "Wait."

"Is there something you wanted to tell me, like your real name?"

Eduard closed his eyes and let his shoulders drop. "Eduard."

"See how nicely this goes." He came back and sat down again on his chair. "You still haven't told me why your clothes are well maintained and why you are so well fed. That burned-down farm doesn't explain a lot."

#

*Eduard — Day 363 (April 19, Camp east of Apache-Sitgreaves National Forest, AZ)*

From *I need to protect Jen*, Eduard was only able to think *Jen* until the next punch hit him. His head flew back and the chair tipped over. He made a hollow with his back and absorbed a part of the fall. Still, when the back of his head hit the cement, he lost his vision for a moment.

"I hate to have him hurt you," said the guy with the clear voice.

Eduard kept his eyes closed, even when he was grabbed by the shoulder and put back on the chair. He didn't have to look; he knew it was the squatty guy. Blood ran down his nose, inside and outside. He couldn't feel his cheek anymore. His body cramped, expecting the next punch, but nothing happened. After a couple of seconds Eduard opened his eyes again. The squatty guy stood in front of him with his hands at his belt and a greasy smirk on his face.

The other guy came over.

"I've told you everything." Eduard swallowed blood.

"You have to help me. I want to believe you, I really do, but I have to report all the details to my boss and he is not as patient as I am."

"Everything."

The squatty guy had moved behind the chair again and Eduard expected another hit any second.

"How is it possible that your clothes are so fresh and that you are so... clean? Your nails are clipped. Hell, you even smell like you had a bubble bath."

The door behind Eduard opened.

"Ah, the master is here," said the guy with the clear voice. "Dan." He nodded to the squatty guy.

Eduard closed his eyes and his body cramped again in expectation of a blow, but it didn't happen. Instead the squatty guy grabbed his left arm and tied it to the armrest of the chair. Wire straps cut into his flesh. Eduard opened his eyes. The guy cut the wire straps that bonded his hands together. Eduard tried to push the guy away, but it ended up more like a helpless wave. Eventually the squatty guy grabbed his second arm and tied it to the other armrest.

"Thanks for your help, Dan. Get something to eat and a drink." The clear voice cut through the air like a knife through vapor.

The squatty guy mumbled something and Eduard could feel him leaving his back. He turned his head to see who had entered, but the person remained outside his view. He could only see the squatty guy stomping out. It was silent after the door closed, but Eduard's hackles rose again. The other guy was coming closer. Eduard couldn't hear him; he just saw a shadow moving and a reflection in the corner of his eyes.

"Eduard, I want you to meet Yelena."

*This isn't a guy. It's a woman.*

Somebody grabbed the chair and turned it around. Eduard looked close-up into staring green eyes surrounded by crow's feet, tattooed eyebrows and eye bags. The smell of smoke in her breath made him nauseous and he turned his head away.

She stood and sneered down at him, her head tilted a little. He tried to stare back, but he couldn't hold her gaze. Then, with a fast movement, she grabbed his hand and tried to get hold of the middle finger, but he clenched his hand into a fist. She pressed her fingernail into his thumbnail right at the point where it went under the skin and pain flashed through his arm. He immediately opened his fist and she managed to fix the middle finger on the armrest with a wire strap.

A smile went over her face and she stood back, breathing heavily.

*She enjoys this.* Eduard tried to free his finger, but the more he tried the more it hurt, and her smile broadened into a grin.

The woman straightened up and picked up a bag that was leaning against the wall. "You know, my mother was a seamstress," she said without looking at Eduard.

He couldn't classify her accent; it could be Russian, but it could also be German.

"Do you know what a seamstress is?" she asked when she turned back to Eduard with a small box. "She was a pious woman. Devoted to worship and rigorous in the education of her seven children. I was the youngest one."

*That is definitively a Slavic accent*, he thought. *What was her name again? Yelena?*

She came closer, supporting her weight on his arms tied to the armrest. He smelled her breath again, but this time he detected a hint of whiskey through the tobacco. He could see the irregularities of her face.

"I hated her. She used to torture me with the needles when I was naughty," she whispered into his ear. "And I was often naughty."

A silent chuckle came out of her mouth and Eduard could feel the warm breath against his ear.

"With time I didn't feel it anymore," she added when she got back up again. "But don't worry, we won't get that far." She opened the box, took out a small needle.

He stared at the needle. *What is she going to do with that?* The needle came close to his finger and he tried to evade the contact, but the wire straps did not yield. The needle touched his finger right between the fingernail and the nail bed.

And then she pushed it into his finger—only a little, only the tip of the needle, but a wave of pain flushed through Eduard's body. He screamed in a mix of pain and surprise and bucked. The chair almost fell over. His fingers tried to bend and blood came out beneath the wire strap, but he didn't feel any pain from that. There was only the pain of the needle.

After a moment that felt like minutes, he got used to it. That's when she pushed the needle a little further in, and this time the chair fell over from his uncontrolled writhing.

#

*Jenny — Day 364 (April 20, Camp east of Apache-Sitgreaves National Forest, AZ)*

Jenny pored over the camp. She lay on the ridge of a hillock two hundred feet away. With the floodlights on, she had a clear view of the barracks and tents as well as the motor pool. Somewhere down there was Eduard. And now CJ too; he had been gone almost twelve hours and Jenny was scared they'd got him as well. He had left her and Max behind.

"It's safer this way," he had said, followed by one of the most frightening sentences she had heard so far: "You leave with him if I'm not back within twelve hours."

Max was sleeping next to her, snuggling close to her body to keep warm. The ground was wet; the heat of the day had gone soon after nightfall.

There had been movement the entire day long. People were coming and going from the camp and moving large equipment around, but there was no sign of either Eduard or CJ. It had started to rain, cold rain. Jenny was glad the trees gave them at least a little coverage.

"Pst."

Jenny looked around. CJ crawled towards them from behind.

A short feeling of relief was followed by worry. "Is he there?" Jenny's voice was trembling.

CJ crawled the last few inches. "Yes. They're questioning him in the barracks over there."

"Questioning him?" Her mouth felt dry and CJ's words reverberated in her head.

"Or rather interrogating him. But he is alive."

"How can we get him out?"

CJ pressed his lips together. "I'm not sure. It will be hard with this many people around—it took me half a day to get in and out unseen." He glanced at Jenny. "Maybe when they go for another raid."

"That could be days! By then he might be dead. He might already be..."

"Shh..." CJ peeked around with a worried look in his eyes. "He's not dead. From what I've heard they want our hideout."

Fear spread over her face. "He'll never tell them. They'll kill him," she whispered.

CJ wasn't listening anymore; something in the camp had caught his attention.

"We need to rescue him," Jenny hissed.

He waved her off.

"What is it?" Jenny stretched her head to see more.

"They're gearing up the engines." He was right. Jenny could now hear the roaring sound of the trucks and see people running around, jumping into the cargo areas of the moving trucks. It was like a parade that passed Jenny and CJ until the camp was deserted.

"I'll be back," he said and disappeared into the night.

Max moved a little his eyes still closed.

"He's going to get Eduard." Jenny caressed Max's hair and added, speaking more to herself, "I hope."

\#

*Jenny — Day 364 (April 20, Camp east of Apache-Sitgreaves National Forest, AZ)*

It was the longest hour Jenny had ever experienced. Twice she had seen CJ moving between the buildings, like a shadow, but that was forty minutes ago. Her eyes already hurt from staring at the deserted camp.

"Pst." The whisper came out of the trees behind them.

Jenny turned around and saw CJ standing behind a tree, waving at them. Her heart jumped. He was carrying somebody on his shoulders. *Eduard! Is it...? It has to be.* She got up and ran over to CJ, closely followed by Max.

Her heart jumped again when she reached them, but this time it felt more like it was jumping off a cliff. Eduard's face was covered in dry blood. "Is he...?"

"He's alive, but they tortured him hard."

"Tort—?"

"Later. Let's go." CJ started to move. He was fast and Jenny had a hard time following. Even Max, who was usually the swiftest, had problems keeping up. The gap between them got larger and larger until CJ finally stopped at an old stable. Jenny had completely lost track of time, but it felt like it had been longer than half an hour. It had rained for a moment, but now the sky was getting lighter, announcing the coming morning. He leaned Eduard against the wall. "We'll get cover here."

Jenny walked to the front of the stable. "It's locked."

"Come back. We'll get in here."

When she turned around the corner, he had already pulled away two boards from the wall and was dragging Eduard inside. Max and Jenny followed and CJ mounted the boards again from inside. It was dark inside and a smell of moist wood lay in the air. The only thing Jenny could discern in the dim light was a ladder to something like an upper floor.

"We have to get dry." He put Eduard back on his shoulder and climbed upstairs.

Max and Jenny followed and were surprised that the upstairs was dry and clean. CJ removed four boards from what seemed to be the back wall, clearing the way to a small compartment—three feet wide and ten feet long—which contained several metal boxes and a worn-out mattress. CJ pulled the ladder up and closed the hatch.

"Get out of your clothes." He turned to the metal boxes and opened one of them. After a glance into the box he opened another one and took out military clothes.

Jenny tilted her head.

"Always have a Plan B that includes shelter and supplies." CJ smirked. "Now, I'll turn around. Just get something dry on and then we'll do the same for Eduard."

Jenny nodded and changed. Max changed as well and sat down by the wall peeking out through a covered hole. It almost seemed like it wasn't his first time in the cabin. The new clothes felt good and the world suddenly didn't seem as bad anymore. In the meantime, CJ had laid Eduard down on the bed and started to undress him. Jenny helped. Tears welled up at the sight of his wounds and injuries, and the more she saw the more tears rolled down her cheeks.

"He will survive. Don't worry." CJ tried to smile. "A week and he'll be back."

After they had put fresh clothes on Eduard, CJ changed as well. Jenny sat beside Eduard, caressing his hair. "Has he been unconscious the whole time?"

"No, he was awake when I found him. He passed out on the way."

"Did he say anything?"

CJ was closing his belt and looking down. "We can't go back. He told them about the bunker."

Jenny almost jumped up. "Never!"

Max startled and looked frightened at CJ, who put a finger in front of his lips and threw Jenny a warning look.

"He would never do that." Jenny lowered her voice to a hissing whisper. "You know that."

CJ pressed his lips together and said calmly, "Everyone has a breaking point. You do, I do and he did as well."

"You're wrong." Her voice got firmer and his eyes got that warning expression again.

He sat next to her. "Did you see his hands?" He took Eduard's hand and showed her his fingernails.

She narrowed her eyes and felt cold again. The last joint of each of the fingers was swollen up and the nails were bloodshot from the tip to the base in a triangle shape.

"What is this?"

"An old torture technique. They push needles up your finger beneath your nail. Doesn't do a lot of damage, but the pain is unbearable."

She contemplated Eduard with mournful eyes.

"But I think pain wasn't his breaking point." CJ showed her the other hand and it had the same marks on all the fingers. "They made him believe they had you, and after what they did to him, he had to protect you. That's what he said: he had to protect you."

CJ's words felt like weights on her chest. "What now?" She was tempted to say she wanted to stay. *But we can't stay. We can't stay anywhere. There is no place to hide. Not for us.*

CJ glanced over to Max. "I have an idea, but I need to think about it. For the time being we stay here, but we have to be careful. As soon as Eduard can walk again we have to move on." He stood up. "Get some sleep. Max will take the first shift and I will take the next one. You can take the afternoon."

#

*Dennings — Day 368 (April 24, Donna's Farm, Apache-Sitgreaves National Forest, AZ)*

Dennings hurried through the corridors of the Apache bunker, passing dead bodies and blood-covered walls.

"This way."

Bruce was leading the way. Adriana was right behind him. They turned into a large hall with two radio stations on the wall. The radios were still receiving signals, only the operators could not listen anymore. Their lifeless bodies were hanging in the chairs or lying on the floor. They turned into a small corridor, passed another door and there it was: a large screen with webcams showing several different places. Dennings stepped closer to the Fairview webcam and turned around with his eyes wide open. Adriana sat down behind the console and started to type.

"It's the moon data center. It's fully operational. This is a miracle—we have access to everything. Here." She pulled another picture up on the screen, showing the deck of a catamaran aircraft carrier. "Say hello to the USS *L.J. Gibbs*." The two flight decks were deserted and it seemed to be going at full speed through rough seas.

"Can we contact them?" Bruce turned to Adriana.

"No, their computer systems were impacted as well; the on-deck camera has a fixed address. Wait. That's it..." Adriana started typing again. Her eyes were glued to the screen and her body was stiff; only her fingers flew over the keyboard. "That guy is a genius," she muttered after a while. "Five satellites have been restored so far."

"Who?" asked Bruce absently.

Adriana didn't answer right away. "That Niklas guy," she said after a moment.

"He was here?" Dennings turned around on one foot.

She tilted her head without taking her eyes off the screen in front of her. "No. At least, I don't know. The restoration of the data was done by a woman, Donna."

Dennings frowned, thinking of a former CIO of The Holding. *Could it be? Funny, how you always meet twice—almost, at least.*

"One second." Adriana raised one finger. With a last tap on the keyboard, a chat window came up on the large screen. '<JEN-SEN>USS L.J. Gibbs, this is Secretary Jensen. Do you copy?' She jumped up and stood next to Dennings. "I know what happened."

He tilted his head and raised one eyebrow.

She smirked and sat down again at the keyboard. "He did nothing but scramble the data."

"Scramble?" asked Bruce.

"Yes, copy-pasted entries around, exchanged my Social Security Number with yours, the USS *L.J. Gibbs'* mainframe address with the address of the coffee machine in your vacation rental, the coding schematics of the New York traffic light controls with the security procedures of the Indian Point Nuclear Power Plant. Do you need more?"

Bruce was still making a face as if he was looking for a light switch. "Shouldn't there be security?"

She made big eyes. "Ohhh, there was a lot of security. Passwords, logical separation, log files, log files of the log files—he scrambled everything. As one of the main database programmers, he had years to plan and execute it." She pulled up another screen, showing a document with the title 'Insurance Policy'. "He documented everything and hid it in the moon data center. They are still recovering data—it's about 40% done."

Dennings turned around. "They must have known what they were doing when they started recovering data. One of them was a data pro, at least one of them." He narrowed his eyes and turned to Bruce. "Did you check that he's not here?"

"We checked every single corner."

Dennings grunted. "Bruce is right. Even with twenty years of preparation, one programmer is not up to certain things."

Adriana fixated back on the screen. "He had a head start. Someone authorized him to build in a back door. That's the way this Donna got in as well."

"Back door?" asked Dennings slowly and put his weight on his fists on the desk, staring at Adriana.

She recoiled. "What?" she asked when he didn't turn away.

"Pull it up." He turned back to the screen with his fists still clenched.

Adriana pulled up the part of the insurance policy that showed the instructions for the back door.

"That bastard!"

This time even Bruce flinched. Dennings turned back to Adriana and pointed to the screen, grasping for words. "I... he..." He pressed his lips together and lowered his gaze, slightly shivering. When he looked up again, Adriana and Bruce were both still baffled.

"That bastard," he repeated with a robotic voice. After another deep breath he glared at Adriana. "Do we still need him?"

Adriana shook her head. "He was nice enough to document everything and the guys here did the rest."

Dennings turned to Bruce. "Change the orders for this Niklas guy: dead or alive. And increase the bounty."

"What about the others?"

"Same, they might know too much. Get rid of the boy. Do it now." The last words he almost shouted. When Bruce was nearly out of the door, Dennings added, "And get Clutsky here. This changes everything."

After Bruce had left, Dennings pressed air through his lips and turned back to the screen. Adriana was still looking at him.

"What?"

"What was that?" she asked with a chortle.

"Nothing."

"Nothing? You shouted at Bruce. You never shout at him. I mean, we shout when we fight. You shout at Frank because he needs it, but you never shout at Bruce. Come on, what's wrong?"

Dennings cleared his throat. His mouth felt dry; it must be the air down here. Finally, he stepped forward and said in a low voice, "This stays between you and me."

Adriana squinted and tilted her head.

"It was me. I ordered them to implement the back door, but I was very clear that I and only I should get access. And I sent the guy who did it to Africa."

"Well, you can't even trust your own employees anymore these days." She raised her eyebrows. "It looks your guy made somebody else do the dirty work. Why did you do it in the first place?"

"Knowledge, leverage. It made me the most powerful man on Earth." Dennings grunted. "This is the last time we talk about it."

Adriana looked back at the screen. Dennings turned his head; he had noticed the movement on the screen as well.

'<BUONO>This is USS L.J. Gibbs, Commander Bushwick.'

'<JENSEN>Glad to hear from you, Commander. This is Adriana Jensen, Secretary of National Intelligence.'

There was a pause from the other side. Adriana frowned and typed again. Seconds later the words '<JENSEN>Switch to Port 5JQ83P for video and voice stream' appeared on the screen.

Soon after, a video stream came through with a picture of the commander standing in his operations room. In the background, as far as they could see in the blueish light, three people were sitting in front of screens. Dennings switched on the light and their own video stream showed recognizable pictures.

The commander frowned. "Give me the room," he ordered the men sitting around him and waited until they had left.

Adriana stood up and was about to say something when Bruce entered the room again.

"Jonathan, is that you? You've lost weight," said Bruce in a tone that was a mix of grumpy and cheery.

"Bruce. I'm glad to see a face I recognize. No offense intended, but I was never much into politics."

"No offense taken," said Adriana and she seemed to be relieved.

Bruce smirked. "This is Adriana Jensen, the only available representative of the Remules administration. The President and the rest of the cabinet are either missing or dead. Jude Dennings is CEO of The Holding and acting as consultant. We were hit by a terrorist attack targeting computer systems and data specifically. This is the first system-based connection we've been able to establish. How are you holding up?"

The commander had listened calmly. "It seems this isn't only us—the Russians and the Chinese were also affected. We had some encounters and we almost started a war, but when we noticed they were in the same position as we were, we used the chance to trade goods. Weaponry works, but only in manual override. We're running out of food; we haven't been able to land in any harbor since South Africa. Now we're north-east of Recife heading home."

Bruce frowned. "Norfolk?"

"Yes."

"Don't. The entire Eastern Seaboard is contaminated. The data outage caused a fusion in three nuclear power plants and there was no one to fix it. We are running the organization through stations in the Midwest and the Rockies. Try to get into Corpus Christi and we will refurbish you to get around to the Pacific."

Dennings could see the commander swallowing. "My family lives in..." After another swallow, the commander replied, "Understood."

#

*Adriana — Day 369 (April 25, Donna's Farm, Apache-Sitgreaves National Forest, AZ)*

"I got it! That bastard took a plane to the Bahamas." Adriana came running into the hall.

Dennings frowned. "He wouldn't have made it. The planes were the first thing to get grounded after three came down in the Midwest."

"Are you sure? The plane to the Bahamas was scheduled to leave that day at 6AM. It could have worked." Adriana ran her hand through her hair. The air was damp and moist and she could feel the sweaty spots beneath her arms.

Dennings rubbed his chin and looked over to Bruce, who was standing with a group getting updates from his subordinates. "It could, but it would have been a close call. Something tells me this is a decoy." He wiped sweat out of his face. "I need to get out of here. I can't think in this air." He stood up. "Look further, but take breaks. This is a marathon, not a sprint." Dennings turned around with the intention of leaving, when Bruce came over.

"Lieutenant Peck is from our cyber forces. He could lend you a hand."

Adriana eyed Dennings until he slowly nodded. She joined in with nodding. "Fine, but I want Captain Stark leading them."

Dennings looked at Bruce. "We need to secure this facility. I want to have an entire battalion stationed here. Get more IT cracks to help, but they have to be kept separate from the others. None of this can leak out."

"Agreed." Bruce waved to the group and two men marched over.

"Colonel Tom, Lieutenant Peck," Bruce introduced the two men to Dennings and Adriana. "Colonel, station your battalion outside. This place has to be defended at any cost. They can use the quarters at the entrance in turns. Lieutenant, you will report to Secretary Jensen. Nothing that you do can be spread to anybody but Secretary Jensen. Any leak will be treated as treason, understood?"

"Sir, yes sir," shouted the lieutenant, while the colonel just saluted.

#

*Dennings — Day 373 (April 29, Donna's Farm, Apache-Sitgreaves National Forest, AZ)*

It had been a few days since Jude had last climbed down into the bunker. The air was still damp, but from time to time he walked through a breeze of fresher air. *They figured out how to ventilate this place.* The rooms nearest to the entrance were a mess; too few beds for too many soldiers. Some were even sleeping in the main hall. At the other end two guards protected the entry to the computer area. He passed them and the air became damp again. *It must be the narrow corridors.*

When he arrived at the computer room, Dennings was surprised to find three more soldiers lying in the corridor. Inside, another soldier was sitting at one workstation, Adriana at another one, while the third workstation was unmanned. The air was astonishingly good in the room.

The soldier jumped up when Dennings entered. Adriana remained seated. "We need the good air in here to cool down the computers," she said.

Dennings took deep breaths. His lungs and his brain welcomed the oxygen. "You got something?"

"Give us the room," she barked at the soldier.

The soldier saluted and left them alone.

"You let them salute you?" Dennings chuckled.

Adriana stepped closer. "They insist on it." She relaxed and her posture became feminine again.

He smiled mildly. "I missed you." Their faces moved closer and he kissed her. "It's been a while," he added after the kiss.

"Not for me—I have my six toy boys here." She turned around playfully and looked at him over her shoulder as she went back to her computer.

He grinned at her. "So, what do you have?"

"I know where he is—or rather, where he was a year ago."

Dennings' eyebrows jumped up and down.

"But first, I need your permission to connect."

"Connect?"

"I can connect to the computers in the Montana bunker and if we move some equipment I can connect with Fairview or your winter camp down here." She smiled mischievously.

He frowned. "That would give away our secret."

"I know, but we would be able to communicate better." Now she frowned. "I understand this is your greatest asset, but we should move ahead. After the arrival of the aircraft carrier this will be a secret you can't entirely control anyway."

"One step at a time. First the Montana bunker, but you have to go there and establish the security. These are Clutsky's men."

"Will you come up as well?"

"Yes, I guess I can move up a little early." He smiled, but his smile was interrupted by a thought. "Where is he?"

"*Was* he. I lost him in Lima... for the moment."

"Fill me in."

She sat down and pulled up a map of the continent on the screen. "First, you were right: the ticket to the Bahamas was a diversion. He crossed the border with Mexico not far from here. Actually, he was clever. He changed his ID to 'Hernández' and let himself get caught by border patrols. You understand? We deported him."

Dennings stared motionless at the lines on map. "He got on a ship?"

"Yes, all ships deporting people from that port release them in Lima for further treatment. He was on one of the ships."

"Hmm." Dennings still didn't take his eyes off the screen, but he wasn't actually looking at it anymore. Then a thought hit him. "How do you know that? There haven't been any updates since the big bang, have there?"

Adriana stood up and smirked. "No, only from systems we were able to reactivate, but he accessed the moon data center."

Dennings turned around on one foot. "He accessed the log from outside?" He was almost shouting.

Adriana didn't react and Dennings calmed down instantly when he realized that it was a good thing. "We have to assume he got off the ship in Lima. Let Clutsky know. He's in Bolivia at the moment. And," he added, talking more to himself, "we have to move our focus back to the rest of the country."

# CHAPTER FIVE

# Sail Away

*Niklas – Day 374 (April 30, Cuzco, Peru)*

Niklas and Marcella held hands while they watched the shadows on the wall across from the window. People were running by. Troops were marching before they spread out, accompanied by the sound of stomping boots, shouting and shrieking, and every now and then the short bellow of a dog or a machine gun.

Their short stay of a couple of days had turned into two weeks. With time, their vision had adjusted to the gloomy light and they had come to recognize more in the room than they wanted to see. They had also learned to eat all food immediately as there was no place safe enough from the rats to leave some for the next day.

It got calmer towards the morning hours. They were dozing when the clicking sound of a key in the door startled them. Niklas jumped up and hid next to the door.

"Pst." The door opened a little and Ezequiel peeked through the gap. Niklas relaxed.

"Got food. Sorry I didn't come for two days, but the purges are heavy. They kill you instantly if they think you have no information to offer. If they think you have, you wish they had killed you instantly." Ezequiel gave Niklas a plastic bag. "I'm sorry, mate, but it's *cuy* again."

Marcella got up as well and took the bag. "I never thought I would actually look forward to eating guinea-pig meat."

"I also have two old coats for you. They don't look as nice anymore, but they are handmade with alpaca wool—warm as hell."

"How long?" Niklas frowned at Ezequiel. "We're going crazy here."

Ezequiel looked back over his shoulder. "Couple of days, maybe even tomorrow. The trains are still waiting for fuel to be delivered. We have to be careful. The searches have gotten worse. They're looking for some guy, Soderstrom."

"Fine." Niklas sighed, but his hackles rose. *Soderstrom!* He glanced over at Marcella, but she was busy with the coats.

"But you have to be ready. Oh, before I forget, here is soap. You should have water in the shower during the next two hours."

Marcella gaped at him.

Ezequiel had a hard time not pulling a face. "You need to. Otherwise the smell will call you out." He looked back again. It seemed something had caught his attention. "I have to go, but I will be back tomorrow."

"Wait," said Marcella.

He turned around.

"Why are you doing this? So far we've caused you nothing but trouble and risk."

He shrugged. "I hate them. Since I was a kid they scoured for people, and whenever they got one you never heard of them again. Innocent people, you know, who were just in the wrong place at the wrong time. It's their system of spreading fear. My dad was the same and one day he disappeared."

Marcella got soft eyes and Niklas had the impression tears were welling up. "Thank you. I know exactly how that feels."

#

### Niklas — Day 375 (May 1, Cuzco, Peru)

They had dozed for a while during the day. Niklas sat up and marvelled at Marcella. Her eyes were still closed. He liked the way her hair smelled after the shower she had taken that morning.

He didn't know how much time had passed; he had given his last watch away to get up to Cuzco. Judging from the sun it was maybe five o'clock in the evening. In two hours the curfew would start. It was the same ritual every day. The police or armed forces—it was hard to tell which through the small window—would marshal on the Plaza de Armas before spreading out to do their purges.

*I still can't believe they have my name. It should have taken them longer. Somebody on the freighter must have blabbed. Hell, there's no other way they would have known my fake identity.*

The room got darker. Niklas looked up to the window. Two people were blocking the light.

*Tourists—funny that there are still backpackers here.*

Niklas frowned as another thought pushed forward in his brain.

*Or, did they fix the... No way. No way they fixed the scrambling. The insurance policy was safe.*

He chewed the inside of this cheek until he tasted blood. *I wonder where Jenny and Eduard are. Hope they survived the prison. I did what I could to help them. I did all I could.*

"What are you thinking?"

Niklas looked over to Marcella. She was still lying down, but her eyes were vivid and inquisitive. She sat up and twined her arms around him.

"Nothing."

"What's bothering you?"

"We've been in here for too long. We have to leave."

She nodded. "Next time Ezequiel comes we have to tell him."

Niklas stopped chewing his cheek, jumped off the bed and walked over to the door.

Marcella sat up. "You won't get it open. I tried it a week ago."

He turned around and raised his eyebrows and smirked. "When?"

"At night. You were asleep."

Niklas inspected the lock. It was an old, heavy lock, like you would see in old mansions or heritage buildings in the South for decoration. He examined the metal frame. It was neatly tied into the stone of the building. Niklas shrugged as he returned to the bed. "Let's wait."

"Yes, Daddy."

Niklas smirked and got on the bed again. "I don't think I ever thanked you for getting me through as your uncle."

"Goes without saying. I'm glad you're not mad we got through that way."

He turned to her and was washed away by her beam. "Anyway, thank you."

She just nodded.

"You never asked who I am."

"You never asked why I was travelling alone to the US."

Niklas gazed at her and suddenly it seemed he had a stranger in front of him. It had never occurred to him that there could be a reason, or that something could have happened that had forced her to leave. "You're better off not knowing who I am."

"And you're better off not knowing what I did."

The sun had gone down in the meantime and twilight darkened the room, but Niklas thought he saw a smile hushing over her face. He opened his arms and they embraced for a long time.

The metallic clicking of the door drew them back into reality. Niklas' muscles tensed and even when the head of the janitor appeared, his subconscious couldn't relax. Tomasz said something in Spanish about leaving. Even though Niklas' Spanish had gotten better, he had a hard time understanding the janitor's accent. Marcella replied and the janitor added something before he left again, leaving the door open.

"Come. They are taking us to the train."

"Where's Ezequiel?" asked Niklas.

Marcella jumped off the bunk bed and shrugged. Niklas crammed their stuff into his duffle bag and got off the bed as well.

The janitor stood at the other end of the corridor, waiting. "*Venga, venga*." He waved with his hands.

"Ask him what happened to Ezequiel," said Niklas when they reached him.

She did and his face darkened. He didn't answer, just shook his head and Niklas saw his shoulders drop. The janitor eased open the heavy door to the street and peeked through the gap. After a second he opened it and went out. Marcella followed him and Niklas lagged behind them.

He couldn't get Ezequiel out of his mind. *He got killed because of my chaos.*

The janitor gestured at them to climb into the back of an old truck. Niklas wiped his thoughts away. The loading bed of the truck was stacked with straw bales, sloppily secured by wooden boards on each side of the truck. Niklas and Marcella got on board and hid between the bales.

The janitor climbed into the cabin on the passenger side. He opened a small window between the cabin and the loading bed and shouted something. Niklas blinked at Marcella.

"It will take a while. They have to drive on side roads to the train station. And we should hide."

Without saying a word, they looked through the opening in the back between the straw bales. It was chilly. With a small bump the truck set into motion.

*We should have put on more layers*, thought Niklas. He put his arm around Marcella and she nestled into his side. The passing streets gave Niklas a strange feeling of being a passenger in his own story. The Palacio de la Justicia disappeared slowly in the distance.

#

### Niklas — Day 375 (May 1, Cuzco, Peru)

They drove for a while, and first the streetlights and then the houses got more and more sparse. The road started to climb the hills around the city. When they turned around one curve they had a wonderful view of the city. Despite solar and hydroelectric power, electricity was still limited and the city looked like a chessboard.

"Something's wrong," he whispered into her ear.

She had been dozing and she looked up with a worried glint on her face.

"We're going east, but we should be going south."

Now she was fully awake and sat up. "What are they up to?"

"I don't know, but it can't be good. Next hairpin bend we'll jump off. The truck should be slow enough on the curve." He got up and squatted in the back of the truck, dragging the duffle bag behind him. Marcella followed.

"We have to climb out and hold onto the outside." Niklas peeked to the front. "When you jump you need to look forward. Don't fight it if you fall; you have to roll away."

"I know how to fall."

Niklas peeked to the front again. "Ten seconds."

They hurried to climb over the board that secured the back of the truck, and stood on the bumper. Niklas was worried that the rusty bumper would give in, but it held. The driver changed gear and the truck slowed down.

"You first," said Niklas. The truck slowed down to walking pace and turned into the bend. "Now."

Marcella let go and Niklas watched her roll away. He let go of his duffle bag. The truck was almost out of the curve and the driver was accelerating again when Niklas jumped off. *Too fast. Should have jumped earlier.* His muscles tensed up and the speed tore away his legs when they touched the ground. He tried to turn his shoulder and curl up to roll away, but his shoulder hit the ground and he scraped along the dirt. A sharp pain flashed through the side of his body. He tasted dust and blood on his tongue. *Still alive.* He jumped up and tried to grab his bag, but his left arm didn't want to obey; instead it just dangled from his shoulder. Marcella came running and grabbed the bag and then him by the right arm to help him up. Together they rushed off the street again and hid behind a boulder on the side of the road, watching the truck disappear.

"Are you alright, *querido*?" Marcella touched his shoulder and pain flashed again through his shoulder.

He twitched away and the arm dangled again. There was not a lot of space behind the rock, only about ten feet until a steep scree slope started. The pain abated slowly. He saw her mouth moving, but her voice sounded as if she was speaking through a muffler.

"Your shoulder is dislocated. Let me try to fix it."

Niklas peered at her, his eyes wide open, not sure what to say. "You can do that?" was the only thing that came to his mind that didn't sound that stupid.

"Jumping off moving vehicles is not the only skill you learn when you try to get into the US illegally." She smirked. "I volunteered as a nurse in one of the refugee camps east of Nogales, just outside the wall."

"I'm glad you did—"

Engine noise in the distance silenced him.

"They're coming back. We have to leave. You can fix my shoulder later." He looked around briefly. "Climbing down there would be suicide." He pointed towards the scree. "We have to follow the road and hide if necessary."

The engine noise grew louder and Marcella narrowed her eyes. "It's too late now. We have to let them pass."

Niklas felt his pulse in his throat. The truck came closer. *Soon they will pass. I hope they pass.* They pressed closer to the back of the rock. Pain wavered through his arm. *We should have gone further away right from the start. This boulder is too small.* The engine sound was now right on top of them and the sound of changing gears indicated that the truck was just before the curve.

Niklas closed his eyes and reopened them with a scared stare when the truck stopped on the curve. Marcella bit on her lips and pressed his healthy hand. A door went and one man said something Niklas couldn't understand, but he recognized the janitor's voice. An urge to pounce on him welled up in Niklas. *He has Ezequiel on his conscience.* His breath grew shorter and faster as the voice came closer. He felt Marcella's body tensing up. *She's going to run, sacrifice herself.* "No!" shouted his eyes. She tilted her head and swallowed; then she nodded and the tension went.

The other guy shouted something out of the cabin. It didn't sound mean, more scared. The janitor replied and Niklas could hear him returning to the truck. The door went and the engine of the truck revved away. Niklas blew out and with the waning strain the pain in his shoulder came back.

"Let's go." He tried to get up.

"Wait. Let me fix your shoulder first."

He nodded.

"But it will hurt."

Niklas shrugged half-sidedly.

"Take this between your teeth." She handed him one of her gloves and he bit on it. A sharp pain flared from his shoulder through his neck when she touched his elbow. With a quick movement she pressed his elbow in and with a round upwards movement back out. The pain burned from his neck up into his head and the world went black.

#

*Niklas — Day 375 (May 1, East of Cuzco, Peru)*

When Niklas came round he was covered by Marcella's coat. Marcella was peeking around the boulder and didn't notice him at first. She was only wearing a T-shirt; Niklas could see her shivering. The cold from the ground was biting and he tried to get up.

Marcella turned around. "You're back, *cariño*."

"How long was I out?" He supported his weight on his right arm and carefully started moving his left. It still felt sore, but the pain was gone.

"About twenty minutes. Do you mind?" She pointed to her coat.

"Of course. Thank you." The cool winter air that swirled around his back when he took the coat off gave him chills.

She nodded and slipped into the coat, still shivering. He moved his arm a little more each time until he was slowly rotating the shoulder. "You did good."

She nodded again, having a hard time stopping her teeth from chattering.

Niklas stood up. "We need to get moving. I hope you can warm up while we walk." He shouldered the duffle bag and they got onto the street.

They walked silently. The curves were close and frequent on that steep part of the hill. Left and right of the street the ground was dry with bare stones and, sporadically, bushes and trees.

Four curves further down Niklas asked Marcella, "Better?"

She wiggled her head. "Yes, but my toes are killing me."

Niklas press his lips together.

Marcella forced a smile. "Don't worry, I've had this before when I broke them all about two years ago. Since then I can't feel them anymore—" Her facial expression froze in the middle of the sentence.

*An engine.* Niklas' eyes frantically scanned the area for hideouts. "Down." He pointed to the outer slope.

They rushed across the street. There was some other noise in the background of the engine sound, but he couldn't say what it was. In the distance, he could already see lights turning around the curve. *Multiple trucks.* The squeaking and rattling sound of tracks came to the fore. *Armed forces.*

"Hurry," said Niklas.

They jumped off the street and ran further down the slope. Niklas almost sprained his foot twice and he was surprised by how nimbly Marcella moved on the rocky ground. Seconds passed while the sound grew louder. Searchlights were randomly roaming across the area.

Marcella poked him. "Cover your face and your hands when they're here. It's the skin that gives you away."

Niklas didn't have time to reply. The cone of the next search-light came rapidly closer. He lay on his hands and looked at the ground. One searchlight passed them, a second and then a third. The sound grew louder and changed its frequency when it passed—a Jeep up front, followed by a truck, two trucks, a tank and another truck. Niklas felt the impulse to raise his head and was glad he hadn't when another searchlight hit them. His heartbeat choked for a millisecond—at least it felt that way—and a tremor went through his entire body.

But nothing happened, no squeaking breaks, no shouting voices, no sound of boots hitting the ground. The convoy continued on its path and minutes later the scare was over. He remained lying there until a couple of seconds later Marcella started to move.

He sat up. His shoulder hurt again, not sharply, but dull and pounding. "Maybe that was just a transport or a patrol."

"You want to bet on it?" Marcella got up.

He shook his head. "Let's go. If they only drive as far as the truck did before they discovered we were missing, they'll be back soon."

They climbed back up to the street and strode downwards. Niklas felt his breath accelerating again, more than usual. *Damn altitude.*

"They'll have dogs. They always have dogs." Marcella was gasping as well. "We need to slow down."

He slowed down. "Those are contradicting statements." He mixed a brief smile between the breaths. "But I agree, we won't be able to keep up this speed for long."

"Dogs will slow them down as well."

They were now almost trudging.

Niklas nodded. "We need to get down to the river."

#

*Niklas — Day 375 (May 1, South of Cuzco, Peru)*

They first heard the dogs when they reached the river. The barking was still far away, but Niklas guessed that they would catch up soon. The river was cold and they were lucky it wasn't carrying a lot of water, just enough to cover their knees. They waded with the current and soon they were out of sight of where they had entered the river. The water made Niklas shiver to the point where his entire body was trembling. His feet felt like they were being pinched by needles. He glanced over at Marcella; she pressed her lips together and continued to wade.

After wading silently for half an hour she grabbed his arm, stumbling from exhaustion. He grabbed her under the arms and she slumped. Niklas almost fell. Step by step he helped her out of the water. They had not heard any barking for a long time, but he still wanted them to take cover under the porch roof of an old shed. They had gone into the river in a deserted industrial area, but now they had reached suburbs with occasional farmland in between.

They sat down on a bench and he took off her shoes. "Your feet are cold as ice." He took a towel out of his duffle bag and started rubbing them.

"We need to move on. Just give me a pair of new socks. We can rest during the day."

Niklas shook his head, but she wouldn't allow him to reply. She took his hand and looked at him. "Let's go."

"Fine." He gave her the socks and they continued on their way, Marcella more stumbling than walking.

#

*Niklas — Day 376 (May 2, South of Cuzco, Peru)*

In the early morning hours they reached train tracks, and with their last efforts they made it to a deserted station building. They had barely climbed to the second floor of the building when a dull rumbling sound reached them through the broken glass of a window.

Marcella didn't notice. She had slumped on a chair, which almost collapsed under her, and was occupied with getting out of her wet shoes. "Can I borrow another pair of socks from you? Mine are already soaked again."

"Shh." He put his finger in front of his lips.

She didn't reply but her darting gaze spoke volumes. The noise came closer and Niklas couldn't get rid of the feeling that it was something massive approaching.

He got down next to her and whispered, "Maybe it's nothing."

She tilted her head. He bit on the inside of his cheek and got up. He still couldn't see anything, but the sound had reached a menacing volume. *A train, it's a train. But why doesn't it have the headlights on?*

"Hurry up, it's a train."

She jumped up and in that moment the passing locomotive made the building shake. That's when he saw the guards out of the corner of his eye and ducked. "Down!" His shout got swallowed by the noise, but watching him she instinctively ducked as well. They held out for minutes until the last wagon had passed. Niklas counted two guards on the roofs of the wagons: one on the first one and the second on the last one. He guessed they were guards but he only saw shadows against the dark blue of the early morning sky.

The absence of the train noise afterwards felt like an absolute silence and it cost Niklas some effort to break it. "We have to be prepared for the next one. I hope that wasn't just a fluke."

Marcella nodded with half-open eyes and seconds later her head fell onto her chest, just to jump up again a blink of an eye later. She repeated this twice before Niklas went over to pick her up and laid her on a dusty desk by the wall.

He had a flashlight in his bag, which he had been keeping for emergencies only to save on battery, but he figured that it would be of good use now. He got it out and for the first time he looked around the room, covering the flashlight so that nobody outside would notice the light. From what he could see, it appeared to be an apartment—probably of the former station master. He walked into the other rooms. The kitchen looked horrible and had no running water, but in the next room he found sheets. They were dusty as hell, but at least he could keep Marcella warm. She thanked him with a murmur. Then he wrapped himself in sheets as well and sat on the chair. Watching sunlight creeping down the mountains on the west side of valley, fatigue slowly crept up his body.

#

*Niklas — Day 376 (May 2, South of Cuzco, Peru)*

The shaking and rumbling noise of an approaching train woke Niklas up again and he jumped to his feet. He was already halfway over to the desk where Marcella was sleeping when he realized that the train was going in the wrong direction. He stopped in the middle of the movement, ducked and crawled back over to the window. The first wagon with a guard had just passed, but the guard didn't seem to have noticed anything, left or right. He was sitting on the roof of the wagon, huddled up. *I would freeze to death up there.*

One other thing caught Niklas' attention: the weapons they carried seemed too modern. With the soldiers in Cuzco he had only seen older guns, Russian or German models, but this guy was carrying a weapon he had only seen on the special forces so far— a great discrepancy from the rest of his uniform.

Niklas frowned while the wagons continued to pass by. Towards the end the shape of them changed from closed wagons to open ones, transporting trucks and even three tanks. At the very end they had attached four fuel tanks. *They must get gas from somewhere around La Paz.* He ducked again when the last wagon with the second guard passed, but it wasn't necessary. Again, the guard was just staring at the tracks where the train was coming from.

After the train had passed Niklas noticed in the bright daylight that the floor was missing in one corner. *Glad I didn't fall down this morning.* He stood up and glanced out of the window. *We need to go into the back room if there are trains during the day. The guards have prime view into this room.*

Niklas picked up Marcella and carried her into the bedroom. Then he walked back to the window and looked out. A dense feeling spread in his chest and he had to go to great lengths to avoid any thoughts that could connect what had happened around him to his scrambling routine.

#

*Niklas — Day 376 (May 2, South of Cuzco, Peru)*

The sun was already going down again when Marcella came out of the bedroom. Niklas had snoozed as well during the day, but he had not been able to sleep long each time. Every noise had made him startle.

"Good evening. How do you feel?"

For the first time in days she beamed. "Evening?" The word was swallowed by a yawn. "Better." She walked up to him by the window, got another chair and sat next to him. "This chair is scary. I hope it doesn't break." She beamed again.

"I thought the same when you crashed on it last night."

Her smile went away. "I'm sorry, I couldn't take it anymore last night. This whole journey is getting to me slowly."

"It's not your fault. This is because of me. I'm putting you at risk."

Marcella sat up. "Stop, before you say anything wrong."

"I just mean—"

"Shh." She put her finger on his lips. "We are in this together and we'll get through it together."

Niklas pressed his lips together.

Marcella gazed into his eyes. "With you I'm brave, but without you the angst will get me. With you I have direction, but without you I'd hole up and crumble."

Niklas stared out of the window again, still clenching his jaw, but his heart was light after what Marcella had said.

"Anything new out there?"

"Yes, we had two more trains pass, each guarded by two guys—one on the first wagon and one on the last. From what I can see, they're just staring in one direction. They have to slow down here because of the switches. We could jump on in the middle."

"Let's try tonight." She stood up to glance out of the window. The evening sun tinted the scenery with an orange tone. "It's beautiful here. I wish I'd seen this before, with you."

Niklas swallowed hard at the way she pronounced 'before'. "Yeah," he replied half-heartedly.

She came back, sat down and leaned on him. "But I'm glad we're here together now."

He put his arm around her and they watched the night fall. The shadows swiftly grew long and soon they were sitting in the dark.

"We should have packed while we still had daylight," Marcella said into the silence. "I'm not sure where all my stuff is."

"I packed it during the day. Everything's ready." He smiled at her.

"You're the best. And thank you for stuffing my shoes with newspaper. They're dry—"

A distant sound interrupted her.

"Here it comes." She jumped up.

He got up as well and peeked out of to the window. "Yeah, it's the right direction." He grabbed their bags and they rushed downstairs. The noise grew louder and they hid in the doorway. "As soon as it's here we have to run fast. I'll check the guards and give you a sign."

Marcella nodded swiftly and they listened to the growing sound. Niklas' heart started to pound as he expected the locomotive to appear any second. To his surprise, the train's brakes started to squeak and when the locomotive finally appeared, it was going at little more than walking speed.

"Back, back," he said and they dodged deeper into the doorway. The first wagon passed and Niklas peeked up at the guard. Just like the previous times, the guard didn't move. Ten wagons later, the train came to a stop. Niklas took another glance at the guards; they were each about ten wagons away. "Let's go."

They ran over to the closest wagon and Niklas opened the door just enough so they could slip in and closed it again behind them. Breathless, they stood in between crates of potatoes and corn randomly stacked around them.

*Food.*

"There." Marcella pointed to an area in the corner with fewer boxes. They climbed over.

Niklas built a small fortress with the boxes. "It's always good to have a hideout."

Marcella smile and kissed him. Another distant rumbling sound interrupted them. *Another train*, Niklas thought. *They're crossing here.*

#

*Niklas — Day 376 (May 2, South of Cuzco, Peru)*

The barren landscape of the high plateau passed by slowly. Marcella was sleeping across from him with her bare feet under his coat to warm them at least a little. Niklas watched the passing shades of brown and yellow that sometimes reached into red or light green. The sunshine added an additional layer, but he wasn't really paying attention. His brain was preoccupied with the events in Cuzco. *How can it be that there are regular trains?* Niklas clenched his jaw. *Did Ezequiel lie to us? Or did they just recently start and only the janitor betrayed us?*

He took a deep breath and glanced over at Marcella. *I'll get her killed if I stay with her any longer.* She twitched in her sleep as if she understood. He turned back to the passing landscape. *Then again, she will insist and it will be impossible to go alone. She's sturdy like an old oak tree.* He smiled at that thought and looked back at her.

She had her eyes open as if she had been awake for a while. "Wanna tell me your thoughts?"

"I just compared you to an oak tree."

She smiled and sat up. "Now that's a compliment."

"How are your feet?" He squeezed them under his coat.

"Warmer, but I still can't feel my toes. I'll probably have to count them every morning from now on." Her smile grew wide and turned into a sarcastic smirk.

#

*Jenny — Day 464 (July 29, Big Sur, CA)*

The sea breeze felt good on the skin. Even though they had been close to the ocean for two weeks, the air in their hideouts was damp. Still, Jenny had been glad to be able to rest after the 860-mile march. CJ had told Eduard, Jenny and even Max to stay and wait while he went to comb the area for a boat. He had been gone several days, coming back only once to bring them food, and Jenny had had erratic panic attacks throughout the entire week. But now, looking down the cliff at that beautiful boat, she finally felt like breathing again. "It's huge."

"It will never float. You'll kill us all on this wreck." Eduard glared at CJ and back down again.

CJ showed no facial expression. "It will float, there's no damage to the hull. We have to see how we can get it out again and how damaged the keel is."

"You've been down there?" asked Jenny, not actually surprised.

Eduard pressed his lips together. "It's too big. There aren't enough of us to sail that thing." He was still looking down, but Jenny could almost read his thoughts. Eduard picked up a stone and threw it.

"It's a cutter. Two are enough to change the sails. Jenny can help me with that, but I need you at the helm, at least until your hands heal." CJ looked at him. "Don't worry, the feeling in your fingers will come back. You just have to let go."

*How much longer does it need?* thought Jenny. *It's been months now.*

CJ's expression had changed after his last sentence. Briefly he checked the deserted cliff road on both sides with a worried look on his face. The sun glared off the stone and dust of the road and made it look as if the road was a snake winding its way around the cliffs.

Jenny frowned. Then she heard the sound as well.

"Back." CJ jumped up and ran to the other side of the road into a small inlet beneath an overhang. The others followed. The sound grew closer.

CJ made a sign upwards and whispered, "Military convoy."

Seconds later, multiple trucks passed by thirty feet above them on Highway 1.

"That's the patrol between LA and San Diego. It passes twice a day." CJ grinned at them. "They can't see the boat from up there. We are safe once we climb down."

They waited another five minutes and then CJ led them to a rope around the corner. He attached it loosely to a set of stones, tied their backpacks to the other end and let them down.

*I hope that holds*, thought Jenny.

"Come. I can carry Max down, but we need to find a solution for you, Eduard."

"I don't need your help. I can get there by myself."

"No way!" Jenny felt blood pulsing through her temples. "You'll fall."

"She's right, but we could try it together." CJ grabbed the rope and swung over the rim. "Come."

Eduard pinched his lips for a moment, but then climbed over the rim as well. From his lumbering movements Jenny could tell he was scared, and from her heartbeat she knew she was terrified. Eduard tried to grab the rope but without strength. Pain flashed over his face. He leaned against CJ, who had been waiting. CJ's muscles tensed up. Slowly they moved down, step by step. With time they gained confidence and their rhythm improved, and then, for a long time, Jenny lost them out of her sight. She couldn't look anymore and turned her head away. Something caught her eye in the distance, something like a long shadow on the water, but she couldn't tell if it was anything or just a reflection. Soon after, Max took her hand and squeezed it. She looked down and saw CJ climbing up again. *They made it.*

"You're next," he said to Jenny when he arrived. "Do you think you can do it?"

Jenny glanced down again, nodded and climbed over the rim. CJ helped her and she started to walk down, holding onto the rope. The first ten feet felt clumsy but not so difficult. *Just don't look down*, she said to herself. Her arms got more and more tired and just when she thought she couldn't hold it anymore, she reached a small plateau where she could rest for a moment. She continued and when she thought she should be close she dared to peek down. Eduard was waiting for her, but it was still far enough to die if she let go now. The skin appeared blueish between the coils of the rope wrapped around her arm. In the last two feet she let go of the rope and her knees gave in when her feet touched the ground. Eduard jumped over, but he couldn't hold her up. The sand felt warm and cozy, a welcome sensation in contrast to the pain in her arms.

He helped her up. "Let's get into the shade. CJ told us to wait there."

From the shade they watched the end of the rope dangling five feet up in the air. After a couple of minutes it dropped to the ground.

*They're falling!* Jenny caught her breath, but nothing happened except the same movement repeated twice more, each time leaving more of the rope lying on the ground in front of them.

"He's keeping the rope—at least that's something smart. That's why he attached it only loosely." Eduard took a step forward and looked up. "They're almost here."

Minutes later CJ's feet touched the ground and he let Max down.

"You guys wait here. Jenny, you're with me." With nimble movements he rushed over and hid behind the rump of the boat, scanning the street they had come down from. He waved at Jenny and she ran over. When she arrived he had already swung over the rail to board the boat, only to throw something into the water and then jump down again.

"When I tell you, you need to push."

She gaped at him with large eyes. "I'll never be able to move it even an inch."

He smirked and pointed to the object he had thrown into the water. "It's a car jack. One of the old mechanical ones. Got it from a repair shop down the road." He glanced up to the road again. "Just stay ducked behind the boat when you aren't pushing."

Jenny nodded and watched him dive beneath the boat. *That's never going to work.*

The boat moved up a little, and after CJ emerged to breathe and dived again, it moved a little more. He repeated the procedure twice more. Jenny peeked once around the corner to check on Eduard and Max; both were sitting in the shade looking over at the boat. When they noticed Jenny they waved, but Jenny didn't dare to wave back.

"The keel was blocked with a stone. I had to remove it first," CJ said when he emerged again. "Now let's push." He stood behind Jenny and they pushed. The boat moved two inches and Jenny crowed. CJ turned around with a frown on his face and Jenny ducked under his gaze.

"Once more," he added and they managed to move it almost a foot before it sagged. CJ dived again and the boat rose two inches more. After three more attempts it began to float and Jenny crowed again. This time CJ didn't throw her a look, but he checked the road above before he waved over to Eduard and Max. Jenny followed his look: all clear up there.

"Get in and hold the helm." He helped her climb in.

The boat had already started to drift off when Eduard and Max reached it. CJ had to help them climb on board before he went back to get the bags. Minutes later he was on board too and the boat was moving out of the bay.

Looking forward to the sea, a thought crossed Jenny's mind out of the blue. *I wonder how Mom is doing.*

#

*Eduard — Day 464 (July 29, Big Sur, CA)*

CJ shouted, "Now."

Jenny let go of the rope and the main sail unfolded. Max clapped his hands. The boat started to pick up speed and Eduard felt it immediately in his hands. Pain pulsed through his fingernails. He had problems holding the helm.

"We have half a tank full, but we should economize." CJ jumped off the foredeck to relieve Eduard of his duties.

Eduard rubbed his hands. "I hope you know what you're doing. I don't want to end up on those cliffs." He sat down next to Jenny and Max on the bench behind CJ.

Slowly they left the bay behind them and as soon as they reached open sea they swiftly picked up speed. The shore got smaller and smaller until it was only a blurry line on the horizon.

"Where are we heading?" asked Jenny, squeezing Eduard's hand. Pain flashed through his fingernails and he flinched.

Jenny threw him a sorry look.

CJ glanced back at the shore. "Out of sight." He glanced over at the compass next to the helm and turned the wheel until the shore was on their left side. The boat started to roll and Eduard felt nauseous.

"South. I know people who might be able to help us." CJ observed the few clouds in the sky. "We have good winds. I suggest you and Eduard go down and get us settled in. I'll need you to take the helm for two hours tonight so I can get some rest."

Jenny got up and Eduard tried to get up as well but he slumped back again on the bench. "Damn!"

"Everything all right, honey?"

Eduard nodded and closed his eyes for a moment, but that made the nauseous feeling worse. *Idiot! How about telling us when you're going to make sudden moves?* He opened his eyes again, took a breath and got up. Unsteady, he followed Jenny below deck.

Actually, there was not a lot below deck: a small cabin, just big enough for a small table that could fit four people if they squeezed in, and a kitchenette. At the end of the cabin there was a door to either a storage room or another cabin. The floor was covered with clutter as if the owners had had to get off in a hurry. Drawers were pulled out and the contents spread over the cabin: forks, spoons, plates and pans in the first cabin, and through the open door you could see clothes and linens spread over the second.

"Reminds me of my college apartment," Jenny chuckled.

He forced a smile. "Actually, it *does* remind me of your college apartment."

Jenny stepped over the mess on the floor and peeked through the door into what was some kind of sleeping cabin, which had several mattresses pushed together to form one large sleeping place that could fit about four people. "How did the owners get out of that bay? They didn't swim around the cliffs, did they? That would have been suicide."

"They might have tried." CJ had come down as well, followed by Max.

Jenny turned around. "Who's steering?"

Eduard had forgotten about his nausea, but now it was back, stronger than before and with a sudden urge to puke.

"I don't think they knew how to navigate without their instruments and they were rescued by one of the ships on the North-South route. Did you see the scratches on the side, up and down? Those are the scratches you get when you dock two ships together on open sea. On top of that, the inflatable lifeboat is still on the foredeck."

Jenny was still staring at CJ.

He shrugged. "I fixed the wheel with a rope. It will do for a while. Don't worry, I'll go back up again."

Jenny relaxed. "We'll get this mess cleaned up in the meantime."

CJ turned around and went up again.

Eduard's urge to puke abated. "Do you know what he has in his backpack?" He glanced over at Jenny. "A gun. He always keeps it with him. Even now he has it upstairs."

Jenny shook her head. Eduard got the feeling she didn't care. He was about to start picking things up when he heard CJ shouting from the deck, "I've found some sea maps. Can you also look for any nautical instruments, like a sextant or something."

Eduard frowned at Jenny and she shrugged.

*What the hell is a sextant?*

#

*Jenny — Day 465 (July 29, At sea)*

Jenny took the helm for four hours in the late evening. She was only supposed to have it for two hours, but she and Eduard decided to let CJ sleep longer. He had explained to her the basics and thumped into her to always keep heading south-south-east; something about trade winds. After four hours she couldn't take it anymore and they woke up CJ. He was upset, but with a hint of appreciation in his eyes.

The exertion meant Jenny slept like a stone. When she woke the next morning, Eduard was already on deck. She could hear him and CJ fighting. Actually, she could only hear Eduard; CJ's voice was too calm to be heard.

"It would be helpful if you could shed more light on where we're actually going. Who are these friends of yours? Some displaced military like you?"

The sea swallowed CJ's reply.

"Who made you decide this anyway? We should elect a leader, not just follow the biggest gorilla."

Jenny frowned. *Not again—what's wrong with him?* She went up on deck. Eduard had his mouth already open to add something, but he swallowed it as soon as he noticed Jenny. She looked alternately at him and CJ. Max was sitting between them, crouching on the floor. Eduard turned his head away—towards the sea.

"Where are we?" Although she was asking CJ, Jenny still gazed over at Eduard, subconsciously shaking her head. Turning to CJ, she glanced over at the compass. It showed they were heading south-west.

CJ's face was stiff as he stared at a point a little left of their heading. The tension in the muscles under his arm indicated the strong pull of the wind.

After a while his face and his neck relaxed a little and he turned to Jenny. "We've been going at seven knots, which makes it about 150 miles. We should be somewhere out of Santa Barbara." His neck got stiff again and his eyes narrowed. "We should replenish food and water. That is, if you agree with me."

"I agree." Jenny blinked at Eduard. He was still standing on the other side. "Max?"

Max nodded and Eduard finally turned around. "How do we ensure we don't get raided ourselves? There must be millions of people out there waiting for us."

"I thought about that. We'll wait until night and I'll try to land at Santa Catalina. Some of those luxury resorts must have food and water left, I hope. It is a bit risky—I could miss it. It's a small island and the maps I've found are useless without instruments..."

Jenny breathed in through her nose. "We found something yesterday. Sorry, we totally forgot." She rushed down and seconds later she reappeared with a kind of decorative object, a tool that looked like a heavy compass, with struts between the two legs and a small telescope attached to it.

CJ grinned. "That's a sextant. Don't tell me you don't know what a sextant is."

Jenny and Eduard smiled sheepishly.

"We have to wait until noon to use it, but it should be enough."

Eduard frowned. "And how do you want to figure out when it's noon? Guess from the sun?"

CJ watched Eduard's expression for a moment, then fixed the helm with a rope and bent down to open his backpack. Jenny and Eduard followed him with their eyes and were surprised when he took out a watch. The joyful feeling in Jenny was dragged down immediately when she noticed the grip of gun.

"It's mechanical and it still works. I keep it in a box to protect it from the salt water. The sun would work as well, but this is more accurate." CJ put the watch back in its box and in his backpack.

Jenny glimpsed at Eduard. He had seen the gun as well and his eyes had an I-told-you-so look she knew well.

\#

*Jenny — Day 465 (July 29, Santa Catalina, CA)*

Jenny and Eduard watched CJ and Max disappear in the dark. With the sextant, CJ had managed to hit Santa Catalina and they had anchored behind a small rock outside one of the coves.

He was already out of sight, but they could still hear him paddling. The island was ghastly dark and quiet, but even more unsettling was the darkness of what should be LA ablaze with light. Now there were only a few spots with what seemed to be floodlights.

"I hope they find something." Jenny sat down on the bench and crossed her arms. She felt that the temperature had dropped and she wished she had more to wear than just a shirt and a hoodie.

Eduard was still standing at the railing and looking in the direction in which the inflatable lifeboat had disappeared. "We should leave."

"What?"

He turned around and there was a look in his eyes that made her blood chill. "We should leave," he repeated with a calm voice.

"Are you crazy? We wouldn't survive one day without him. And he's our friend." Jenny's breath was rasping and her pulse racing. Her head suddenly felt hot.

"We're safer without him. He's the bigger risk. You've seen the gun as well. What's preventing him from using it against us?"

"What possesses you?" She wanted to get up, but a sudden move of the boat threw her off balance. She slumped back on the bench. "Why do you think he's a risk? He saved you, for heaven's sake, risking his own life."

"Right, and by the way, he killed two guys in front of my eyes. I could tell it wasn't his first time. He didn't even bat an eyelid. I tell you, he is a monster." Eduard peered out again towards the island. "There will be situation when it's him or us."

"He's not a monster. Fine, we don't know anything about his past, but nobody asked about anybody's past on the farm. From what I've seen he's risking his life every day for us. Why would he do that if he wasn't a good guy?" This time Jenny managed to get up. She went over to Eduard and touched his arm. "Hey, tell me what happened."

She took his hand and guided him over to the bench. He sat down and it felt as if he had collapsed at the same moment. After a second of silence, he started to cry, and there was no holding back anymore when Jenny took him in her arms. They sat there for what felt like hours, holding each other.

Finally Eduard started to talk. "I thought I lost you. They had me and I gave them everything. I thought maybe they wouldn't do the same to you as they did to me if I told them all I knew. I betrayed our friends, Tank, Jason and the others—I killed them."

"You did it because of me."

"It doesn't make it better." His body stiffened up and he tried to get out of her arms. "I killed them and I gave away our home. It's my fault that we're here now, lost on this boat."

Jenny noticed the same rage she had seen in the cell after the arson attack in Burlington. "It's not your fault. Everybody would have given in to what they did to you."

He relaxed again, but it felt more like resignation than understanding.

"You don't understand. They had me. I was actually glad when I heard the other guy ordering my guard to kill me. I was relieved. And then CJ jumped out. I hadn't even seen him come in. He was just there and seconds later the guard was dead. They went down without a sound. I should have died, not them. I should have died and everything would be over."

Jenny took him in her arms again and this time he didn't resist. "It's ok. It shouldn't have been you. We didn't survive the prison, the flooding and so many other things just to give up like this. And we should be glad to have a friend like CJ who protects us."

Eduard nodded.

"But," Jenny gazed deeply into Eduard's eyes, "we should ask him about his past. We deserve to know the truth."

Eduard nodded again, but in the middle of the movement he turned and tilted his head. "Shh..."

Jenny had heard it as well and they both ducked behind the railing. There was a paddling sound coming closer.

#

*Eduard — Day 465 (July 29, Santa Catalina, CA)*

Jenny helped Max to climb on board while Eduard grabbed the heavy items CJ lifted up to them. Eduard was surprised that the pain under his fingernails wasn't as pinching as before. After everything was on board, he tried to lend CJ a hand, but CJ shook his head.

"I have two more rounds to go. I even found fuel," he said and disappeared again.

Eduard looked around at the bags and boxes he had just lifted into the boat. Jenny kneeled down and opened one after the other. "This is like Christmas. We have white rice, honey, corn starch, corn syrup and check out at all those cans."

*Something is missing.* He couldn't say what it was, but it hit him when Jenny said something about powdered milk. "I hope he brings water."

Max poked him and nodded.

"You're injured." Jenny grabbed Max's arm. A deep, ugly lesion reached from his elbow down to his wrist. The blood was already dry. "We have to disinfect it, immediately. Wait." She rushed below deck while Eduard inspected the lesion.

"How did you get that?" Eduard rubbed his neck.

Max only shrugged, and before he could do another mime, Jenny came up again with a small white box with a red cross on top.

"I found this downstairs." She got out a flask, poured some liquid onto a white cotton pad and started to disinfect the lesion.

"Come. Let me finish it up downstairs," she said and they went below deck again.

Eduard heard a noise. *CJ.* He headed towards the railing. CJ appeared with the lifeboat full of boxes. *No water.*

CJ started to hand over the boxes. When he grabbed the last box, he added, "Be careful with this one—this is very sensitive equipment." Before he handed it over he added, "Really sensitive and really important."

Eduard frowned and almost tripped over another box he had placed on deck. *Damn, that's what happens when somebody tells you to be extra careful.*

"And don't open it—not yet," CJ said from the lifeboat, already taking off again.

Eduard followed CJ with his eyes until he was out of sight and then turned back to the boxes. He opened all of them, except for the one CJ had told him not to—no water yet. A sound caught Eduard's ears; Max was whimpering downstairs. He saw Jenny finishing up dressing the wound when he got down. She raised her head when he entered the cabin. "They only had this old acidy disinfectant. You know how this shit burns." Jenny caressed Max's hair. He stopped whimpering immediately.

"We still have no water." Eduard flicked his head up to the deck.

Jenny straightened up. "I'm sure he would bring it if he found some." Her eyes took on a defiant glance.

"I'm not doubting him, but we need water to survive. It's a pity this isn't a modern boat or we would have solar panels woven into the canvas and a desalination plant on board."

Jenny didn't reply. What could she say anyway? All these if-then thoughts didn't actually solve any problems. Eduard's cheeks hurt and he realized he had been chewing on them all along.

Max twitched Eduard's shirt and Max nodded. Eduard frowned. "Do you know what he means?"

Jenny shook her head. Eduard hunkered down and looked at Max. "You got water?"

Max smiled and nodded again. Eduard pressed his lips together and Max hugged him. Eduard gasped. His eyes were wide open, but his mouth was smiling.

They all startled when something hit the boat. Eduard rushed back on deck as the bang was still echoing through the hull. It didn't sound like a big thing, more like a small boat. He could hear voices on the other side of the railing. He recognized CJ's, but there was another one—a female voice. Eduard bent over the railing. CJ was sitting in a small skiff; with barely enough space for two passengers and all the tanks and boxes, it lay deep in the water. The lifeboat they were dragging behind them was full as well, but he couldn't see the contents as they were covered with a large, folded piece of canvas.

CJ glanced at Eduard. "Can you help Lin? But be careful, the skiff doesn't allow for too much movement."

The woman stood up and held her hand out. Eduard couldn't see a lot in the dim light, but he could tell she was of slender build with straight hair. The skiff was already shaking dangerously and CJ was having difficulties keeping the water out. Eduard grabbed the woman's hand and helped her climb into the boat. Her grip was weak and he was surprised by how light she was. He had guessed her to be about his age, but when she was sitting in the boat and he could see her closer, he noticed the wrinkles in the corners of her eyes. Jenny appeared on deck and stopped when she saw the woman. Eduard let go of Lin's hand and turned back to CJ to help him with the other boxes and the canvas. He could hear Jenny talking to Lin behind him, but he only got fragments. Lin didn't reply. He flicked his head to the side when CJ handed him the next box.

"I found her in the naval research center. She was the only one left. It's her equipment. I leave nobody behind," said CJ.

Eduard continued with the boxes without answering. The last thing CJ handed over before he got into the boat himself was a metal box with cables attached to it.

"Battery." He had guessed Eduard's question. "And the box I told you not to open contains portable desalination equipment— that means unlimited water. Help me get the lifeboat back on the foredeck."

Soon after they were ready to go. With their new passenger, they had to squeeze together on the bench. Eduard watched the island disappearing in the dark. The skiff, attached with a rope, was dancing on the waves made by the boat.

#

*Eduard — Day 466 (July 30, At sea, West of Los Angeles, CA)*

Jenny and Eduard took the helm again for four hours in the early morning. Lin had been up with CJ and went to rest with him. Jenny threw Eduard a look. Eduard didn't react, but he had noticed it too—it was as if there were earlier ties between those two, or new ones. Max slept on deck like he always did. Jenny checked on him while Eduard took care of the course and the helm.

A small sickle of light announced the sun on their left. A fine line between the light and the reflections of the sea indicated land.

Jenny came back and hugged him. "What do you think of her?"

"Not sure. She seems awfully attached to CJ."

Jenny held him closer. "I trust him."

Eduard didn't reply. He looked over to the east. The light was getting brighter by the minute. He wondered where they were. *I have to ask CJ when he gets up. He needs to involve us more.*

"Honey?" Jenny tore him out of his thoughts. "What are you thinking?"

He squinted at her. "We need to ask him about his past— alone. I do trust him, but I want to know."

Jenny nodded and they both silently watched the sun rise. Two hours later CJ came up, without Lin in tow.

"Where are we?" Eduard stepped away from the helm and CJ took over.

He glanced over to the shore. "South of Tijuana, I guess. We'll have good winds until Panama. Afterwards we'll be slowing down."

Jenny frowned at CJ "Why's that?"

CJ looked at the compass and slightly corrected before he answered. "We are hitting the tropics. It's mid-August—that means that the trade winds are changing. So far we've had south-easterly winds so we could go south, but when we hit north-easterly winds we'll have to zigzag our way south. It will slow us down by half, at least."

Eduard cleared his throat. It didn't help; it still felt dry. "You need to tell us more about your plans and how to get there."

CJ scanned him and although he didn't frown, Eduard had the feeling that he was close to it.

"Don't get me wrong. It's not that we don't trust you, but what if you get sick or hurt and we have to carry on? You know all this from... wherever, but you hardly share."

CJ looked down and then alternately at Eduard and Jenny, standing to the left and right of him.

"You're right. I have to tell you more. Please accept my apology, but I'm not used to this."

Jenny smiled, but Eduard couldn't. "What is 'this' to you? You're very resourceful, but we know so little about you."

CJ stared forward for a long time before he answered. "Yes, I'm not used to talking about me, but you're not very talkative yourself, Eduard, are you?"

Eduard got goosebumps looking into his piercing dark eyes.

"What do you mean?"

"I never heard you actually say that you were in prison for that bombing in Burlington. Fine, Donna told me, but I never heard you say that you were there, or that you were innocent." CJ glanced back at the compass and again corrected the course a little.

Eduard felt nauseous again and his fingernails were pinching. "I..."

"Yes?" CJ turned back to him.

"I..."

"He's protecting me." Jenny's voice from the other side sounded firm and weak at the same time. "We're scared that if people know who I am, we'll become a target."

"And who are you, if I may ask?"

"My full name is Jenny Remules. I am the daughter of August Remules."

CJ whistled through his teeth and eyed Jenny, tilting his head. "Yeah, I think I saw you once on TV, but you looked... different."

"I was heavier... and angry, back then."

CJ turned back to Eduard. "I guess your questions come from when I got you out of the camp."

Eduard nodded and bit on his lips.

"I'm an ex-Navy SEAL, if there is such a thing as an ex-SEAL. I got injured twice in Syria and Iran, but after the Pan-Arabic civil war I couldn't take it anymore. I was diagnosed with PTSD. Why do they even have to give it an acronym? Maybe it's less scary to them, but for me it was hell." He paused and blew out air.

Eduard listened, his legs growing weaker by the second.

"After they had pumped me full of medicine in the hospital, they released me and I wandered across the country until Donna found me one morning, sick and exhausted. She took me in on her farm and I grew calmer working in the fields and the woods." CJ took another deep breath.

Eduard glimpsed at Jenny. She was listening, staggered.

"Don't get me wrong," CJ fixated on Eduard, "I had to rescue you, but since I..." CJ swallowed hard. "There is a reason I don't want to sleep. I'm happier standing here, holding the helm. It gives me direction."

184 | G.D. LEON

"I'm sorry." Eduard swallowed. "I had no idea. Let me know—I'll do whatever I can."

CJ turned to him. "Just let me have the helm. And trust me; please just trust me."

"I do." Eduard blinked at Jenny.

She nodded. "We do."

#

*Dennings — Day 580 (November 22, Fairview, MT)*

Jude was walking up and down his office on the 75th floor when Adriana arrived.

"What's wrong?" she taunted him with a mix of worry and amusement.

"Nothing. It helps me think." He stopped and sighed. "And it keeps me warm. We were too late. It's freaking November and we're already in the 40s. Damn Clutsky—when the hell will we get full heating back?"

"I agree. I can't wait to get back into my warm bunker, but why don't you stay in the Convention Center or on the lower floors? They're heated well."

He frowned. "Are you kidding? With that smell? I'm actually glad we haven't had a mutiny yet."

She strolled over to the window and watched out. The early morning sunlight gave the scenery something peaceful and serene. "It should go up to the high 60s today."

Dennings chuckled. "Who says that? The weather channel?"

"No, my satellites—we've recovered 60% now." Several dark tails of smoke indicated barrels burning in the streets. The city had grown tremendously in the past two years; motor homes and trailers had moved in from all across the country. Every time she came up here and watched it, she had the feeling it had grown since the last time. *I'm glad it's not my problem to feed them all anymore.*

"When are Frank and Bruce coming up? They don't expect me to go down, do they?"

Adriana turned around and laughed. "How dare they."

Dennings forced a smile. "Fine, let's go to the Convention Center, but we need privacy. And next week we're moving back to New Mexico for the winter. Clutsky should inform the guys on the Holloman Base."

#

*Dennings — Day 581 (November 23, Fairview, MT)*

"He what?" Dennings jumped up, shouting at Frank, who looked small despite his natural size.

"He escaped. Don't shout at me. I only heard it today."

"When?" Dennings leaned forward and narrowed his eyes. His ears picked up noise outside the door.

"Seven months ago, right after he gave away the secret bunker." Frank straightened up a little. "I was in Bolivia back then. How was I supposed to know all the details?" he asked with a quaking voice.

Without listening any further to Frank's prevarications, Dennings started to march around in the small room. *We're losing it.* His body felt heavier than when he had been walking in his office earlier that day. He turned back to the table. "We need to ramp it up."

They looked at him with question marks in their eyes.

"Our leadership team is too small. Well, except Bruce, who has the luxury of having inherited a chain of command. We need to expand, set up roles and responsibilities."

Bruce and Adriana nodded.

"But how?" Frank was the only one who still had the questioning look in his eyes.

"We do it the old way. Bruce, you take care of defense outside the US; Frank is in charge of law and order inside the US. Adriana ensures intelligence and information. I'll lead the efforts to re-build the infrastructure." Dennings turned to Bruce. "And we need resources: metals, sugar, bananas, rice, whatever you can get overseas."

Frank crossed his arms and lowered his gaze. Dennings frowned at Adriana, but she only chuckled at Frank's reaction. *What a big baby.*

"Spit it out." The noise outside the door got louder, or was it only in Dennings' mind? He pinched his lips and scowled towards the door.

Frank took a deep breath. "I should be responsible for the continent. I already have the connections in Latin America."

Dennings turned back to the others. Adriana reacted first. "It would be difficult to maintain the relationships with military power. They tend to react strangely to a US military presence."

Dennings sighed. "Bruce?"

Bruce shrugged. "As long as we can use their ports, I'm fine."

"I can guarantee that," said Frank quickly.

"Fine, but..." Dennings waited until Frank's attention was back, "you need to split to get some support." He stepped closer to the table, took out a paper and a pen. "I need seven names from you: in Latin America, one for the north and one for the south, then the West Coast, Rockies, North Plains, South Plains and Canada, or however you split it up. Those will be your deputies, governors or whatever you want to call them and you will spend half of your time here in Fairview coming up with rules and regulations."

Frank had already straightened his back and taken in air to protest, but Dennings wouldn't allow him to utter a word.

"Or do you want me to appoint all security issues to Bruce? You can have a SWAT team, bounce around the continent and blow people up. Your choice." Dennings leaned forward, supporting his weight on the back of a chair, and simply stared at Frank. He was surprised to find that he would feel relief if Frank chose the latter.

Frank didn't reply.

"I thought so." Dennings turned around. "Tomorrow, same time, I get the names."

# CHAPTER SIX

# Strike

*Adriana – Day 600 (December 12, Donna's Farm, Apache-Sitgreaves National Forest, AZ)*

Adriana frowned at the picture in front of her. "You intercepted that how?"

The young lieutenant stared at his screen and typed frantically on his keyboard. Adriana turned around to him and he winced. She felt impatience bubbling up inside her. Shaking her head, she stomped over to the door and shouted "Captain!" She loved to stomp; certain guys winced with every stomp.

She was still holding the door after a second and she tilted her head. "Stark! Now!"

Captain Stark appeared in the door. He was dressed only in a towel and half shaved. "I'm sorry, I was..." he stammered.

"Never mind. Your rookie is having some difficulties." Adriana still held the door, leaving Stark barely enough space to squeeze through. He almost lost his towel and Adriana chuckled as she watched him waddle over to the lieutenant, who whispered something to him. A new view appeared on the big screen showing the same picture, but sharper and with coordinates.

The captain looked at the screen. "It's a TEL." He turned his head towards Adriana.

"Is that what I think it is?"

"Mobile rocket launcher, somewhere in Siberia."

Adriana tilted her head. "How did we get this picture? Does this mean their cameras work as well?" She turned to the lieutenant. He ducked behind his screen and peeked over at the captain. Stark waddled over with a pinched expression on his face, still holding his towel with one hand. Adriana had a hard time holding her laughter back and she was sure the corners of her mouth were constantly twitching.

He peered at the screen and frowned. Then he slowly got up and turned to Adriana. "They have set up a rudimentary network. We tapped into it by accident."

"Where?"

Stark looked back at the screen. "Somewhere north-east of Yakutsk. We also have satellite images."

On the screen a second image appeared. The lieutenant pointed to something and the captain added, without looking up, "Communication indicates that they loosely cover half of the Yakutsk province, and it's half-baked military jargon as far as the translation AI can tell." A glimpse of worry showed up in his eyes. "This doesn't look like Russian troops—it looks more like a local warlord."

Adriana took a deep breath and blew out through her mouth. Both the captain and the lieutenant were staring at her when she turned around, but both looked down when her eyes caught them.

"Get dressed and alert the others. Meeting in fifteen."

"Yes Ma'am." Stark was almost out of the door when Adriana called him again.

"You still have shaving cream behind your ear."

He blushed and disappeared. Adriana walked over to the lieutenant and bent down to him. He showed difficulty in concentrating on the screen. "Never hold back. A simple 'I'm not sure, but...' would do it. You are entitled to a couple of mistakes. One's already gone now."

The lieutenant swallowed hard. Adriana turned back to the large screen and smiled. "Get me Dennings and Bruce."

#

*Dennings — Day 601 (December 13, Donna's Farm, Apache-Sitgreaves National Forest, AZ)*

Dennings arrived one day later and wrinkled his nose when he entered the computer room. Two soldiers jumped up from the floor and saluted. Adriana got up slowly.

"This must be super important, obviously more important than hygiene." He grinned.

Adriana's reply was eaten by a yawn. She scratched her head. "We need Bruce as well."

"He's with the fleet. They gathered all the ships they could reach in Hawaii."

Adriana grunted and walked over to one of the computers. "Is that smart? They could blow up the entire fleet with one strike."

He tilted his head and felt the urge to stretch his neck. He always felt like that when something seemed wrong. "Who are 'they'? There is no 'they'."

Adriana brought up the picture of the TEL on the screen. "Warlords in Siberia. And there are more in Northern China."

For several seconds, Dennings stared at the screen. He clenched a fist and rubbed it in his other hand.

Bruce came up on the screen.

"Howdy." Bruce was standing on the bridge of the USS *L.J. Gibbs*. Behind him, the two flight decks of the catamaran aircraft carrier plowed their way through what appeared to be a rough sea.

"We need a secure environment. This is confidential."

Bruce nodded and the screen went black again.

"That wasn't Hawaii." Adriana had got rid of her jacket and he could see the sweat patches under her arms. "Do you want me to get Clutsky as well?"

"No. This is international. I don't want him to mess with Bruce again. That incident was enough."

Adriana smirked. "Which one do you mean? The one where he kept one of Bruce's aircraft carriers in port, arguing that he wanted a toy as well, or the one where he hit on Bruce's mistress while he was out?"

Dennings didn't feel like joining in with her smirk.

The picture of Bruce came up on the screen again, this time in his captain's quarters.

"Where are you?"

"In my quarters. Why?"

Dennings shook his head. "Not you. Where's the fleet?"

"Ah. Half of it is on its way to Indonesia—we need food re-plenishments—and I am on my way to meet our friends."

Dennings glanced at Adriana.

She tilted her head. "Russians or Chinese?"

"Actually both. I got a call two days ago. It seems they're having problems at home. We will meet them in the Philippine Sea."

"And why are we only hearing about it now?" Adriana's expression had moved from puzzled to annoyed.

Bruce leaned forward and got a pinched expression on his face. "Do you want to tell her?" He looked at Dennings and raised his eyebrows.

Dennings could feel Adriana's gaze, but he took his time to turn around. "Need to know."

Adriana's shoulders dropped and it took her a split second to get her act together. "Well, it was nice talking to you Bruce, but this is need to know as well." She turned around, strode to her computer and severed the connection.

Dennings turned around on one foot. "Out," he barked at the military staff. They jumped up and rushed out.

"Before you start—" began Adriana, but Dennings interrupted her with a wave of his hand.

"Get Bruce back on."

Adriana didn't move.

"Do it. This is for both of you." Dennings thought he heard a low rumbling, but a second later Bruce came back on.

He was leaning back and his feet were on the desk. "It almost feels as if we're married."

Adriana opened her mouth to shoot back, but Dennings was faster. "Stop it, both of you." He paused to make sure he had got their attention. "Where on the way did we lose the trust, guys? Yes, he told me two days ago, but I had no way to communicate it from New Mexico. You didn't expect me to tell you that over radio, did you?" Dennings glowered at Bruce. "And you, don't try to divide us. This is not a game. We have to rely on us, otherwise this will break apart and we will lose what we've built. Including Clutsky, even if he has acted a little strange lately. He's still part of the team and I expect both of you to give him an update if you have contact. Is that clear?"

"So why did you say it was need to know, then?" Adriana put on a resilient stare.

"It was a joke, for heaven's sake."

"Fine," she replied and pressed her lips together.

"Well then. But actually, I didn't expect him to already be on his way."

Bruce took his feet down. "They said it's urgent and that it's a homemade problem. Still, I don't trust them. I have a drone boat with a radio scheme magnifier going ahead of us. If they are ill willed we will be on top of them before they can even say Vladivostok." He grinned and scratched his chin.

Adriana shared her screen and Bruce's eyes widened. "What the hell?"

She filled Bruce in on the details. In the middle of her explanation he jumped up, and by the time she was done he was walking around his quarters with a fierce grin on his face. "We need to take the warlords out." He looked up. "That's what they want from me—they can't handle it themselves."

"Be careful, this is not our war. I don't want to be retaliated at by them."

"We only have a limited a number of conventional cruise missiles anyway. I'm hesitant to sacrifice any planes or pilots." A pensive shadow covered his face. "I hope they don't propose a nuclear strike."

Dennings and Adriana both jumped at the word 'nuclear'.

"No way will you use nuclear weapons." Dennings felt heat boiling in his head. He didn't look over at Adriana, but he could feel her thoughts jumping around in her mind.

Bruce got serious again and glared back into the camera. "I won't, at least not against those warlords, but..."

"No nuclear weapons!" Dennings hadn't heard himself shout in decades. *Not another Phoenix—not on my account.*

"Hear me out. What we see here is a new development. Right now they're warlords, but soon they might gang together. Think this out: in a year from now we might have to face a recovered Chinese or Russian government and they will be more dangerous than these warlords. We should hit first, before they're able to react. We have calculations available from before the blackout: six big warheads and EMP-bomb coverage of the rest will run no risk of a nuclear winter."

"For the last time, no nuclear weapons!"

Bruce grumbled something before he said out loud, "Fine, but mark my words."

Dennings jutted out his chin. "Keep us posted when you know more about their plans."

Bruce nodded, hesitant.

#

*Adriana — Day 605 (December 17, Donna's Farm, Apache-Sitgreaves National Forest, AZ)*

Adriana jumped out of bed at the first knock at her door. The young lieutenant lying next to her only grunted when she grabbed the blanket to cover her nudity.

Outside, Captain Stark stood with a chalk-white face. She had only opened the door a slit. He didn't even bother to notice the blanket or peek into the room. "There has been an incident. You need to come."

"I'll be there in two."

The captain nodded sharply. She closed the door and woke the lieutenant. "Out. Now," she said while slipping into her trousers and shirt. He looked at her as if she was speaking in riddles, but the missing blanket helped him to regain his senses. "Out. I need to go. Get out. If somebody sees you, I'll have you executed."

He flinched and hurried to get dressed as well, but she barely noticed as she ran out.

One minute later she entered the main computer room and was confronted with satellite images of burning cities, woods and landscape: a total of fifteen screens.

"We have multiple large-scale explosions all across Russia and China, including Moscow, Beijing and other major cities." Captain Stark was having problems finding his words. "Smaller cities and rural areas got hit with EMP bombs, mainly in Russia and Northern China. Ma'am, this was a nuclear and EMP strike targeting Russia and China."

Adriana swallowed. "Do we know the source?"

"Not with 100% certainty. It originated somewhere out of the Philippine Sea." He ducked with a face that was begging not to beaten.

"Can you get me satellite footage?" Adriana felt as if her face was frozen, incapable of moving to show any expression. For the first time she felt the air conditioning blowing against her neck and her left ear started to hurt. It took forever for the pictures to appear. Thoughts of *That's not true* and *It wasn't him* were dashing in her brain, but the latter gave her a sting in her stomach. *If not him, who else?*

Then the images came up.

*Better him than the Chinese or the Russians*, she thought.

"We had a satellite in range for about five minutes, starting two minutes prior to the detonations." Captain Stark watched Adriana as if waiting for a reaction.

She stepped closer to the large screen. "What are these three groups of ships? Can you go closer?"

He moved the picture closer to the group of ships that was furthest away from the rest. Judging by the scale, it was over thirty miles to the west of the other two groups, who were almost merged.

"This appears to be the USS *L.J. Gibbs* with the usual cruisers and destroyers, but what are the others then?" He concentrated on his computer and the images moved to the two other groups which were closer together. "These are Russians and Chinese. There's a Shtorm-class carrier, probably the *Kamchatka*, and over here the *Guangdong*..."

Missile launches on the screen interrupted him. All the ships in the Russian and Chinese fleets showed launches; Adriana guessed at about 40. The captain scrolled out and the image now showed a multitude of launches. *There must be more than a hundred.* All the launches pointed in a similar direction, north to north-west, towards the area of the warlords. All but two, launched from the US carrier group, which were pointing towards the east. Seconds later, while the majority of the missiles were still underway, the first two hit the Russian and Chinese fleets. Two domes rapidly built up until they grew into one single, eight-shaped dome. *Hydrogen bombs. This asshole took out the other fleets before taking out their entire countries.*

He switched screens and showed pictures of missiles impacting targets all across Russia and China. A dozen domes from hydrogen bombs grew where major cities were, but most impacts appeared to fail: EMP bombs. One satellite in a lower orbit got knocked out. As the domes collapsed, they left rings of fire.

Adriana opened her mouth to say something, but her dry throat prevented it. She swallowed and cleared it. "Get me Dennings. Tell him it's urgent. I expect him within the next six hours." She closed her eyes and breathed deeply. Then she turned around and let herself fall into her chair. After a second she got the key to the bottom drawer, opened it and took out a bottle of bourbon. She grabbed her coffee mug and filled it halfway, walked over to Captain Stark and filled his as well.

"This screws everything." She shook her head and took a gulp.

He shivered and took a sip as well.

# CHAPTER SEVEN

# Vineyard

*Jenny – Day 634 (January 15, Valparaiso, Chile)*

Sitting at the bow, Lin saw the lights first. She frowned briefly and shrieked when she realized it was Valparaiso. Jenny and Max jumped up at once and brachiated carefully to the front of the boat. Eduard remained in the back. The sea was rough and since CJ had changed course towards the continent an hour ago, the waves had been hitting it from the side, causing a constant rolling of the boat. After half a year at sea with only very few stops to replenish their supplies, Eduard still had not gotten used to the rolling.

"That's more light than just from solar cells. They have power." Lin said what Jenny was thinking.

"Why do they have power? Not even Lima had power."

Lin shrugged. "I don't care. Power means civilization and civilization means we get off this sloop." Her lips curled. "Aren't you happy as well, CJ? You don't have to take care of a bunch of kids anymore," she added and glared at Jenny.

Jenny wanted to reply, but Eduard was faster. "Stop, pitting us against each other," he said in a low voice. "We've been through much more with CJ than you can imagine."

Without losing any further words, Lin's gaze turned back to the lights.

The boat turned to the right and the rolling eased. Jenny turned back to CJ at the helm, but not without throwing another angry look at Lin.

*Did she just smirk?* Jenny's neck stiffened.

"I don't want to land in the city." CJ explained without being asked. "There's a beach a little south. Around this time of the year there should only be fishermen doing their business."

"Why do they have power?" Jenny glanced over at the dim lights that were now a little more to their left.

CJ shrugged. "An outdated power grid in combination with hydroelectric plants, I guess, but it's not as bright as I've known it. Seems they were only able to rebuild some of the power." He frowned. "We have to be cautious."

Eduard had a forced smile on his pale face. "Will your friends still be there?"

"I don't know." CJ only took his eyes off their heading to glance at the compass. "That's why we have to be cautious."

"How do you know them?" asked Jenny.

CJ pressed his lips together. "I was stationed here." His grip of the helm got tighter as the boat started rolling again with the waves hitting from the side. "A classified mission during the Pan-Andean war when they found crude oil in the south." He paused for a second and looked down at the compass, as if he still needed it with the coast that close. "Let's say I trust them but nobody else."

Eduard glimpsed at Jenny and she nodded. *Sometimes you don't want to know more*, she thought.

Nobody talked for quite a while. The lights passed unnoticeably slowly on their left. CJ turned the boat back left and the lights disappeared behind the dark mass of a headland.

"No lights on deck anymore from here on." He flicked his head to the deck lights.

Eduard switched them off. Only a small light right next to the helm remained, allowing CJ to monitor the compass.

"Cape Docas. The town of Quintays is right behind it." CJ blew air through his nose with a nostalgic expression his face, as far as Jenny could see in the light of the small lamp at the helm. "The best fish I ever had."

Jenny smiled at him. "Not the only good thing that happened there."

The nostalgic gaze in CJ's face turned melancholic. "It was the best time of my life—nothing but fish, sun and wine." The melancholy disappeared and he put on his usual inscrutable face. "I'll go and check out the situation."

They were now close to the shore. A small cliff loomed on their right and to their left a single light indicated that they had entered a bay. The darkness in front of them provided a gloomy contrast to the brightness of Valparaiso one bay further up. CJ let down the anchor and turned around to reel in the skiff.

"I'm coming with you." Lin had come back from the front of the boat.

"No, I'm going alone." CJ caressed Max's head. "You stay as well this time. It's safer."

Max nodded, CJ climbed over into the skiff and disappeared into the night.

#

*Jenny — Day 634 (January 15, South of Valparaiso, Chile)*

CJ came back half an hour later. In the meantime the offshore wind had brought wisps of fog towards the boat. They heard the paddling and minutes later CJ boarded.

"They're still there. We can hide the boat in the boathouse of the old diving school." His face came into the light at the helm and it seemed to be beaming. "Eduard, anchor, please."

Eduard lifted the anchor and CJ steered the boat towards the land. In front of them, a little to the left, a beacon appeared. It constantly moved up and down, and judging from the speed, it had to be a strong flashlight. The light was blurred a little by the fog and it got denser the closer they got to the shore. CJ steered the boat towards the light and soon the shapes of buildings came up in front of them. The light disappeared and CJ whispered to them to take the ropes at the bow and the rear and throw them to the guys on the quay. Jenny could see neither the quay nor any guys, but she climbed to the bow and grabbed the rope anyway. Not too late; seconds later there was the quay and a guy silhouetted against the dark. Jenny threw him the rope and he attached it to a cleat. In the dim light she thought she saw Eduard doing the same in the rear. The ropes stretched and the boat came to a halt. Afterwards, the only sound remaining was the waves beating against the quay.

The two men climbed over and started working on the mast. Jenny could not see a lot, but she heard the wood of the mast moaning. Only minutes later, the sails were removed and the mast folded to a third of its original height. Without having said a word, the men jumped back onto the quay and removed the ropes from the cleats. The boat moved forward again towards the building in front of them and a large hole appeared out of the darkness. Slowly, the hole swallowed the boat. The fog made Jenny cough and the dry baying echoed from the building.

As soon as the boat was entirely in the boathouse, one of the two men closed the doors behind them while the other attached the ropes again at the cleats.

"Get your stuff and follow me." Even though CJ uttered the words in a low voice, it sounded unnatural after the minutes in silence.

Jenny moved back to the rear of the boat, where Eduard had already started stuffing their bags. They got off the boat, right behind Lin, who had made sure she remained close to CJ. She stumbled up the first steps; after months on the boat it took her a couple of seconds to get used to solid ground enough not to stagger anymore, but the reeling sensation remained.

"Come," whispered CJ and they followed him and the two men past abandoned houses to a building a little uphill. Nobody spoke while they were walking. From time to time moonlight broke through the clouds and created a white wall of fog around them. Somewhere a small bell jingled in the wind. The closer they came, the more Jenny could see of the building. It had two stories, with its front towards the sea and a little terrace. The main entrance was on the side and they were let inside without a word being said.

Jenny first had to get used to the light. The only thing she saw at first was somebody hugging CJ. When it became clearer, she saw an elderly woman, dressed in black and with a small, crooked posture; in CJ's arms she appeared even smaller. Jenny couldn't understand what she was saying, but between words lost in sobbing or muffled by CJ's clothes she recognized the words "*querido hijo*"—beloved son.

The two guys were about Jenny's height and were built more on the bulky side, but it could also have been that the sweaters and coats they were wearing made them appear that way. Jenny guessed one of them to be around forty and the other in his late teens; probably father and son, judging by the similarity of their faces.

When the elderly woman let go of CJ, he hugged the older of the two guys, followed by the younger one. The woman turned to Jenny and hugged her as well. She was surprisingly strong. She hugged each of the others while CJ introduced them to the family in Spanish. "This is Max. I picked him up out of a totaled car. His parents got killed in the accident; he miraculously survived."

Jenny examined Max's face. A veil of sadness covered his eyes.

"I met Jenny and Eduard on a farm we worked on together, and we rescued Lin from an island outside Los Angeles."

Lin's back stiffed up when CJ explained to her what he had said. "Given that you wouldn't have gotten far without my equipment, I would rather say I joined you than you rescued me," she snapped.

"Fair enough." CJ didn't react to her comment.

The elderly woman guided them into the main room of what appeared to be an old restaurant. "*Hambre*?" She smiled and repeated in broken English, "Hungry?" Only then did Jenny notice the plates and the food on the table. They all rushed over and started eating. Jenny had never imagined that boiled potatoes, corn cobs and spinach could be such a meal. Only the fish was left over. *No wonder, after six months of fish on the boat.*

When they were all done and leaning back in their chairs, the older of the two guys brought out wine and CJ started to answer the questioning looks on Jenny and Eduard's faces. "This is the Roca family. They grew up here. Fishermen since you can remember. Maria's husband," he pointed to the elderly woman, "opened this restaurant as an additional business. During the war, they were on the federal side, in favor of sharing the oil with Argentina and prospering together. Franco fought in the militia and when the nationalist squads found out they tried to hunt his family down. This is Francisco, Franco's son."

"They got my father when he was out fishing." Franco, the older man, had good English with a light accent. "That's when I asked Cornelius for help."

Jenny tilted her head and saw Eduard's eyebrows go up. CJ chuckled. It was the first time they had seen CJ chuckle. Lin answered with an artificial snigger.

"Cornelius James. I shortened it to CJ when I was eight years old. Franco and I met before his father was killed. He helped me several times with critical information, and when he asked me to help protect his family I couldn't say no. The nationalist squads tried twice to kill them, but gave up afterwards, because they were on the retreat anyway. Since then I've had family down here."

Franco stood up and refilled their glasses. "It has gotten worse again. The squads are back, but instead of being nationalists, they raid whatever they can. The entire town has fled. Valparaiso is safe because it is under the control of the army, but there is no food there, except for the army's."

"But you're still here," said Eduard.

"We are. Again, they raid for food. Every morning when I get back in they are waiting. Two guys up here, two down at the pier, all armed to the teeth, to get whatever I've caught. If we have a good day, they leave us with five fish. If not, they get everything. Then we have to go out again to get more, but too many days we remain without."

Eduard leaned forward. "Why don't you fight?"

"Fighting, *si*, fighting." Francisco had been listening quietly so far, but the word 'fighting' had triggered something. His English was cruder than his father's.

"*Cállate. Tonto.*" Franco rebuked his son and turned back to Eduard. "I'm sorry for my son. He hasn't seen what war can do. We don't fight because there is nothing that would protect us. Back then there was some kind of organization, government or whatever, that provided stability. Now there is no law. People get shot for nothing. Our only protection is the usefulness we have for these people."

"What about the army? They ensure some safety, you said," asked Eduard.

"Yes, but only in Valparaiso and only because it's a harbor. They cover the strategic points. Also in Santiago there are districts that are worse than anything I've seen during the war. But I'm glad you are here—we can use a helping hand."

CJ stood up. He had to tilt his head so as not to hit the ceiling. "We can't stay too long. We endanger you and your family."

Lin frowned at that comment and opened her mouth, but held off whatever she wanted to say. Eduard tilted his chin downwards and for a second Jenny had the impression he was blinking back tears. But then he clenched his jaw and his fists.

Franco hesitated a second and then nodded. "But you are going to stay a couple of days, my brother, right?"

CJ nodded and sat down again.

#

*Eduard — Day 634 (January 15, South of Valparaiso, Chile)*

The atmosphere grew familiar and the family talked about old times, at least for some. Eduard did not feel at all in the mood to participate. *Where will we end up? We can't just run for the rest of our lives.* He glanced over to Jenny who threw him back a worried look. *I hate who did this. Niklas. It was Niklas.*

When it got quieter again, Eduard took Jenny and sat next to CJ, who was laughing with Franco about coups they had achieved. "CJ, we need to talk."

CJ's face got serious. "Anything wrong?"

"We were just wondering why we can't stay longer? I mean, we can help them, and except for the raids in the morning it seems quiet enough." Eduard put his hands on the table palms up and eyed CJ.

Franco stood up, but CJ held him back. "This is important for you as well."

He sat back down again.

"Tell me, do they search for people? I guess you have flyers for some wanted people."

Franco hesitated for a second and bit his lips before he got up and took a tattered paper out of the cupboard behind him. CJ's face darkened when he looked at it. He took a deep breath and handed it over to Eduard and Jenny. It said 'Dead or Alive'. Eduard immediately recognized four of the five pictures: Jenny, her parents and himself. The fifth one he could only guess must be Niklas.

"You are safe here for the moment, but you can't trust anybody." Franco frowned at Jenny and Eduard. "One million *dollares* is a lot of money. People would sell out their families for this money."

Eduard slowly lowered the paper. "How did you know?"

"I didn't, at least not that, but I guessed after they found out about the farm that they would search for us." CJ's face tightened. "I'm surprised though that I'm not on the list."

"What now?" All the hope and happiness of the past hours had disappeared from Jenny's face.

Lin got up from the other end of the table and walked down to them. Before CJ could answer she grabbed the wanted poster and scowled at it. "Now I have questions." When she lowered the paper her brows were wrinkled and her lips pressed into a line.

"I can explain," said CJ, but Lin waved it away with a brusque movement of her hand.

"I want to hear it from her." She pointed to Jenny. "Now, I recognize you. You're the brat of that idiot president. He was never my president."

Jenny jumped up. "Don't you dare talk that way about my dad."

Lin sneered at her. "Try me. I know everything. You were involved in that arson attack. And now look at this." She pointed to the wanted poster. "It almost seems as if you had something to do with all this." She pointed around.

Jenny let her shoulders drop. "No, I didn't. We didn't." Her voice broke down.

Eduard jumped in. "We were innocent of that arson attack. Yes, it was her car, but we were not involved. They just needed a scapegoat. We escaped prison in the chaos. Since then we've been on the run."

Lin didn't lose the scornful expression on her face. "And what about this one?"

Jenny opened her mouth, but Eduard was faster. "We don't know him."

Lin narrowed her eyes and Jenny lowered her eyes. Lin looked back at the paper. "Fine. I hope this is all the truth."

"It is," said CJ, still sitting at the table.

Lin nodded carefully, but somehow there was a wall that had not been there before.

#

*Jenny — Day 635 (January 16, South of Valparaiso, Chile)*

When Jenny woke up the next morning, she was alone. The family had given them Franco and Francisco's rooms, while they crammed together in the grandmother's room. Jenny found Eduard sitting with a cup of coffee and a Thermos flask in the main room downstairs. The main room didn't look very different in daylight. The small windows only allowed a little light to enter, creating bright light cones while the rest of the room remained dim. Pan and kettle sounds from the kitchen indicated that they were not alone.

"Good morning, my love. You have no idea how I missed coffee. Want some?" Eduard took another cup and poured her coffee out of the Thermos.

Jenny kissed him. "You know what I miss? Peppermint hot chocolate."

Eduard closed his eyes and licked his lips. "Followed by a cream cheese bagel."

"Where are the others?" She glanced around. Now that her eyes had got used to the dim light she noticed that the room had needed paint for a long time.

"I don't know, let me ask Maria." Eduard stood up to go into the kitchen, but he turned back to Jenny. "CJ left his backpack here. I guess we really are safe here."

Maria appeared in the door. "*Hambre, querida?*"

Jenny nodded. "Where are the others?

Maria put on a questioning look on her face.

"CJ?"

"*Afuera, pescando.*" She pointed towards the sea outside and Jenny understood. "*Con Franco, Francisco y el niño.*"

"When will they be back. When?" Jenny pointed to the clock on the wall.

"*Tres o cuatro horas.*" Maria held up three fingers and returned into the kitchen.

Jenny sat down. "Shall we walk a little after breakfast? Just a little way up the hill. I need some exercise."

"Great idea, but let's not go too far."

"No, just up the ridge at the back of the house."

Maria came back with bread and butter. Eduard moved two chairs to the window and, watching the sun reflecting on the water, the world was good for the moment.

#

*Jenny — Day 635 (January 16, South of Valparaiso, Chile)*

Jenny and Eduard had been strolling for about an hour along the cliff and were already on their way back when they heard the engine sound. They rushed back, but they didn't get far. From a distance they saw dust rising from the street; it looked like multiple cars. When they reached the ridge above the house they saw three military Jeeps and a pick-up truck stop at the end of the pier. The fishing boat had returned and Franco and CJ were unloading the catch; it appeared to be a good one. Eduard crouched down behind a stump and Jenny followed him. From above they could see Max hiding in a box on the boat. Francisco was already standing on the pier.

"Where is Lin?" whispered Eduard.

Jenny tilted her head, but before she could answer, men started getting out of the cars—a total of about a dozen, all heavily armed. They moved in groups of two to several points along the pier, almost as if they were chessmen. When they were all positioned, another man got out of the car; judging by his golden epaulettes he was a superior. Right behind him, Lin got out of the car.

"She went to them, that bitch," said Eduard with a dark, shaking voice.

Jenny couldn't reply. Her mouth felt dry and she felt the urge to clear her throat. Her heartbeat was racing. The superior was walking over in a relaxed manner, almost strolling. Lin was plodding behind him and Jenny thought she was limping a little. The superior approached Francisco outside the boat and glanced over the catch. He looked up at Franco and CJ and said something. The two got out of the boat and soldiers surrounded them.

"I'm glad we're not down there," whispered Jenny. "Maybe they'll leave again when they don't find us."

Eduard mumbled something without taking his eyes off the scene. The superior climbed on board and scanned around. From far away Jenny could see CJ duck and spread his legs a little.

*He'll attack.* Jenny's heart jumped with that thought.

The superior bent over the box. Max jumped out and tried to run away, but the man caught him. CJ leaped forward. Two soldiers tried to hold him, but he escaped their grip. Two more jumped in. CJ struck them down. Other soldiers ran towards CJ; one hit him with a gun butt on the back of his head and the other kicked his legs away to hinder him from getting on the boat. Three more soldiers were necessary to keep him on the ground. The superior waited until CJ calmed down to say something. CJ shook his head. Franco looked down at his feet. Max used the superior's inattention to get free from his hold.

He didn't get far. The superior drew his gun and shot Max in the back. The dry sound of the gun echoed in the bay. Jenny covered her mouth to prevent herself from shrieking, and a jolt went through Eduard as if he wanted to run down there, but he stopped in the middle of the movement. They could hear CJ braying and bellowing; he had freed himself and was fighting with the soldiers. From the first one he had struck down he apprehended a gun and shot all around. The soldiers shot back. Six men were already lying on the ground, including Franco, and blood flew off the pier into the sea. The superior took cover in the boat and the remaining soldiers covered the area with bullets. Francisco got hit right away; CJ got hit two or three times before went down. Multiple echoes were thrown back from the buildings and the rocks around the bay.

It was all over in less than a minute. The silence afterwards had a ghastly touch.

The superior got up from his cover and barked some orders. The remaining soldiers loaded the fish into the Jeeps. The superior went from body to body and shot a bullet into each. When he got to Max on the boat, it was as if he shot Jenny in her heart.

The soldiers were waiting in front of the cars. Lin had taken cover behind one of the Jeeps and came out now after everything was over. The superior marched towards her, grabbed her arm and tore her out into the open. He barked something to one of his men and Lin started to yell. The soldier who was standing next to her pointed his gun at her and pulled the trigger. Lin tried to duck away, but she didn't stand a chance.

The superior barked orders and most soldiers rushed to their vehicles. The pick-up truck and two of the Jeeps drove off. The two soldiers that remained with the third Jeep started throwing the dead soldiers into the water.

Jenny and Eduard sneaked down to the house, carefully making sure they were not seen by the remaining guards. The dust of the Jeeps had settled when they arrived behind the house. Just then, Maria came running out of the door. With loud moaning and whining she ran down to the pier. One of the soldiers caught her and hindered her from getting to the bodies of Franco and

Francisco. The other soldier took out his gun and pointed it at her.

Eduard ran into the building and grabbed CJ's bag. With CJ's gun he ran down to the pier as well, making sure to always stay covered by the buildings. Jenny had difficulties keeping up with Eduard's speed, but she finally reached him at the last building before the pier. He peeked around the corner and signalled her to stay. The men were still fighting with Maria. Ducking, Eduard ran over to the Jeep. Covered by the car, they did not notice him. They had thrown Maria to the ground and the one with the gun narrowed his eyes.

*He'll shoot.* Jenny saw Eduard leaving his cover. *Don't.*

One of the soldiers had his back towards Eduard and the one with the gun pointed at Maria stood side on to the right, but he didn't look up. Eduard slinked along the car, pointing the gun at the soldier on the right. The soldier was slightly bending his finger and his grip on the gun was getting tighter. Eduard pulled the trigger and hit the guy in the torso. He fell backwards and tripped over the rim of the pier. The other turned around and ducked behind the Jeep. He tried to level his weapon, but Eduard was faster. He pulled the trigger again and hit the second soldier in the shoulder. With a short gurgling sound the soldier fell behind the car. Eduard followed him around the corner of the car and stood over him.

"*Me rindo. Me rindo*," he shouted and Jenny could see him putting his hands up.

The tension went away and she was about to come out from behind the corner when Eduard pulled the trigger again. Jenny ran over to him. "What did you do?"

His hands were shaking. The soldier lay in front of them with blank eyes.

*He killed him*. Jenny felt as if she had to throw up. *We're alive. He killed him!*

Eduard lowered his weapon. It was as if he had not noticed Jenny next to him.

Jenny tore her eyes away from the dead soldier over to Maria, who had gone to Franco's body. She leaned over him, crying. They went over and Jenny took her into her arms.

"We will bury them properly. Right, Eduard?"

Maria shook her head. She wiped the tears out of her eyes and her face got firm. "*Querian ser inhumado en el mar*." She pointed towards the ocean. "Sea."

"We will help you."

She shook her head again. "*Ajudame con los cuerpos*." She pointed to the bodies and the boat. "*Despues*." She gesticulated again. "*Se anda, con el coche*. Jeep." She pointed to the Jeep and waved with her hand.

"Are you sure?" asked Jenny.

Maria nodded and Eduard, still trembling, walked mechanically over to CJ's body, picked him up and dragged him on board. He almost tripped when he looked down. *Max. He must have seen Max. I can't go up there!* thought Jenny. He came back and did the same with Franco and Francisco. In the meantime, Jenny went to the house and packed their bags. When she came back, she grabbed whatever useful gear she found in the boathouse. Maria was already on board and Eduard had removed the ropes when Jenny came out again. Maria waved as the boat started to move.

216 | G.D. LEON

Jenny swallowed and took a breath. "We have to go." Jenny took Eduard's hand and the tension fell off him. He nodded and followed her like a puppy.

#

*Jenny — Day 635 (January 16, East of Valparaiso, Chile)*

"Do you know where you're driving?" Jenny was being thrown around in the seat.

The dusty street in front of them was climbing up a hill. Evergreen trees lined the road on both sides, reminding Jenny of the woods around Donna's farm. That seemed centuries ago. Eduard had been following the road for hours, only switching onto tarmac roads for a couple of minutes at a time.

"Edu?"

Eduard continued to stare at the street in front of them until he abruptly turned the Jeep into the woods. Jenny was thrown around once more until the car came to a halt two yards off the track under a tree. He switched off the engine, jumped out of the car and looked up. Jenny followed him. Seconds later a helicopter flew by, towards the shore.

"I hope they didn't notice the dust," said Eduard.

The helicopter continued on its way and he exhaled without releasing his clenched jaw.

"Honey." Jenny walked around the Jeep and held Eduard's arm.

It was as if he melted under the touch. His legs failed, he sat down on the floor and cried. Jenny sat next to him and held his head. Tears were running down her cheeks as well, but it felt more like she was weeping inside. Eduard's crying turned slowly into sobbing and Jenny let go of his head. He tried to say something, but she put a finger on his lips.

"I know. We stay together and nothing can separate us." Jenny caressed his hair.

Eduard shook his head.

She held his head again, feeling his heavy breathing on her arms. "What is it?"

He shook his head again, stood up without looking at her and walked towards the road. Jenny followed him and he peeked out from under the trees. The sky was blue with brushes of clouds. Wind in the trees was the only sound. Jenny squinted down the road both ways. Wafting dust and heat clouded the view in the distance.

"We'll drive towards the mountains." His face had that ferocious look again, but it had a touch of pain mixed into it.

Jenny scanned his face, trying to get through the mask, but she soon gave up and looked back down the road. "Why there?"

"I overheard Franco telling CJ that there is a pass across the Andes to the Argentinean provinces. There's more space and he suggested we would be safer there. In Chile we'll always be squeezed between the mountains and the sea." Eduard peeked out again. "We should look out for a town called Los Andes in the north-east. We might be able to hop on a train across the mountains from there."

Jenny opened her eyes. "I saw a sign right before we turned into the dust road. It said Los Andes 70 kilometers."

Eduard nodded. "I know. I tried to stay away from open roads, but maybe you're right—we should stay on the roads. I just don't like the risk."

"Could we drive by night, without light? If we only had a map."

Eduard slapped his forehead. "A map." He ran back to the car, Jenny right behind him; she almost stumbled over a root. Eduard opened the passenger door and rifled through the compartment. With an exclamation he held up a map and opened it on the engine hood. "Los Andes is here and we were on F-10-G; no, it was G-10-F. Here, I turned over into the dust..."

A sound shut him up and he stretched his neck. Jenny tilted her head. *The helicopter.* The sound came closer and browsed over their heads, following the side street.

"They saw the dust." Eduard's face was fierce. "They know where we are and in which direction we're going."

"Then let's go back to the paved road and follow that route. They wouldn't expect that and we won't leave a dust cloud."

Eduard folded the map so that the square showed where they were in one corner and Los Andes in another. "Great idea. Let's first check what else we can find in the car." He walked around the car and opened up the back. A whole arsenal of tools and weapons appeared in front of them.

Jenny crowed. "Oh my god."

"Let's take the flashlight and the rope." Eduard took them out and closed the trunk again. "I don't want to start a war here."

"CJ would know what to do with those."

"I'm not a soldier," barked Eduard.

Jenny startled and opened her eyes wide. "That's not what I meant."

"I'm sorry." Eduard's shoulders slumped. "I didn't want to shout at you." He turned around. "The helicopter is gone. I guess they'll send a patrol and I don't want to be here when they arrive. Let's go."

They got into the car and drove off towards where they had come from. Twenty minutes later they were back on the main road and driving towards Los Andes.

#

*Jenny — Day 635 (January 16, East of Valparaiso, Chile)*

Two miles before they reached Los Andes, they ran out of gas. Night had fallen in the meantime and, from what Jenny could see, they were on a deserted road between a copse and a dry arroyo. In front and behind she could see sparse light from the two towns they were between: San Felipe behind them and Los Andes in front of them.

"Let's get it off the street." Eduard jumped out of the Jeep. "Take the steering wheel." He pointed to the copse.

Jenny moved over and Eduard pushed the car into the copse. The gentle slope helped a little and minutes later the Jeep was covered. They took their bags and Eduard stuffed two more guns and some ammunition into them.

"I may not want to start a war, but I'll be damned if I'm not prepared for one," he said with a grim face when Jenny looked at him. She opened her mouth; she didn't know if she liked it or not, but didn't know what to say.

"Come." Eduard crossed the street and Jenny followed.

When he climbed down into the dry arroyo, she hesitated. "Shouldn't we stay up here?" she asked from the rim.

"Down here we are protected. It's much safer down here," he said without looking up.

"I just mean, are you sure the creek is dried out?"

Now he looked up. "No, I'm not... but I'll take that risk over being detected. One million dollars—did you forget?"

Jenny closed her eyes and breathed twice. Eduard was already walking when she opened them again. Jenny got down into the creek bed and rushed to catch up with him. They walked silently and the lights of the town came slowly closer. Twice they passed a deserted house right on the bank of the creek. The first time, Eduard had Jenny take cover while he checked out the house, but the second time she insisted on just walking by in cover. When they came closer to town, they noticed that the creek did not go through town but flowed around it. The town was dark with the exception of what they guessed was a square in the center that was ablaze with light.

Eduard stopped at the town entrance and climbed out of the creek bed. "The town is deserted. Except—" He pointed to the light. "I guess the train station is over there."

Jenny saw a movement in the corner of her eye, over by one of the buildings. *Flashlights.* She poked Eduard and they ducked behind the wall of what used to be a kindergarten. The flashlights came closer.

"I hope they don't have dogs," whispered Eduard.

The flashlights passed the wall. Jenny counted two guys. *No dog.* Jenny blew out when they were out of sight.

Eduard got up again. "Let's see what we can find at that place in the center."

Jenny remained ducking. "Isn't that too dangerous?"

He mumbled something.

Jenny stood up and tilted her head. "What?"

"Nothing. Let's go." He turned around and walked away, making sure to stay covered. Jenny hesitated for an instant and peeked around the corner. Eduard was already two yards away and she rushed to catch up. He took several detours and approached the lighted area in a wide circle. As they got closer, they sneaked through a narrow alley between several two-story buildings. Jenny could hear engine sounds as they came closer to the center, and something else, something popping. *Is that gunfire?*

Eduard stopped at a corner of the square in the center. The wall across the alley was lit by the floodlight from the square in front of them. He waved Jenny to stay in the doorway of one of the houses. "Your shadow," he whispered.

She nodded. Eduard peeked around the corner, startled and rushed away from the corner. He turned his head left and right; his chivvying made her nervous.

"What's—"

"Inside." He opened the door behind Jenny and pushed her through.

Steps came closer and seconds later two men drudged by. Jenny wasn't able to speak; her heart beat in her chest as if it wanted to jump out. One of the men made a loading sound with his rifle. Jenny picked up a few words: something arrives in half an hour, meat and four men to protect it, and twice the word 'wine'.

Eduard peered out of the window. "Let's get upstairs. Maybe we can see more from there." He went over to the stairs.

"How do you know there's nobody living here?" whispered Jenny, still standing at the door.

He shrugged and glanced around. "Not locked. And no clothes hanging, no shoes." He shrugged again and went upstairs.

Jenny followed him. The kitchen was located towards the light. Eduard positioned himself at the corner of one of the windows, and Jenny peeked through the window from below. The floodlight lit the area in front of them like daylight. Jenny had a good view, except for the two closest corners left and right. There was no train, but there were train tracks. Several Jeeps were positioned at one end. Men stood in front of them around barrels containing open fires, although Jenny didn't have the impression that it was cold outside. From time to time one of them shot into the air. On the other side, several pick-up trucks were ready to take on whatever the train was carrying, and close to the tracks containers and boxes were piling up.

"I heard 'four men to protect it'," whispered Jenny.

"No need to whisper. Nobody will hear us with those maniacs out there."

"And it should arrive in half an hour." Jenny didn't know why, but she was still whispering.

"I heard the same. What do you think—how fast will it go when it leaves town?"

Jenny bit on her lips. "Not sure." She glanced over the area again. "What about that area on the other side of the tracks?"

"Too much light."

"At the moment, yes, but as soon as the train is standing there it should be in the dark."

Eduard narrowed his eyes and pressed his head towards the wall to see more into the corner. "Could work. There, at the end."

He fixated on the guys in front their Jeeps once more and clenched his fists. "Let's go."

#

*Eduard — Day 635 (January 16, East of Valparaiso, Chile)*

They hid in the dark, just outside the light, until the train arrived. Jenny was right—it provided perfect cover. She wanted to run straight over, but he grabbed her arm at the very last moment. Jenny frowned at him and he pointed towards the end of the train, where two guys were patrolling.

As soon as they were out of sight, he whispered "Now" and pointed to the end of the train. "That one's already loaded."

Jenny took a short breath through her teeth and they rushed over. The first wagon was locked, the second as well, but the third was still open. They jumped inside and hid behind a pile of boxes. They had barely settled when the door opened again and a handful of men carried more boxes in. Eduard pressed himself against the wall and touched the grip of one of the guns in his bag. Jenny was clinging to his arm.

*I should have given one to her. I could take down three, maybe four if I jump out now and surprise them.* He pictured himself shooting them down. *It wouldn't be hard—just jump out and pull the trigger. They wouldn't stand a chance.* His jaw hurt from clenching his teeth.

More and more boxes piled up and soon covered their view. Eduard sensed Jenny shivering and he put his arm around her. Soon after, the wagon closed and he could hear a metallic clicking.

"They locked us in," he whispered. He couldn't see a lot in the dim light, but he noticed Jenny chewing the inside of her cheek.

He took a breath to say something like, "Everything will be al-right," or, "We will make it," but he didn't. He didn't know why, but before he could rethink it, the train started to move.

#

*Eduard — Day 636 (January 17, Across the Andes)*

Eduard's ears were crackling when he woke up again; they must have gained altitude. He stood up when he realized Jenny was not sitting next to him anymore. She was moving around and opening boxes. Judging by the number of open boxes, she had not slept at all.

"You shouldn't have done that. Now they'll know we were on the train," he snarled at her and regretted it a second later. "Is there something good in there?"

She shook her head. "Batteries, bags of sand and—hey! There's food." She held up a bag from the box she had just opened. She ripped it open and shouted, "Dry meat."

They sat down again and for quite a while the only sounds they made were chewing noises.

"They would have known anyways, or did you want to wait for them to open the door?" Jenny picked the last piece of dry meat out of the bag.

"You're right. I hope it goes slow at some point." Eduard got up and grabbed a dozen more bags out of the box. "We should keep these as provisions."

Jenny stood up as well. "I was wondering what these trains run on. I don't hear any diesel engine and there were no power wires."

"Solar power maybe." Eduard staggered a little. "We must have passed the saddle point. It's going down again."

A muffled sound came from the wheels beneath them.

"And it seems they use the brakes to feed the batteries," he added.

They sat down again and Jenny snuggled into Eduard's side. He put one arm around her. With the other hand he grabbed the grip of CJ's gun in his bag.

Jenny's breath flattened soon after, but Eduard could not find sleep. *Why did Lin do that? One million dollars? What can you do with one million dollars? Nothing! It's worth nothing if you can't find a bigger moron who'll take it.* The monotone *tadam-tadam* of the train tracks that had been in the background moved to the fore. He clenched his jaw. Heat built up in his head and he started sweating. *Damn Niklas. Without him we would still be in our Burlington Resistance cell, lamenting how bad the world is without knowing how good we have it.* Eduard leaned his head back against the wall of the wagon and the vibration transferred to his skull. The *tadam-tadam* of the train got louder when he did this. He moved his head away and the *tadam-tadam* faded into the background again. *Funny...*

Jenny moved a little and he pulled her closer.

*Where do we go? What should we do? We should have fought on the farm. At least that way it would be over.* The heat in his head faded away and what remained was the cold sweat around his neck and on his forehead, and the pain in his jaw.

The sound of the train tracks moved to the background again and Eduard slowly dozed off.

#

*Jenny — Day 636 (January 17, Mendoza, Argentina)*

"It's slowing down. Can you see anything?" Jenny looked up at Eduard. He was standing on a pyramid of boxes and looking out of the only small window the wagon had.

"Hard to say." He coughed.

Jenny could see him narrowing his eyes. He turned his head a little to the left, in the direction the train was going. "We're in a large vineyard. Wait..."

"What?"

"It's a sharp curve. The first locomotive is already around the curve."

He tottered a little when he got down from the boxes and staggered over to the bags.

Jenny frowned. "Everything alright, hon?"

Without responding, he got down, grabbed his bag and took out the gun.

Jenny jumped back. "What are you doing?"

"There's no other way out." He went over to the door. "Get your stuff."

Jenny nodded and got her bag. Eduard pointed the gun at the lock and shot twice. The door was still locked.

He swore and shot once more. Still swearing, he joggled the door. They were almost at the curve. Jenny could feel that the train wasn't slowing down anymore.

Finally the door opened.

The train was going slowly, but still faster than a man could run.

"On three," Eduard shouted.

"No time for that." Jenny jumped. The sound of the train and the wind disappeared and she felt light. For a second she had the impression this wouldn't be a hard landing. Then her feet touched the ground and it felt as if somebody had pulled a carpet away beneath her. Her shoulder hit the ground hard and she almost flipped over.

Before she got back all her senses, Eduard was standing next to her. "Up. We need to get to cover."

Jenny got up, slower than she expected. Her side and her shoulder hurt and she limped over to hide between the vines.

"Everything ok?" The last part of the 'ok' was eaten by coughing.

Jenny nodded and they watched the train disappear.

Eduard coughed again. "Damn dust."

She frowned. *That sounded deeper than just the throat.*

He turned around and started to move away from the tracks. She followed him and was glad he didn't walk too fast. Her hip still hurt.

#

*Jenny — Day 636 (January 17, Mendoza, Argentina)*

They had been walking for about half an hour, through fast-changing surroundings: scattered vineyards, dry grass and dusty stony areas. In the distance she noticed a shed or a shack.

The silence around them was only interrupted by Eduard coughing. Jenny felt that it was getting worse by the minute. He further reduced the pace; now it felt even slow even with her limping.

"Are you ok, hon?" She peered at him from the side.

He didn't turn his head. "We must go further. We can't—" Coughing interrupted his sentence. He swallowed and breathed heavily before he continued. "We can't stay here."

"You're getting sick. You have to rest."

Now he turned to her with a painful look in his eyes.

She glanced around. "Over there. We could try to get into that shed. It's not far."

Five minutes later, they stood in front of the small shed.

"It's not locked." Jenny peeked inside. The smell of motor oil and soil dust made her almost cough. "And it's empty."

She held the door and he trailed inside. He faltered and almost fell. Jenny rushed inside to support him and the door closed. The shed had two small windows, providing only dim light. Eduard sat down in the middle of the room.

"Come on, you have to get up again. You'll get pneumonia on that cold floor." Jenny dragged him up again and sat him down by the back wall on a pile of gunnysacks. He moaned and she put her hand on his forehead. It was glowing. Jenny bit on her lips.

She got up again and looked around. A ladder led to something like a small attic, where she found old blankets. He coughed again and his entire body writhed in pain when she covered him up with the blankets.

Jenny looked around again, hoping to find something else she could help Eduard with, but she didn't see anything. *Water, I need water*, she thought and went to the door.

He moaned again.

"I'm just going outside for a moment to see if there's water around here." Thinking of water made her notice how dry her own mouth felt.

Eduard didn't reply. She opened the door a little and peeked out. The sun was still high—she guessed it was mid-afternoon—but clouds had started to cover parts of the sky. After another glance out, she slipped through the door and walked around the shed. At the back she found a barrel of foul-smelling water. She looked up. Against the bright snowy peaks of the Andes in the background, the brownish hills in front seemed even dustier. She had the feeling she could see houses between the hills. She ducked behind the vines. Should she go over? *No, that's too dangerous.*

The sun from earlier in the day had left and it had cooled down. Jenny had not noticed before, but now she was almost shivering. Slow-moving, lead-colored clouds covered the sky, crumpling up against the mountains. She sneaked back to the entrance, careful not to lose the cover of the vines. She was barely in the shed when the first heavy raindrops fell.

Eduard had stopped moaning, but he was still shivering and he was covered with sweat. She took her coat off and put it over the blankets that already covered him. She sat down next to his head and caressed his hair. Heavy rain poured down outside. The roof leaked and drops came down inside. Jenny scanned the inside of the shed again for something else that would help Eduard, *anything*, but with the covered sky it was even harder to see.

*We should have taken more medical supplies. CJ had everything in his bag, but we idiots only thought of our own stuff. CJ—if only he was here. He'd know what to do.*

She got up again and opened their bags. With a mix of respect and alarm she took out the guns, holding them only with two fingers by the grip. The bags of dried meat reminded her that she should be hungry by now, but she wasn't. Under the bags, her finger touched something plastic: a bowl they used to eat out of. She dug it out and placed it in front of the shed, trying not to get too wet. The bowl soon filled with water and Jenny went back inside. She gave Eduard some to drink before she took a gulp as well. Then she got out one of her shirts, dipped it into the water and put the wet shirt on his forehead. He moaned as if he wanted to say thank you.

The dull light and the pelting of the rain made her sleepy. She couldn't recall when she fell asleep, but she woke up several times. Each time she had the feeling she had heard something outside, but before she could grasp another thought she slipped away again.

When she woke up the next time a light of a flashlight dazzled her and the room seemed full of Spanish-speaking voices.

*They got us!*

#

*Jenny — Day 637 (January 18, Mendoza, Argentina)*

A shadow came closer and Jenny reached out to where she thought she had put the gun. Quick steps rushed towards her and the beam of the flashlight twitched across the wall. Somebody grabbed her before she could get hold of the gun and threw her to the ground. More men and more flashlights entered the room.

She wanted to jump up again, but a man put his hand on her shoulder and pushed her down. "*Pará chica.*"

In the back she heard Eduard coughing. Jenny's strength began to weaken and her resistance ceased. The pressure on her shoulder released a little. One of the men gave commands in Spanish, but not in a military way. They sounded more like orders from a boss. She picked up some words, like "get the gun", "put them on the truck" and "infirmary". The last word especially made her relax.

Somebody grabbed her under the arms and put her back on her feet. A man looked into her face. In the light of the flashlights Jenny could only recognize contours. One of the flashlight beams wandered across his chest; he was holding her coat. Realizing that it had cooled down, Jenny shivered.

"English?" asked the man.

Jenny nodded.

He grunted, but Jenny couldn't make out if it was scornful or just grumpy.

"*Venga.*"

He waved and nodded, like waving at a puppy to come out of a hideout, and lured her with her own coat. She followed blunderingly. In the meantime they pushed a cart into the shed.

It was still raining outside, not as heavily as before, but still enough to dampen her clothes within seconds. They had already lifted Eduard onto the loading bed of a truck and Jenny climbed on as well. A canvas held by a metal grid stopped the loading bed from being flooded, but it didn't prevent everybody from getting wet.

The truck moved off. A small lamp at the back of the cabin provided a little light. Eduard was lying in the middle on a wooden board under some blankets. Five men were sitting on benches on each side of the truck and Jenny felt them looking at her. She ducked a little into her wet coat. The men all had heavy coats on and two of the men were bearded. All somehow had a scruffy look.

One of them got out a cup with a straw and filled it with water out of a Thermos flask. He passed it on to another guy who drank out of the straw. The cup found his way back to the first guy, who refilled it and the same procedure was repeated.

"Where?" asked the guy across from Jenny, who had drunk first from the cup. He spoke in broken English and he added something like, "*Schankee?*" She didn't understand a lot of the discussion that followed, but it seemed to be something about pronunciation. They continuously repeated "sh" and "e" until finally one said, "*Iankee.*"

"America."

The guy said something in Spanish that sounded as if he was singing swear words. The others chuckled. Jenny watched the cup with the straw go back to the guy with the Thermos.

He looked at her. "*Quieres?*"

"What is it?"

"*Mate. Toma.*" He handed it over to her.

She frowned briefly. The guys were all looking at her and she realized she couldn't go back now so she took the cup and sipped. The taste was bitter, but her body welcomed the warmth of the water. She took another gulp. The warmth spread through her body and gave her goosebumps, immediately followed by a shiver from the bitter taste.

The guys laughed. She gave the cup back and the guy across from her asked, "*Te gusta?* Like?"

Jenny made a waving movement with her hand indicating so-so-la-la. The laughter continued and Jenny's mood lightened. They were good guys.

#

*Eduard — Day 640 (January 21, Mendoza, Argentina)*

A staccato of coughing caught Eduard when he woke up and it only got better after he had sat up in the bed. He glanced around. Several beds were lined up against a half-painted turquoise wall, which gave the room the appearance of a hospital, although it didn't smell like one. Only the medical machines and the triangles above the beds to pull oneself up on were missing. Both sides of the elongated room had windows.

The last thing he recalled was walking through the vineyard, and he had the feeling he had heard voices speaking Spanish. He felt better; still weak, but better. The hot feeling in his head and the aching of the limbs were gone. Only his breath was still rattling a little. Eduard cleared his throat and got up. The white shirt he wore was far too big for him. He almost tripped over it when he went over to the window. There was a terrace in front of the window, but he only saw a wall of white laundry that was hung up to dry in the afternoon sun. Through the opposite window he oversaw a busy square between a handful of buildings. The one to the right had to be the main building, given the size, the veranda and the busyness of the people entering and leaving. In the back he thought he saw stables, and right in front of him there was a factory building with concrete walls and the typical glass roof with diagonal windows on top resembling the teeth of a saw.

A chattering noise from the next room reached his ear. Somebody was laughing. *Jenny!* He rushed over and opened the door. Jenny immediately jumped up and ran to him.

"I'm so glad you feel better. I was worried to death."

"Yeah, I can see that," he replied with a smirk and pointed to the plate of cheese and the two glasses of wine on the table.

The woman who had been sitting with Jenny stood up and came over. "Still, you should rest. Your coughing is not better yet." Her handshake was firm and surprisingly strong for her small posture. "I'm Joanna."

She wore a lab coat, but underneath he could see jeans and riding boots. Her brown hair already had broad waves of grey. Eduard guessed her to be around seventy.

"And when do I get a glass of wine?" He raised his eyebrows.

"Tomorrow. Maybe." She took him by the arm and guided him gently but determinedly back to the room with the beds. "You just got over a fever and you can count yourself lucky. There are no antibiotics available anymore."

Jenny was right behind them and carrying her plate with the cheese and bread.

"Where are we?" Eduard asked after the woman had left and he had grabbed some cheese and bread.

"This is the winery of the vineyard we walked through. It's their shed we hid in."

*Shed*, thought Eduard. *Which shed?*

"They're the nicest people ever. Joanna is the owner's wife—his name is Jorge. She was born in Connecticut and came down here fifty years ago. Isn't that amazing? She only wanted to travel around and she met the love of her life. They make good wine but times have been better, they say. All exports to Europe and the US broke away. Now they have too much wine, she said."

Eduard had been munching throughout her entire monologue. Now that the plate was empty, he lay back again. "She's right. I still need time." He turned his head. "What do you think—can we stay here? At least for a while?"

"I guess at least for the autumn. They're short-staffed for the grape harvest. She already asked if we would be willing to help, for a salary, obviously."

Eduard breathed deeply and triggered another cough. "I'd be glad to be able to rest for a while," he said after the coughing abated.

"That's a good idea." Joanna had appeared in the door. "You should let him rest. You can come back tomorrow."

Jenny half turned her head towards the door. "Five more minutes." Joanna left and Jenny took no answer as a yes.

"If they have too much wine, why don't they replace some of the vines with other stuff?"

"They already did that, Joanna said, but it always kills them. These vines have been out here for decades. They built up all this; it's the highest vineyard in Argentina."

He grunted. "Crazy night. I hardly recall anything from yesterday."

"Yesterday?" Jenny opened her eyes wide. "You were passed out for three days."

*Three days?* He felt weaker again.

"Your five minutes are up," shouted Joanna from the next room.

Jenny stood up and kissed Eduard on the forehead. "The boss is calling. I'll be back tomorrow."

Eduard looked after her as she left the room. Alone, the pictures of the shooting in Chile came up again. They still hurt, but now they were accompanied by an empty feeling of desultoriness. He took all those feelings and threw them at Niklas. *If we ever meet again, he'll pay for that.*

# CHAPTER EIGHT

# Reunited

*Niklas – Day 642 (January, Uyuni, Bolivia)*

Running felt easier. They didn't have to pant that much anymore after almost one year at altitude.

Niklas and Marcella had started working. Cleaning solar cells was strenuous, but that way they could sustain themselves without using all of Niklas' money. After they had left Cuzco, they didn't want to stay in another big city and so they decided to go to Uyuni. Right before the blackout an immense solar power farm had been built here and Marcella had overheard that they were desperately looking for people to clean the cells after the cleaning robots had packed up.

Marcella turned around the corner at the first gong of the church bell. There were only a hundred feet left to the door of the hostel.

"Hurry," she shouted to Niklas, who was right behind her.

Two police officers in a Jeep were watching them and obviously enjoying the scene.

Marcella reached the hostel at the fifth gong, Niklas at the sixth.

The owner held the door and closed it behind them. "You guys are lucky. One more minute and I'd have had to leave you outside. They were already waiting," he snarled in broken English and flicked his head towards the cops outside the door. "You wouldn't be the first *extranjeros* to get killed just for disregarding the curfew."

"Thank you, Hector," replied Marcella, giving him her usual wink.

While walking away, he snarled something else, leaving Niklas and Marcella alone in the foyer. It sounded like, "Watch out for the drunk."

Niklas peeked around the corner into the common room of the hostel. The usual crowd was hanging around the fireplace, but unlike usual the mood was overly cheery and chipper. They rushed past the door, but they didn't get far.

"Hey, what are you guys up to?" shouted a male voice from the common room when they were already two steps down the hallway on the other side. Marcella pulled a face. Niklas shrugged. It wasn't that they didn't like the other stranded ones, but their company was usually just depressing.

"Nicolas, Marcella," shouted the voice again, this time a little closer to the door.

Niklas took two steps back to the door. They were all there; Roberto, who had called to them, was from Italy originally and travelling around.

"Why not use the chance to get around?" he had gloated when he arrived two months ago. "My currency is worth a hundred times more now."

Dragana was leaning on him, giggling. She had heard from neither her family nor her boyfriend back in Serbia for over two
years and had stopped caring a while ago. Dan and Hanna were
from Canada, and Niklas had a hard time understanding their
French accents. There were also two other girls from Asia, but
they usually kept to themselves. Hanna told Marcella that they
had tried to hit on Roberto and that Dragana had almost beaten
them. Right now they did not seem happy at all.

The only person missing was Jason, a young backpacker from
England.

"Come, my friends. Have a drink." Roberto tried to start a par-
ty every night, usually with mixed success, but this time he
seemed to be on a roll.

Niklas frowned at the box next to them. It was filled with bottles of wine, whiskey and some other clear alcohol that he wasn't
able to determine. "Where did you get this?"

"There was a delivery to the local grocery store today—finally,
after weeks. It was crazy. All those people got some kind of food,
but I got this little treasure." He filled two cups with wine and
gave them to Niklas and Marcella. "And by the way, don't try to
get anything from Hector today. He's really moody."

Marcella raised her eyebrows. "Probably because he needed
groceries for our dinner."

"Maybe, but come, celebrate with us. We have to say good-
bye to Jason."

"Where did he go?" Niklas threw a glance at Marcella, and
although she hid it pretty well, Niklas could tell she was surprised.
Nobody ever left from here. It was like the Hotel California: you
could check out anytime but never leave.

Roberto got up, almost hitting Dragana with his shoulder, put a hand on his chest where his heart was and put on a solemn face. "He got taken in by one of those police gangs. Poor soul. They thought he looked like the guy on the flyer."

Roberto got a piece of paper from the table and gave it to Niklas. Niklas' heart dropped and his head felt hot. 'Dead or Alive' was printed on top, with a bounty of one million US dollars—as Roberto had said, worth a hundred times more than before the blackout. The pictures on the flyer were blurry and the obviously ancient printer made it worse, but Niklas clearly recognized pictures of August, Olivia, Eduard and Jenny. The last picture was even worse; it showed a young man and seemed to be taken from a badge or company photo. The young guy looked handsome and had nothing to do with the worn-out, bearded face Niklas saw when he regarded himself in a mirror. He glanced over to Marcella and he could tell by the poker face she had put on that she had recognized him as well.

"To Jason." Roberto raised his glass and one of the Asian girls started to cry. Roberto immediately turned to her and started to comfort her, which made Dragana jump up and drag him away.

Marcella tapped Niklas' arm. He nodded and they used the confusion to sneak out of the room.

They didn't get far. Further down the hallway they got dragged into Hector's office. He peeked down the hallway once more and closed the door behind them. "I told you to watch out for the drunk. I'm just waiting until they kill themselves when we run out of food here." Hector sat down at his desk and put on a fierce face that they had never seen on him before. He could be snappy and grim, but never fierce.

Marcella remained close to the door. Niklas glimpsed over to her, but her face didn't release any expression.

"We have to leave. I will leave because this town is dead—sooner or later they will stop carrying food up here—and you have to come with me... well, you know why." He pointed to his own copy of the flyer.

Marcella stared at Niklas and he had the impression she shook her head.

"I know this guy who runs trips through the desert and further down to the Chilean border. He would carry us, but I don't have the money." Hector sneered into Niklas' face.

Niklas heard the blood rushing through his ears, but he didn't react.

"You guys have money, US dollars, I know it, in the side pocket of your bag."

"You sifted through our stuff?" Marcella's voice got a gruff undertone. She moved her chin forward.

"I go through everybody's stuff. I need to know who sleeps here. Girl, you haven't gone through dictatorships. I never sold anybody out, but I'll be damned if I go under for somebody. So, are you in or not?" Hector raised his eyebrows. "I for my part don't want to end up like Jason."

Niklas relaxed. Marcella's lips were still pinched together, but her clenched fists relaxed a little. She nodded subtly to Niklas.

"How much?" Niklas turned back to Hector.

"How much do you have?" He pretended to be occupied; first he put all his pens into a penholder and then he searched for something in the bottom drawer of his desk.

Niklas tilted his head and his nose felt itchy. "I thought you went through my stuff."

Hector put on a surprised face. "Ok. Well, you can give me five hundred now and three hundred more when we reach Chile." Hector put on a smirk. "I need to live as well."

"I can't spare that much." Niklas stretched out his palms and raised his eyebrows.

Hector shrugged and went back to his bottom drawer. "Did I tell you that they're starting to search the hotels? Yesterday they were at the one across the street and I hear that they'll be here tomorrow," he said absently.

Niklas glimpsed again at Marcella. She had lost her narrowed eyebrows.

"Fine," he said when he turned back.

Hector grinned. "2AM. Be on time."

#

*Niklas — Day 645 (January 26, Between Bolivia and Chile)*

The salt desert was long past them, more than two days back. It had been the most beautiful thing Niklas had ever seen in his life when the red of the rising sun was reflected by the white of the salt. They had stopped at a deserted mass accommodation block by a red lake. Niklas had never seen such red in a lake before. Now that they were approaching the border to Chile, he felt for the first time that they could actually make it. They only had food for a couple of days and Niklas felt his stomach protesting.

"How long?" he asked. The driver didn't react. He had not said a word since they had gotten into the Jeep.

Hector turned around. "One hour until we switch cars. I hope he will be there."

"You hope?" Niklas raised his eyebrows.

"It's not really like we can call him up," Hector snarled and flicked his head over to the driver. "Julio has his doubts. Last week he had to wait for an entire day until he showed up."

The driver grunted something.

"Getting through the checkpoints is getting more and more difficult. They try to catch smugglers." Hector grinned and pointed to the rifle between the passenger seat and the driver seat. "Sometimes the only things they catch are bullets."

The driver chuckled.

*So he does understand us*. Niklas leaned back and crossed his arms in front of his chest. Marcella reached out for his hand and squeezed it. He squeezed back and they watched the reddish stony landscape passing by.

Half an hour later Julio slowed down. They had been driving alongside a mountain. Niklas tried to recognize anything, but all he saw was the dusty plateau to their left. Right before a sharp bend around a large boulder, the driver stopped and got out of the car. The three in the car followed him with their eyes. Standing behind the rock, he peeked around the corner into the open. He waited for another minute and then came running back.

"He's here," said Hector when he got back into the car, visibly relieved.

The car moved again and only minutes later they stopped a yard away from a pick-up truck. Their driver got out and waved at the other driver. Niklas and Marcella got out of the car as well and the other driver's face darkened. He turned around and tried to get into the car, but Julio moved fast and grabbed him by his arm.

*He didn't know about us at all*, thought Niklas. *They'll leave us in this desert.*

He and Marcella watched them gesticulating vigorously. Hector joined them and tried to settle the situation, with success; the driver calmed down and started to unload stuff from his truck. Julio and Hector came back and Julio started to get boxes out of the back of the Jeep as well.

"We need to share with him. I can offer fifty from my part and Julio is willing to do the same, but we need another hundred to calm him." Hector avoided looking at Niklas and squinted out into the valley.

Niklas looked over to Marcella and tilted his head. "He can have my watch. I don't have any more money." He showed his wrist.

Hector didn't turn around. "Not sure if that's enough."

"It has to be."

This time Hector looked up and narrowed his eyes. After a long stare into Niklas' eyes he sighed and sauntered over to the two drivers who were occupied loading the boxes Julio had brought onto the pick-up truck. The full-blooded discussion picked up again and Niklas got the feeling it even intensified. He threw Marcella a glance and noticed her poker face again. She was still standing next to the open car door, peeking in to the driver's seat.

*She's checking the car keys. Good, that way she can jump in if anything happens.* Niklas took a deep breath.

"*Boludos!*" shouted the other driver and trudged over to the pick-up.

Niklas' hackles rose. His muscles started to jump under his skin. He turned around just enough to see the driver getting something out of the car.

*A gun.*

The entire world seemed to slow down in front of Niklas' eyes. Julio looked the other way and Hector seemed surprisingly passive.

*He knew!*

The driver made two steps towards Niklas and pointed his gun at him.

*They planned this.*

A shot tore the silence apart and echoed from the mountains around them.

*Why can I still hear the echo?*

The scene resumed its normal speed. The driver dropped onto his knees and fell over. Julio and Hector both startled and gawked over at Marcella. She came around the back of the Jeep with Julio's rifle levelled.

"Down."

They remained frozen.

"Down!"

They got on the ground and put their hands behind their heads.

"Quick, get our stuff."

Niklas grabbed their bags and threw them into the loading bed of the pick-up. He rushed back and also grabbed the excess canister of gas and the other driver's gun. Niklas slowed down; an irrational alarm caught him that the driver would grab his gun and shoot him. Nothing happened. He looked up. Marcella moved slowly towards the pick-up. Niklas reached it before her and started the engine. Hector raised his head above ground. Marcella fired the rifle and he jerked, but she only hit the Jeep's tire.

"That will slow them down," she said to Niklas when she jumped into the car. He hit the gas pedal and the pick-up quickly gained speed. In the rear mirror he saw the others jumping up and running to their car. Then he only looked forward.

#

*Niklas — Day 645 (January 26, Between Chile and Argentina)*

They had not been driving for long when they hit the main road. Niklas stopped even though there was no traffic at all. He checked the rear mirror before he turned towards Marcella with a questioning look on his face.

"Left," said Marcella with a pinched face. "Change of plan. We go to Argentina."

"Didn't you say you would never go back?"

Marcella ignored his question. "Let me drive."

Niklas checked the rear mirror again and shrugged. "Fine with me."

They changed seats. He was barely in the car when she turned left and hit the pedal.

"I know people who could help us."

Niklas nodded. "How long?"

"Six hours. We should be there before nightfall." Marcella didn't take her eyes off the road, even though it went straight for another couple of miles. Her hands almost strangled the steering wheel and Niklas saw her cheek muscles contract and not release. He checked the rear mirror again.

"They're not following us. I checked already." She pressed her lips together.

"Everything alright?"

She didn't reply. Only after a few seconds did she force a smile. "Sure. Why shouldn't it be? We got away." She turned her head, still smiling with her lips, but her eyes were not. He smiled back and she turned her head back to the street.

They drove for about an hour, Niklas guessed. Looking at the sun it had to be around noon. The landscape had not changed; rusty and yellow colors took turns. Niklas could almost taste the dust the wind blew up. He turned to Marcella, who was still driving as if she had to break through a door. "We should stop and check out what we're carrying. I don't know how far the border is, but I don't want to be taken for a smuggler."

"That would be the least of my concerns," she replied snippily, only to recoil right afterwards. "You're right." She drove off the road and directed the truck behind a small dune.

"Let's see. Maybe there's even something to eat. I'm starving." He opened the door.

"I'm not hungry." Without looking at him she got out.

He raised his eyebrows and had some difficulty in fighting down a feeling of annoyance. He got out as well. She was already standing on the loading bed and had pulled back the cover. Half the bed was covered with the boxes they had transported in the Jeep through the salt desert, and the other half was covered with other bags. First Marcella opened one of the boxes and one of the bags inside it. Niklas peeked into the bag. It contained a white substance.

Marcella licked her finger, stuck it into the substance and licked it again. "Salt." She blew out air through her nose. "Funny what gets value in these times."

Still standing on the side of the truck, Niklas opened one of the bags the truck had brought. His eyes opened wide. He reached in and took out a plastic bag. It contained dark reddish pieces, like randomly melted plastic. "This isn't..." he said more to himself and ripped the bag open. He plucked a piece out and smelled it. "Dry meat." Without another word he bit into it and tore a piece away. Munching, he held the bag towards her. She climbed over and grabbed a piece as well.

They both ate silently until Niklas, after his fifth or sixth piece, studied her face. "Peace?"

She stopped chewing. "No need, we didn't fight."

He tilted his head and raised his eyebrows. She pouted, bit on her lips, let her shoulders drop and nodded, all within a second. Then she reached down and hugged him and kissed him on the cheek. "Sorry. Just don't ask."

Niklas nodded. "So what's next?"

"I don't know." Marcella took another bite of the meat. "I see three scenarios. Actually, four: they catch us and take us in for being smugglers, take all our stuff and throw us into prison. They could also just keep part of the salt and the meat and let us go with the rest."

"And the third one?"

She shrugged. "Well, we get through with it."

She didn't mention the fourth and he didn't ask, as promised. He examined the surroundings and turned back at her. Her entire demeanor had calmed down and she almost seemed serene. "Let's try it."

She jumped off the loading bed and they covered the boxes again. After they got back into the truck, before she drove off, she threw Niklas a sly smile. "I'm glad we found the meat. I was starving."

#

*Niklas — Day 645 (January 26, Between Chile and Argentina)*

They had driven for hours without seeing another car or human. Niklas figured that they must have passed the Argentinian border hours ago when the gradient of the road moved from slightly upwards to slightly downwards. Also, the vegetation had changed from almost nothing to nothing.

Niklas had fallen asleep and woken up once or twice, just to open his eyes for an instant and go back to sleep again. The third time he woke up a parked car on the side of the road caught his attention. "What was that?" he asked, still a little dozy.

"Probably nothing."

The moment she said that, the car put on its siren and followed them. Niklas and Marcella gaped simultaneously into the rear mirror.

Marcella had her worried stare back on her face. "Local police. Let me do the talking."

Niklas nodded and briefly squeezed her leg, not sure if he wanted to comfort her or himself.

She slowed down and directed the car to the side of the road. The other car came closer and Niklas could see that there was only one guy in it. They both stopped and the guy got out of the car. Niklas got a strange feeling of being in the wrong place; with the yellow-reddish stones around them, and a cop with a light brown uniform, a cowboy hat and slightly oversized sunglasses, this could just be any side road in the Rocky Mountains.

He glanced over at Marcella and frowned. Her worried mien had switched to a broad, expectant smile.

"What?" Niklas whispered.

She released the seatbelt. "Today is Christmas and Easter for us."

The cop reached their car and walked slowly along the driver's side, carefully keeping his distance and one hand on the holster of his gun. Marcella opened the door a crack. The cop flinched, drew his gun and pointed it at the crack. She held her hands out of the crack and shouted, "*Primo*." The cop relaxed a little. Without taking her hands back into the car, she opened the door with her legs.

"Marcella!" The cop put his gun away and took the sunglasses off his eyes.

She jumped out and hugged the cop. Niklas released his seatbelt as well and got out of the car. The cop stiffened up a little.

"He's with me," explained Marcella quickly.

The cop nodded. "You still can't show up in Jujuy. Follow me. You can stay at our house for the moment, but we have to drive off the main roads." Despite a heavy accent, his English was astonishingly good.

"Thanks so much." Marcella hugged him again. When she let go she walked over to the truck. "We've got freight, just to let you know." She pulled back the cover and he glanced over the loading bed.

"This isn't a problem, is it?" Marcella raised her eyebrows.

He sighed. "Yes and no. It's not a felony, but these days it raises a lot of questions." He glanced over to Niklas before he turned again to Marcella. "However, I think we can use this as a pawn to appease some of the people here."

Marcella covered the back again, avoiding looking at Niklas it seemed. The cop walked back to his car and Marcella and Niklas got back into the truck. The cop passed them slowly and Marcella followed his car, making sure to keep a decent distance.

The road was still flat with large curves to the left and right. Niklas had his hand on Marcella's leg while she drove and he could feel the tension in her body. After a while they reached an extended white field—another salt desert. The white glared in his eyes. He turned his head towards Marcella.

"He's my cousin, Ignacio," she started without him needing to formulate a question. "I grew up here... well, here, in Mendoza and Buenos Aires. After my mom died I was raised by my uncles. One lives in Jujuy, one in Mendoza and one in the capital. I always loved the one in Mendoza the most, but Buenos Aires was my favorite place." Marcella beamed at the thought of that.

"What did he mean by appeasing some of the people?"

Marcella pouted. "You promised me not to ask."

"You're right. Sorry."

She turned to the side window and Niklas looked at the road ahead.

"There was a man. He was the son of the local power man. You know, the one every town has."

Niklas turned his head; her eyes remained on the road ahead and the car they were tailing. His eyes hurt from the glare of the salt desert, but it didn't seem to affect her.

"The family was rich, fingers in everything and thinking they could get away with anything." Marcella's expression turned blank, but her eyes had a fierce glow. "I was working for one of his daddy's companies. His dad had the idea that I would be perfect for his son."

Her grip on the steering wheel got tighter again. Niklas could almost feel the tension in her chest.

"He tried to rape me." Her fierce expression took on a wounded dash before it turned fierce again.

She did not say a word for several minutes and Niklas did not want to ask her. In the meantime they left the salt desert. For a long time the mountains that surrounded the high plateau had not seemed to come any closer, but now Niklas could clearly see them ahead.

"I killed him," she started abruptly again. "They all knew what he was after and they let him do it. His whole family turned their heads that night." Marcella breathed heavily. "I ran. I took all their company cash and ran. Ignacio helped me." Her chin made a pointing movement to the cop's car in front of them. "I swore to never come back."

"We can still turn around if you want." Niklas squeezed her leg again.

Her facial contours got a little softer. "No, it's fine. We'll be fine." She turned back to the street. "But thanks anyway. I know we'll be ok if we're together."

The police car in front of them slowed down and stopped on the side of the road. They had almost reached the mountains, which looked more like hills now that they were closer. Ignacio got out of his car. Marcella wound down her window. "What's up?"

"I think you'd better hide in the back. It's only two hours, but for now it's better nobody sees you."

They got out of the car.

"You know how to drive?" He looked at Niklas and turned back to Marcella without awaiting an answer. "Take the gun." He pointed to the side door compartment where Niklas had put his gun. "You're still a good shot, I guess."

Marcella nodded. "He taught me to shoot," she said to Niklas.

"And she was a hell of a talent," Ignacio added.

Marcella climbed onto the loading bed and Niklas helped her to move the boxes and bags around so she had a nice nook to hide in. Niklas handed her the gun and her cousin gave her a bottle of water. Niklas noticed how dry his throat was when he saw the water and swallowed hard.

"I only have one," said Ignacio to Niklas.

Niklas swallowed again and blinked up and down the empty road. "Let's get moving again."

"*Vale*," said the other and returned to his car.

"In case we have to stop, I'll knock when we're safe."

She nodded and kissed him. Then he pulled the cover back so he could only see her when he was really close and got back into the driver's cabin. Shortly afterwards they were on the road again.

#

*Niklas — Day 645 (January 26, Jujuy, Argentina)*

Finally they left the high plateau. After one last long bend Niklas looked down an almost endless serpentine road. It was an astonishing view and he would have loved to share it with Marcella, although he was sure she had seen it before and even now, lying in the back of the truck, she would recognize where they were. At the bottom of the curves, they turned into a valley that had at least green bushes on both sides of the road, and the more they drove down that valley the greener it got. After an hour, trees started to border the road. He couldn't recall when he had last seen green trees—at least not the solitary trees of the high plateau. It must have been before Cuzco—in Lima—ages ago. A little further down, even the hills to the left and right of the road were covered with woods, and with the returning green around him Niklas' spirits lifted. *Maybe we can stay here.*

Further down, the valley opened and the density of houses increased. A city grew up in front of Niklas. He wondered if his Chilean license plate would draw attention. The police car turned away from the main route into side streets and after another hour they reached a small residential area outside the city. Niklas read 'Los Alisos' on a sign, and two blocks later they turned into the backyard of a house surrounded by high walls.

Ignacio got out of the car and guided Niklas into the garage. Then he closed the doors to the backyard and came back to the truck. Niklas was barely able to knock in time before Ignacio uncovered the loading bed. Marcella jumped down from the truck and ran towards the main building; obviously she knew her way around.

"Wait," shouted the cop and she stopped before entering the house.

She turned around. "What?"

"You've been away for quite a while."

Marcella tilted her head and narrowed her eyes, like she did when something was wrong.

He reached her and held out his hands as if he wanted to stop traffic. "You know who helped me with your escape back then. She did it because she knew what he did was wrong, but he was still her brother."

Marcella took a step back from him and frowned, but no words came through her lips.

"She's my wife. Let me talk to her first."

Marcella took another step back. Ignacio bit on his lips and disappeared through the garage door into the main house. Niklas got out of the car and walked over to Marcella. She leaned on the car with her shoulders down, looking at the tips of her shoes.

"Everything ok?"

Tears welled up in her eyes. Shaking her head, she stumbled two steps right into Niklas' arms.

The door opened again and a woman stood in the doorway; her hands stemmed into her hips and her back was bent like only pregnant women bend.

"*Entra*," she said in a tone that mixed harshness with impatience. Slowly Marcella let go of Niklas and entered. Marcella didn't look at the woman when she passed her and slid into the living room.

Her gaze wandered around the room and when it hit an empty chair in the corner, she turned around. "Where's Uncle Alfonso?"

Her cousin sighed. "He died last year—pneumonia. They had an issue with getting enough antibiotics at the hospital, like everything around here."

Niklas lowered his eyes and felt his throat thicken. *What have I done?* He glanced over to Marcella, but she was somewhere else. He swallowed hard.

"*Sentate*," said the woman and pointed to the table. Niklas was glad to be torn out of his thoughts, but the dense feeling in his chest remained.

The woman's tone had changed; it was warmer, more merciful. "*Soy Belén.*" She pointed towards herself. "*Teneis habre?*" A little helpless, she looked at her husband. "Eat?" She made a sign with her hand to her mouth.

Niklas swallowed empty. "Water? *Agua?*"

She nodded and got two water bottles. Niklas grabbed one and drank eagerly.

Marcella was still standing in the room, a little lost, and only slowly did she start to move. She sat down at the table and drank as well, followed by a "*gracias*". For the first time she looked at Belén, who walked over, bent down and hugged Marcella.

With the hug, Marcella broke out in tears and spluttered a gush of Spanish words. Niklas only understood "*Disculpame.* I'm sorry."

The woman said nothing. When she got up again, she caressed Marcella's hair. "*No hay disculparse, querida.*" She turned to her husband and said something in Spanish.

He turned to Marcella and Niklas. "You can stay here, at least for the night, but not for longer. Her family is still after you and the moment they know you are here, they'll hunt you. But one night should be ok."

He glanced at his wife and after a second of hesitation she nodded and Marcella and Niklas relaxed.

"Eat?" asked Belén.

Both nodded and only shortly afterwards the kitchen was filled with chopping sounds and the smell of sizzling meat floated into the living room. Marcella went in and Niklas heard her asking if she could help.

"You have to excuse her. Her family is not the easiest and she tries to keep everything together, especially now that we'll have a family of our own." Ignacio sat down as well and he looked at Niklas as if he had to apologize himself.

"Supplies are not easy to come by and most of the stuff that is hard to get we get because of her family." Outside the windows the shadows of the surrounding mountains had dimmed the light inside. He got up again. "Beer, wine?"

"Wine would be fine." With the meat smell in the air, that decision came easily.

Marcella's cousin got up and came back with a bottle of Malbec from the region and three glasses. "Any idea where you'll go? I might be able to convince her that you can stay a couple of nights longer..."

Niklas shook his head. "Don't worry, we don't want to put you into a dangerous situation."

The other guy pulled a face as if he had a sudden back pain, but before he could answer, Belén and Marcella came back from the kitchen with cheese and bread.

"She made us fresh empanadas. You have no idea how I missed them." Marcella was beaming with happiness and Ignacio poured her wine and his wife water as they sat down.

"When is it due?" asked Marcella in Spanish.

"In four months. Mid-March."

Belén smiled and he caressed her belly. Then her face went firm again and she said, "I'm sorry we can't help you more, but..."

"It's ok. I understand." Marcella tried to smile. "At least we have empanadas."

"You could try your uncle's winery," said Ignacio, chewing on some bread.

"I thought about that as well, but we need gas. Can you spare food in exchange for the salt and the dry meat? I mean, I love meat, but it would be a bit unbalanced nutrition-wise."

"Goes without saying," said her cousin. "Right, my love?"

"Salt is a good trade, thanks to the Rojas," said Belén. "They control the salt flats on the high plateau."

Niklas' understanding of Spanish had improved even further in Peru, but he still had some difficulties following their conversation.

Marcella turned to Niklas. "The Rojas are the other big family here."

The smell of baked dough from the kitchen intensified and Niklas' stomach grumbled. "You wouldn't have another license plate by any chance? I'm not sure how far they will allow us to go with the Chilean plate."

"I can grab one tomorrow morning in the office. There are more than enough plates around from car wrecks. We have to collect them and they're just lying around."

"Let's not talk about that now." His wife stood up. "The empanadas are ready and I think we can spend the time better."

Marcella wanted to stand up as well, but Belén told her to stay and said that they for sure had a lot to catch up on. "He." She pointed to Niklas. He got up and followed her into the kitchen, accompanied by cackling from Marcella and Ignacio.

In the kitchen, Belén opened the oven and a warm wave of wonderful smell surrounded Niklas.

"*Dos más*," she said, closed it again and turned around. "*De donde conoces* Marcella? Meet?"

"We met on a freighter outside Lima. I helped her to keep nasty sailors away."

She nodded, but Niklas had the feeling she had not understood a thing. "*Barco*... Lima."

She nodded again with a more lucid glance in her eyes. "*Ah, sos un marinero.*"

Niklas hesitated a moment. "Right."

She smiled and opened the stove again. "*Ahora*," she said and took two baking sheets full of half-moon-shaped stuffed pastries out of the oven. They returned to the living room where the other two were chit-chatting in Spanish. Marcella switched to English and a lively mixed-language discussion started.

"I just told him how they tried to rip us off on the journey through the *salar*." Marcella smiled innocently at Niklas. Ignacio repeated the story of the confrontation in the desert to his wife in Spanish, repeatedly interrupted by chuckles.

*Funny, how naked fear can trigger silly laughter afterwards*, thought Niklas.

"I taught her to shoot, you know," he said to Niklas. "She was a good shot back then, but hitting that tire—woah!" He shook his hand as if he had burned it.

In the blink of an eye Marcella's innocent expression changed and she threw Niklas a glance. Niklas looked back at the two others; Ignacio was still preoccupied with chuckling, but Belén narrowed her eyebrows almost unnoticeably.

*She suspects something. Hope she doesn't poke around.*

Belén turned back to her husband and told him something in Spanish.

"You are a sailor?" he asked Niklas. "There's not a lot of use for that here in the mountains."

Now Marcella got a questioning glance and Niklas explained. She translated and they all laughed. Belén asked something in Spanish again.

Marcella stammered something before she turned to Niklas. "What were you actually working as before... in the old world?"

Niklas smiled mildly. "I was Professor for Information Technologies at a small US college, and in today's world there's not a lot of use for that either."

They laughed again after Marcella had translated and she added that Niklas was doing a pretty good job as a handyman.

"Lucky me, I'm good with practical stuff: home improvements like wiring, plumbing, cement work, you name it. I worked for a construction company during college," Niklas added.

There were other cliffs to circumvent during the evening. Niklas got goosebumps once or twice, but jokes and laughter helped. Apparently they decided to let it go for that one night, especially Belén.

#

*Niklas — Day 646 (January 27, Jujuy, Argentina)*

The next morning, Marcella was already downstairs when kitchen noises woke Niklas up. He searched for his clothes, but they had disappeared. In the bathroom he found a blanket to put around his waist and went downstairs. The women were in the kitchen, Marcella doing dishes and Belén sitting at a table drinking something with a tin straw out of a wooden cup.

"Anybody seen my clothes?" He looked at Marcella, who was dressed in sloppy gym clothes.

Marcella grinned. "She laundered them last night when we were already sleeping, but it will take a while until they're dry. We'll take some of their old clothes so we can get rid of some of ours—the tramp ones and your piggy-pink shirt."

"What's wrong with my shirt?" he asked, but without expecting an answer he turned around to Belén and added, "*Gracias*."

"*No hay de que*." She waved it aside and got up. "*Venga*."

Niklas followed her to the master bedroom, where she gave him a pile of clothes. He thanked her, but she didn't even want to listen and waved him off again. He went upstairs to take a shower and when he came down again Marcella snorted with laughter.

"They are... a little big." She came over and twitched on each side of the shirt and the pullover. "But they work for the moment. Maybe you'll grow into them."

Niklas grinned. "Shut up, you don't look better in your gym stuff."

"I bet I do." She posed and they all laughed.

Niklas eyed the wooden cup with the tin straw that the two women were sharing. Marcella noticed.

"You want to try? It's mate."

"I know. I had some in Mexico. No thanks, it's too bitter for me."

Marcella translated and Belén smiled knowingly. Marcella turned back to Niklas. "Well, I got two bags for the trip and my own cup and straw. I lost my old one somewhere on the way."

"Do you have any plans for when we should leave here?" Niklas asked. "How far is it to this winery of your uncle's?"

Marcella hesitated with an answer, but Niklas got the feeling that it was not because she didn't know.

"Two days, I guess. Anyway, we have to wait so we don't have to rush right now." She squinted at the clock on the wall. "Noon? *Mediodia?*"

Belén nodded.

"Good, by then the clothes will be dry as well. Ignacio already unloaded the bags and boxes and she prepared us provisions for the way. Cans of beans and water—lots of water," added Marcella.

"Fine." Niklas sat down as well. "Then let me try again. Maybe it's less bitter the second time." He pointed to the mate and made a face at the first sip he tried. They all laughed again heartily.

Three hours later they were back on the road, Niklas driving and Marcella back in the trunk, at least until they reached the border with the province of Salta.

#

*Dennings — Day 647 (January 28, Fairview, MT)*

When Dennings entered through the back door, the conference room was full of high-ranking military personnel: the regulars to the left, looking depressed; Clutsky's direct reports to the right, most of them with broad grins on their faces, except Clutsky whose face was motionless.

*He realizes what this is.* Dennings sat down behind the main desk, four judges to the left of him and the jury to the right. They had all been wisely selected to represent all four parties, including Bruce. Each got to select three jurors and one replacement in case one of the main jurors fell out, but Dennings had made sure they had all gotten the briefing of what was at stake. Bruce was sitting in front of him, accompanied by a pro forma lawyer who was supposed to defend him. Adriana stood in the back; three of her officers were supposed to testify.

Dennings gazed provocatively through the crowd for a minute. He turned towards one of the judges, who hammered the gavel on the table. "In matters of the United States of America against Bruce Warner, former Admiral of the US Navy..."

"Objection." Bruce's lawyer stood up. "This is not a court that could represent the United States."

Dennings scoffed at him with pity. "This court was called by the elected US government and therefore is entitled to represent the United States."

The lawyer shook his head. "There is no member of the government left alive—"

Adriana stood up and interrupted him. "I am Adriana Jensen, Secretary of National Intelligence. I called this court and if anyone doubts the regularity he should speak up or shut up." With her chin forward and her hands on her hips she stood there like the Statute of Liberty in New York, large and unyielding.

Dennings waited for a second before he continued. "Now that we have clarified that, please read the charges."

One of the judges to the right stood up and read from a paper. "Bruce Warner, you are charged with treason and first-degree murder in twenty to forty million cases."

The judge continued for another ten minutes, but Dennings faded out and focused on Bruce. He didn't seem to be too concerned. He was leaning back in his chair and had an almost jolly grin on his face. From time to time he glanced over to the jury and each time he rested on one face a little longer, just a millisecond, but enough for Dennings to notice it, and when he looked over to Adriana he knew she had noticed it as well. *So the rumors are true—he's got his loophole sitting in the jury.* Dennings glanced over the jury. Bruce's men, all military, sat in the second row to the right: two colonels Dennings didn't know too well and Bruce's old mentor, Admiral Bushwick. *Damn, Bushwick—he's double-crossing.*

After the judge was done with reading the charges, the main judge hammered the gavel again. "We'll take a quick break and reconvene in fifteen minutes." He got up and left the room. Out of the corner of his eye Dennings observed the jury being guided to the room next door.

#

*Dennings — Day 647 (January 28, Fairview, MT)*

Dennings didn't bother to look around when he entered the room he had reserved next to the improvised courtroom. The only things that were his in this room were the bar and the sofa in the corner he had brought down from his office in the tower.

He stepped over to the windows. The square outside was filled with soldiers lining up in lines and squares. Only Adriana's company was not in order. They were lurking around in the back of the square.

*Enough for all eventualities.*

Somebody knocked on the door.

"Come in," Dennings said.

Andrews, Commander of the USS *L.J. Gibbs* after Bruce had appointed Bushwick to admiral, appeared in the door. "Sir."

"Thanks for taking the time." Dennings still watched the soldiers on the square.

"Is this about my jury appointment?" Andrews cleared his throat. His feet were pointing towards the door as if he wanted to leave again. "If yes, I'm not actually on the jury. I'm just a replacement."

Now Dennings turned around. "For Bruce Warner, I know. How well do you know Admiral Bushwick?"

Andrews' face turned red and pale within seconds. "Not that well." His voice was shaking. "He has not been visiting the fleet a lot recently, but I heard good things about him," he added quickly. His body was slightly shivering.

Dennings looked back out of the window. "Interesting." There was movement in the square. The clear lines had fallen apart. A group of men were taken away in a truck. "I didn't hear anything good. Well, except for what Bruce Warner told me. Anyway, he's no longer playing a role." He turned around. "I will split the fleet. You will command the catamaran carrier group. I'll give you two more cruisers and destroyers. I just wanted to let you know before you join the jury."

Andrews relaxed a little. "Thank you. I will not disappoint you."

"No, you won't."

Adriana entered the room. "It's time."

"Let's go back. Admiral Andrews, you won't disappoint me."

The newly appointed admiral started to shiver again.

#

### Dennings — Day 650 (January 31, Fairview, MT)

Bruce had gotten nervous when Admiral Bushwick did not re-appear in the jury. When Dennings had started to line up the wit-nesses for the prosecution, Bruce had been having a lively discussion with his defense counsel, until the counsel had gotten up and required an explanation for the exchanged jury member. One of the judges had waved it away with a simple, "He got sick and we replaced him."

With delight, Dennings observed how Bruce got more and more strained with every witness. In addition, the defense coun-sel was doing a perfect job of being ineffective. In the middle of the second day, Bruce lost it and jumped up, shouting and screaming, until the judges had him removed from the room.

The court case was done after two days. Bruce was found guilty on all counts and sentenced to death. When the gavel fell at the end, Dennings got up and approached Clutsky.

"We need to talk."

Clutsky nodded and stood up. His men observed them with a mixture of insecurity and restlessness. Clutsky calmed them down with a wave and then followed Dennings at a distance of four feet.

Dennings closed the door behind them. "Bourbon?"

Clutsky grunted and Dennings filled three glasses. Clutsky raised his eyebrows, but got the answer to his question immediately when Adriana entered the room.

"Now we are three." Dennings handed one glass to Clutsky and one to Adriana.

Clutsky sneered at Dennings. "How long will you wait until you amnesty him?"

Dennings swigged down his bourbon and refilled his glass without looking at Clutsky. "Which of your guys would take over the fleet?"

Clutsky almost dropped his glass. A brief grin hushed over his face, followed by a scowl and a deep breath. "Why is this your decision?"

"It's not. Sit down, please."

Clutsky and Adriana sat down on the couch in the corner of the office. Dennings remained standing.

"Bruce went too far. He personally decided to kill millions and he was sentenced to death for it."

Clutsky took a swig from his glass.

"But this has also shown us that we have deficiencies," added Dennings.

Clutsky wiggled his head and Dennings assumed he was nodding. Dennings grabbed the bottle of bourbon from the bar. While refilling the glasses, he continued. "We need to establish a government. I was glad that junior defender didn't pick on our legitimacy. Adriana has had some ideas and she's convinced me."

He pointed to her and she got up. "We'll establish a transitional government—a triumvirate. Additionally, we'll elect a kind of senate, representing all seven regions, which will act as legislators. Each of us will nominate fifteen people. Also, each of us will nominate three judges. If a nominee dies, the original nominator gets to re-elect a replacement." She paused to let the words settle.

Dennings stepped in. "When I asked you before if you have a good guy that could take over the fleet, I didn't mean that he would report to you. While we still have to decide how we split responsibilities among ourselves, we will have the forces report to the triumvirate, including the armed forces on the ground. They have to believe they are getting their orders from the three of us."

Clutsky didn't show signs of understanding what this would mean.

Adriana, still standing next to Dennings, spelled it out. "We decide among the three of us and the responsible person executes the decision, even if it's against his or her own vote."

Slowly, Clutsky got it. He opened his mouth to say something, and judging from his face it would have been a complaint, but he seemed to abandon his thought before he said it. He gulped his bourbon down. "Fine with me, if I keep control of the Americas."

"I guessed so." Dennings refilled Clutsky's glass again. "But let's call it 'Safety and Protection'. I thought foreign affairs, including the fleet and all the economics and production, would be for me: agriculture, industry, etc. That would leave everything people-related and intelligence for Adriana."

Clutsky nodded. "Triumvirate, you say?"

"We can also call it a 'troika'." Dennings chuckled down at Clutsky. Him and Adriana standing in front of a sitting Clutsky like this felt like parents talking to a child.

"No way, too Russian."

"How about Cerberus?" Adriana threw into the discussion. "The three-headed Greek dog guarding the door to Hell?"

"I like that." Dennings put on a smirk.

Clutsky shook his head. "Fine with me. What's next?"

"Now we make our first decision." Dennings waited until Clutsky looked up. "Do we amnesty Bruce?"

Clutsky opened his eyes wide.

"I told you, it's not my decision." He tilted his head. "So, yes or no?"

Clutsky waited a moment, then he stood up and said with a firm voice, "No."

"Adriana?"

"No as well."

"Then it is decided. Frank, I guess that's your department."

"Consider it done." Clutsky got up and pounded towards the door, but turned his head midway. "And the three of us are equal in this triumvirate, right?"

#

*Niklas — Day 650 (January 31, Mendoza, Argentina)*

The trip took longer than she had estimated. They took the back roads through Salta, Catamarca and two other provinces Niklas couldn't remember, and had to hide once or twice when they got suspicious. It was already late at night and a little February fog was skulking through the valley when they arrived at the winery, and even though they had shared the driving, Niklas was exhausted. 'Estancia Colome' was written on a sign when they turned off the main road, and five minutes later they reached a handful of buildings.

He had difficulty making out details in the sparse light of the lamps. The buildings surrounded a square and Marcella parked in front of what Niklas guessed to be the main building.

Marcella had gotten more excited the closer they got, but now she was almost lolloping. Before they reached the porch a grim-looking guy came out. He was holding a rifle, and in his worn-out clothes he appeared more like a robber than somebody guarding a house.

"Juancho," shouted Marcella and added to Niklas, "He organizes everything for my uncle and my aunt around here," before she jumped up the steps.

The guy frowned for a second and then his grim look yielded to a broad smile.

"*Señores, es* Marcella!" he shouted inside and his face was beaming when he opened his arms to hug her. Niklas had the impression the grim-looking guy would start crying soon. Two faces appeared in the door, a man and a woman, both about sixty years old. The man had a metal-rimmed glasses. They also welcomed Marcella with extended hugs and shouts of "*querida*" and "*amor*". Niklas got completely forgotten in the hullabaloo.

"*Venga.*" The older woman waved them in and Marcella took Niklas by the hand. Now the others paid attention to him and the older man put his hand on Niklas' shoulder as they entered the house. Behind them, Juancho closed the door again, but not without peeking out one last time.

Inside, Marcella introduced Niklas to them in Spanish and he had to smile internally that she used the word for 'boyfriend'. Jorge grabbed Niklas' hand and shook it wildly while patting his back with the other. "Welcome, my son." He had a little accent, but he used colloquial words he could only have picked up if he had been to an English-speaking country. "This is my wife, Joanna."

Joanna came a step closer and hugged him as well. "Welcome. I'm glad you two are here." Her English was perfect, as if she was from the US. "You two must be hungry. Come into the kitchen. I have cheese and bread, and a glass of wine."

Niklas didn't have a chance to say anything before she turned around and walked towards a door in the back of the room, so he directed his words at Jorge. "I'm glad we're here as well and thank you for your warm welcome. Let me know if I can help with anything around here."

He waved him off and Marcella poked him. "Don't be so stiff." She grinned, linked arms with Jorge and went into the kitchen. It seemed to Niklas as if she was ten years younger than before, light-hearted, as if all the worries had fallen off her.

He glanced around. It was an entry hall, dining room and living room all in one. On the left side there was a fireplace with a sofa in front of it. Chairs surrounded the sofa randomly; at least ten people could sit there. When he turned his head, he just caught Juancho leaving through another door on the other side of the room, behind a monstrous dining table with even more chairs than on the other side. The kitchen was almost as large as the living room and, judging by the size of the pots and pans, they cooked for the entire farm here. Right now it smelled of tomato sauce. The room was twice as long as it was wide and a large work surface occupied the middle of the room.

Marcella was already sitting on a bar chair at the work surface with a cheese and charcuterie plate in front of her. Jorge had poured four glasses of wine and they were looking at him with beaming faces.

He went over to them and Joanna hugged him again.

"She already told us. Thank you so much for looking after her. We love her like our own daughter."

Jorge took his glass and raised it. "*Salud, amor y dinero.*"

"That's 'health, love and money'," added Marcella and winked.

"My Spanish is not that bad."

"Of course, that's why I was a living translator the entire trip."

Niklas smiled, but it was interrupted by a yawn.

Marcella smirked. "Tired? Come on, you slept through the entire province of La Rioja."

"I need to go to bed as well," said Jorge and added to Niklas, "It's harvest and days are long."

"Again, let me know how I can help."

Jorge waved him off again. "No, please, get settled first and then we'll talk. Tomorrow night." Having said that, he turned around and left the kitchen through another door in the back.

"You want to see my old bedroom?" asked Marcella with big eyes. "It's over in the small house."

Niklas wondered for a second why she had her room in another building, but before he could ask she took him by the hand and dragged him out of the kitchen, through the same door Jorge had disappeared through before. A second later they were outside and she walked towards a small building a few yards away. Somebody had just entered that building and Niklas guessed it was Jorge.

"The main building is a guest house. You have no clue how many people want to take a vacation in a winery. Must be some romantic, nostalgic feeling, although I can see now how it would be beautiful here." Marcella talked like a machine gun, striding ahead with the same pace.

Niklas almost had to run to keep up and more than once he stumbled on the uneven ground.

She paused for a second and the worried voice came back. "The living room was actually pretty empty for this time of the year." Then she switched back to the carefree sing-song. "The quarters for the permanent staff are in the right wing of the house, over there." She pointed to a part of the main building with some lights behind the windows. "And behind the winery there are the quarters for the harvesters. They're only occupied during this time of the year." She pointed to a single lighted window in the main building. "They have at least one guest."

Niklas was too tired to interrupt her. They entered the front garden through a small gate. He couldn't see a lot, but there were about twenty vegetable beds on each side and in the corner there was a construction that looked like a greenhouse.

Standing on the porch, Marcella stopped. "When I was a kid, we had breakfast on this porch. I so miss that time. Or at night, we would sit together having mate or a glass of wine." She smirked at Niklas. "Jorge let me have a glass once in a while after I turned fifteen."

They entered the house. The rooms were small, not just in contrast to the main building. She led him upstairs and through the first door on the right. Inside, Marcella switched on the light. They were standing in a girl's room. Two large posters with soccer players were hanging on the wall, both with yellow-and-blue shirts, the same colors as the flag pinned next to the posters with the word 'Boca' printed on it.

"I was so in love with them, both of them at the same time." Marcella beamed. "Can you imagine? That's only six years ago." Her smile faded away a little. "It might as well be a century. I'm surprised they kept the room untouched."

At the window there was a desk and a book was still flipped open there, next to a notepad and a pen, just as if the girl who lived here would be right back. She sighed and sat down on the single bed that was placed on the right side of the room. Niklas glanced over the bookshelf next to the desk. Heavy stuff like *War and Peace* and *The Count of Monte Cristo* was mixed with Dorothy Parker and Spanish books like *Martin Fierro*. He picked up one with a blue cover. *The Frigorifico* was the title.

"You have a nice collection here." He turned around and smiled mildly. Marcella had fallen asleep on the bed. He went over and covered her with a blanket. He yawned, took the other blanket and lay down next to the bed on the carpet. Seconds later he had fallen asleep as well.

#

*Eduard — Day 650 (January 31, Mendoza, Argentina)*

Eduard was still sitting at the window looking out into the night. His body was tired, but his mind was playing tennis. He had hoped that the work in the vineyard would help him to get rid of his anger, but it had nourished it instead. He could only see as far as the owner's house in the back, but the darkness behind it was like a canvas that his mind used to replay the past years over and over again.

*All this would not have happened if I had took better care of Jenny better—but I took it lightly. What was supposed to happen?* Eduard clenched his fist. *No! This is not my fault. We would be free and back in Burlington by now, thanks to Jenny's father. The breakdown of the world, the contamination of Burlington and the bounty on us is all Niklas' fault.*

Jenny moaned in the bed behind him and turned towards the wall.

*Where shall we go? Could this be the place to stay? Probably not. At some point they will recognize us as well, or worse, somebody else will, and then they'll kill them all.* Eduard looked back out of the window just in time to see Jorge walking over to the small house. *The best thing would be to ride off and kill ourselves. That way the nightmare would end immediately.* Two people were following Jorge: a woman and a man. The guy almost fell twice. Somehow Eduard had the feeling of familiarity, but he wished it away.

He shook his head. The couple disappeared into the house. It was quiet again outside and the pictures reappeared on the black canvas: CJ and Max at the marina, the killings on the farm, the prison and a feeling that had accompanied him for a long time that he was now able to articulate in his mind—the fear of losing Jenny.

#

*Jenny — Day 651 (February 1, Mendoza, Argentina)*

When Jenny went fetched their lunch bags in the kitchen of the main building she encountered a new face. A girl was standing at the counter preparing two bags. She seemed to be the same age as Jenny, give or take a couple of years. Jenny caught her singing, and when she noticed Jenny she stopped and blushed for a second.

"*Hola, que tal?*"

Jenny tried to gather the little Spanish she had learned from the workers. "*Bueno. Soy Jenny.*"

"Seems you're from the US." The girl grinned.

Jenny was relieved. "Yes."

"I'm Marcella, Jorge and Joanna's niece." Marcella's English was almost flawless, but she couldn't hide a little accent.

"Nice to meet you."

Eduard shouted from outside.

"My fiancé," said Jenny. "I have to go. The truck is waiting."

"Oh, you're one of the harvesters." Marcella handed her the bags and Jenny rushed towards the door.

"It was nice meeting you," Jenny added over her shoulder.

"Same here. We can catch up tonight when you're back from the harvest. My boyfriend is from the US as well."

Jenny almost ran Joanna over on her way out. A truck was waiting outside for her; the others had already departed. She jumped onto the loading bed. Eduard grabbed her hand and helped her up. Jenny just managed to grab hold of one of the benches when the truck started to move.

"I just met somebody new in the kitchen. Marcella. She was nice, about our age. Her boyfriend is from the US as well. She wanted to catch up tonight."

Eduard pulled a face. "Let's just hope he doesn't recognize us."

Jenny opened her mouth to throw him a snippy answer, but she just sighed and closed it again. She turned around and watched the vines pass by.

#

*Niklas — Day 651 (February 1, Mendoza, Argentina)*

Each limb and joint hurt when Niklas woke up, especially his hips and his shoulder. Somebody must have shoved a cushion under his head during the night. He also had more blankets covering him.

He sat up and moved his shoulders; it helped a little. Marcella was not in her bed anymore. He got up. It was still early morning and everything was awfully quiet. Niklas got dressed, but even downstairs he encountered nobody. Only when he went over to the main building did he find Marcella sitting in the kitchen with a coffee and one of her old books.

"*Amor*, you're up, finally." She got up and kissed him. "Coffee?"

"Yes please. How long have you been up?"

Marcella refilled the coffee-maker. It was one of those ancient ones you fill with water on the bottom and coffee powder in the middle. They had become trendy again years ago. "About two hours. I helped Joanna prepare the food for the harvesters." She put the coffee-maker on the stove and sat back down.

Niklas sat next to her. "What are you reading?"

"*The End of the World as We Know It*. It's a dystopian story about the Earth after a war. None of the infrastructure is working and they're fighting against each other to survive. Kind of what we're in now."

The coffee was ready. She got up and poured him a cup. "By the way, one of the harvesters is a girl from the US and I think her boyfriend is as well. I told her we can catch up tonight."

Niklas didn't reply right away and Marcella's eyes darkened. "Oh. But at some point, we have to lay down the fear. We are safe here."

He sighed. "You're right. I don't want to be on the run forever either. I'm sure they're nice."

Marcella smiled. "They are. Her name is Jenny. I don't know his name—she had to run for the truck."

Niklas wasn't listening anymore. *Jenny? No, that's not possible*. He started sweating and stood up.

"Everything alright?" Marcella frowned.

"Sure, I just need water." He got some soda from one of the large water bottles on the other side of the counter. His head was spinning and he drank the entire glass in one go. "They live with the other harvesters behind the winery?"

"They live upstairs." Joanna had entered the room. "I couldn't put them with the others—they were in pretty bad shape when they arrived and I think they'll stay for a while." She came over to Marcella and Niklas. "How do you feel? Jorge wanted to move you to another bed last night, but we just couldn't wake you up."

Niklas tried to smile. "My shoulder and hip hurt a little, but other than that I'm fine."

"We'll put you in another room tonight with a king-size bed. That should help."

This time Niklas smiled for real. "Thank you so much!"

"So what are your plans today?"

Marcella shrugged at Niklas. "I don't know. Maybe I'll show him the winery and the vineyard."

Niklas nodded. "That would be nice. If you'll excuse me for a second, I'll be right back." He turned around and walked into the living room. He waited for an instant and listened carefully as if he had heard something. The stairs to the upper floor were to his right. He glanced over his shoulder and to the left—nobody visible. He hurried upstairs and started opening the doors. None of them were closed and all of the rooms were unoccupied. It was a sad sight, but Niklas was too stirred up to lose any thought on it.

Behind the fourth door he found what he had been looking for. The room was roughly in the middle of the building, where he had seen the light last night. Clothes were scattered around the room and the floor. Two half-empty bags were stuffed into the corner. He raced over and started digging carelessly through the bags. He paused when his fingers touched a gun. He got it out and put it on the bed. A little further down he found a piece of paper. He took it out and unfolded it. The same five faces that he had already seen in Uyuni looked back at him. Niklas studied the faces, and although the pictures were the same, they seemed more desperate. A sound from the door startled him. He looked up.

Marcella was leaning on the door with her arms crossed.

Niklas faltered over and showed her the flyer. "I know them."

"That's you, isn't it?"

"Let me explain—"

Marcella interrupted him. "No need. I watched you in that radio room on the ship. You did something that caused this chaos."

He swallowed hard, having trouble fighting back the tears. "I'm so sorry for all this," he was barely able to choke out.

She hugged him. He collapsed into her arms and there was no holding back tears anymore.

#

*Eduard — Day 651 (February 1, Mendoza, Argentina)*

The trucks entered the yard of the winery in the evening, when the sun was low over the Andes behind the buildings. Eduard was standing in the front of the loading bed of the truck, holding himself up on one of the poles that held the cover in place when it rained. He was exhausted, but he still felt pumped up; he clenched his jaw and his fist. Maybe there was some after-work he could do. Jenny, sitting next to him, touched his arm. He looked up and tried to smile. She smiled back, but her eyes had a glance of despair, as if she was missing something. Eduard jumped off the truck when it stopped in front of the house and rushed over to Juancho who had driven in another car.

"You need any help, Juancho?"

Juancho sighed. "You embarrass my guys, *chico*," he answered in Spanish.

Eduard had picked up some Spanish while working with the guys after hours. "I'm just grateful to be staying here and it's the least I could do."

Juancho flicked his head to Jenny who had just gotten off the truck. "You might also think about spending an evening, just the two of you. There are some romantic spots on the farm around this time of the year."

Jenny looked at Eduard with eyes half pleading, half full of bliss.

He sighed. "*Disculpame*, Juancho." He walked over to Jenny.

"I'm excited to meet Marcella's boyfriend." She smiled at Eduard, but he only grunted.

While they were strolling over to the main building, he made all possible effort to suppress his urge to run over to Juancho, take his gun and shoot around wildly. He achieved it when they reached the stairs to the porch. Every step felt like a step up, and at the top he was calm and the only thing that could have given him away was his clenching and unclenching fists.

They entered the main room and Jenny immediately turned left; a girl with black frizzy hair jumped off her seat and came over to them. While her behavior was extremely welcoming, Eduard caught a hesitant glance in her eyes. She and Jenny exchanged some greetings. The scenery seemed fake and Eduard felt the urge to turn around and leave. He only turned his head and froze when he saw Niklas in the kitchen door.

It all went very fast.

Jenny turned her head as well and shrieked with joy.

Eduard's stomach dropped. *You!* His fist clenched and all the rage of the past years emerged. Before he could think, he was over by the kitchen door, sitting on top of Niklas and frantically hitting him with his fists.

He had hit him half a dozen times, without feeling Jenny or the other girl trying to drag him off Niklas, when two strong hands grabbed him and pulled him away. The first thing he remembered was Jenny's face looking into his eyes and constantly repeating the words, "It's alright."

Her eyes were calm and warm like he had not seen them in years.

"You're ok?"

He nodded and looked over to the living room. The other girl and Joanna were taking care of Niklas; he seemed to have a few bleeding cuts to the face. Joanna came over to him. Eduard didn't feel guilty about the blood, but he felt guilty in front of Joanna.

"We've seen some fights in here, but most of them are because of alcohol or women. I guess this one is different." Joanna fixated on Eduard.

He bit the inside of his lips.

"Why don't we go into the kitchen and have a talk?" She got up again and was about to turn around when Eduard said, "We should all go. I'm just not as good at lying as he is."

He put on a dark face, but his eyes remained determined.

Joanna looked back at him. "Yes, all. I never thought otherwise." She went into the kitchen and Eduard followed like a puppy.

Marcella reached the door first and Jenny second. Niklas and Eduard reached the door at the same time and Niklas let him go ahead, but not without bowing first.

Eduard grunted and felt the impulse to hit him. Inside the kitchen, Joanna was sitting at the front end of the work surface and Marcella and Jenny to her left and right. Eduard felt abandoned and for a millisecond his rage pointed towards Jenny.

"So tell me," started Joanna, "what was that all about?"

"Why don't you ask him?" asked Eduard right away, pointing towards Niklas.

Niklas swallowed and opened his mouth. Marcella didn't give him time to answer. "Whatever you think, he's a good man."

Niklas lowered his gaze for a second and then said to Joanna, "Maybe you want to call Jorge. He should hear this as well."

Joanna nodded. "I can leave you guys alone without killing each other?" she added and left the room without waiting for an answer. Eduard stared fiercely and Marcella concerned.

Two minutes later, Joanna was back with Jorge. "Well then, amuse me."

"This is all his fault." Eduard pointed to Niklas. "All this, the nightmare he has thrown the world into."

Joanna glanced over at her husband.

Jorge narrowed his eyes and said with a calm voice, "I can't believe that it's one single person's fault. Usually it isn't."

Eduard felt anger boiling up with every word Jorge said. "Why don't you ask him?" he said through his teeth. Jenny squeezed his hand.

Jorge paused for a second and turned to Niklas, who had been standing quietly on the other side of the work surface. Marcella had placed herself in front of him as if she wanted to protect him.

"It's actually funny that you're angry with me. I did what I did to protect you, Jenny." He took a deep breath. "I had to promise your dad."

Eduard could feel Jenny's body tensing up. "That's bull," he said in a dash of wanting to defend her. "Now it's her fault?"

"No, that's not what I meant."

"Let him speak. I want to hear this." Jenny scowled at Eduard.

He blew air through his nose. Then he looked up again at Niklas who had stepped out of Marcella's cover.

"You know what I told you back then in Jacob's basement. About a week before his inauguration, your dad contacted me. It was out of the blue after we had that blow-out after he left... after the whole thing. I promised to watch over you."

Jenny was listening suspiciously and subconsciously shaking her head.

Niklas continued, undeviating. "I came back to the Resistance meetings to tell you and to warn you. Do you remember what I said that night?"

Now Jenny shook her head consciously.

"They were trying to use you to gain leverage over your father. I don't know if it would have helped to walk away like he suggested, but that explosion with your car gave them exactly what they wanted."

"She had nothing to do with it!" Eduard jumped forward and leaned over the kitchen island. Slowly his tunnel view opened again and he noticed how frightened the others were.

Jenny was the first to say something into the silence. "I gave Martin the car key that night. I put us all in this misery."

Eduard turned around and rubbed her arms. "No, I left you alone that night."

The tears in Jenny's eyes almost killed him. The picture of them laughing in Jacob's basement flashed through his mind. Eduard bit on his lips; he wished to go back and stop everything back then, but how? It all felt as if it had had to happen the way that it did. As if it was destined.

Jorge cleared his throat. "So far I see young people who made mistakes. Nothing that threw the world into the abyss."

"Those were the dominoes that started everything."

"Ok, but before you continue, how was your father involved?" Jorge pushed his glasses up.

She swallowed and opened her mouth, but she closed it again and glanced pleadingly at Eduard.

"Her dad was President of the United States." He frowned at Jenny and continued when she nodded. "Her parents were separated."

Jorge nodded slowly and the communication ceased for a moment.

"After that explosion they took in our entire Resistance group," said Niklas into the silence. "I was smart enough to use a fake identity for the Resistance meetings—that's why I got away. When I heard what would happen to you, I started a program I coded that would scramble up the data a little. I hoped to get you free that way or at least buy you time."

"But why?" asked Jenny with a weepy voice. "My dad came down to get us out."

"Your dad signed your death sentence." Niklas blinked at Jenny with a mix of determination and helplessness.

"What?" Jenny's voice went two octaves higher. "No. No."

Niklas' eyes turned watery as well. "I guess he didn't know. They might have slipped it into his papers, I don't know. The only way to save you was to stir up the system, change some of the data, identities, bank accounts, locations. And—" He paused and glanced at Marcella as if he wanted to say sorry. "And I wanted to hurt them. Those guys who think they get away with everything." He swallowed. "But I never wanted this."

The words 'change identities' were still hanging in Eduard's mind when it hit him like an epiphany. "That might be the reason why they didn't know who we were, in the prison." He glanced at Jenny.

"That would mean you actually saved us." Jenny stared at Niklas.

"But at what price?" he replied looking at Jorge and Joanna, who were still silent. He took out the flyer with the five faces and put it on the table. "I don't know if you've seen this, but that's us."

Jorge took the flyer and eyed over the rim of his glasses. "I would not have recognized you." He looked at the four and then at Joanna. "We've all done stupid things when were younger. Me as well, during the Dirty War here in Argentina, but we can only move on and live with the decisions we made."

Joanna held his arm as if he needed support.

"For now I suggest we all go to bed and sleep on it. Tomorrow we decide what's next."

*Tomorrow*, Eduard thought. *Tomorrow? How do we know what tomorrow will bring?* He glimpsed over at Jenny. *I'm just glad I have Jenny.* And with that thought a feeling of gratitude towards Niklas rose up within him; gratitude for having given up the comfort of his own life to save theirs.

#

*Niklas — Day 651 (February 1, Mendoza, Argentina)*

Joanna had already gone over to the small house and Marcella and Niklas were on their way to the back door when Jenny came around the kitchen table. Marcella stopped and he could feel the tension in her hand he was holding. Jenny looked at her first and after a second the tension dropped and Marcella nodded. A smile dashed over Jenny's face and she hugged Niklas. After she had let go, she whispered, "Thank you for risking your life to save us."

"Your dad was a good man. He had his faults and made his mistakes, but he cared for you."

Jenny swallowed hard and Niklas could see the tears welling up in her eyes again. She turned around and fled the kitchen, immediately followed by Eduard.

Marcella was halfway out of the door when Jorge grabbed Niklas' arm. "Can I talk to you for a moment?" He nodded at Marcella and added, "Alone?"

Niklas followed him back into the kitchen and the door closed.

"Do you care for Marcella?"

At first Niklas didn't know what to say. *Of course, he loved Marcella, but why ask that way?* "Of course," he simply replied after a couple of seconds.

"You can't stay."

Niklas frowned. *What? No.*

"And you need to leave Marcella behind, for her own safety."

Niklas felt as if he had stopped breathing for a moment. He opened his mouth and closed it again, just to open and close it once more.

"I'm sorry. You are a nice guy and we all make mistakes. I can protect the other two as they were only involved on the edge. Nobody will really care about them, but they will try to hunt you down for the rest of your life."

Niklas opened his mouth again, but Jorge just continued without waiting for what he had to say.

"I've been there. My father bombed a police station in Buenos Aires during the Dirty War. My mother was not involved, but they searched for her for ten years until they eventually gave up after 1983. They did not give up the search for my father until they got him after forty years. He was a wise man; he left my mother to protect her, my brother and myself. Be a wise man, Niklas. You're already on that path, but you can still protect her."

Niklas tried to swallow but his mouth was too dry. He could only nod. After a moment he found his voice. "The car and my stuff... and I need provisions and a gun."

"All prepared. The truck is outside, filled up, and Joanna is already in the other house packing your stuff." Jorge pointed to the pantry. "Take whatever provisions you want."

Jorge went into the living room. Mechanically, Niklas opened the pantry door and gaped at the shelves. There were cans and glasses full of vegetables—some pickled, some not—accompanied by corned beef in cans and a bag of potatoes. They all seemed to grin scornfully at him. It was all so meaningless. He grabbed the cans of beef, two cans of beans and a couple more of corn. He put everything on the table; it looked like a desperate band of brothers.

Jorge came back and regarded the food. "You'll need more." He went over, got out more cans and three large bottles of water. "And here's a box."

Niklas nodded emptily. As if it was happening in slow motion, he filled the box can by can.

Jorge put a gun on the table and ammunition. "You might also need this and I've got you money. It's not a lot, we don't have much, but it's the least we could do."

Niklas just looked at the gun and only slowly realized that it was for real. Maybe he could use it on himself. He grabbed it and put it into the box, together with the money Jorge had given him.

"Where will you go?" asked Jorge.

"I don't know, maybe to the end of the world." Without look-ing up again he headed for the door to the living room.

"Niklas."

He stopped, but didn't turn around.

"I'm really sorry, son."

Niklas nodded and left. The truck was parked in the driveway. He opened the door and put the box on the passenger seat. He didn't even bother to check if they had packed everything. With-out once looking in the rear mirror, he drove off.

#

*Jenny — Day 652 (February 2, Mendoza, Argentina)*

It was quiet in the kitchen when Jenny and Eduard came down the next day. Joanna was packing the lunch for the harvesters. Her eyes were reddish as if she had been crying. Jorge entered the room and Joanna looked up briefly. He went over to her and patted her on the arm.

Eduard frowned at Jenny. She bit on her lips. *He noticed it as well.*

"Do you know where Niklas is? I think I owe him an apology," asked Eduard.

Joanna lowered her eyes. Jorge replied, "He left yesterday. I asked him to. I have to protect the family."

Jenny swallowed and her chest felt tight.

Joanna came over and took her into her arms. "Don't worry, darling. You two can stay as long as you want."

"Thank you." Tears were rolling down Jenny's cheeks, but the tightness in her chest ebbed away. She looked Joanna in the eyes. "Where's Marcella?"

Joanna shook her head. Her eyes were red as if she had cried.

"He took her with him?" Eduard's voice sounded surprised.

Jorge grunted. "She wouldn't allow him to leave without her. I found a note this morning. She is strong-willed, you know." Outside a truck honked.

"We'd better go," said Eduard and out they went.

"One more thing." Jorge looked at them. "You two have to agree to stay on the farm for now. Maybe you can go to the village later, sometime."

Jenny nodded and swallowed. Eduard hesitated for a second but nodded as well. Her throat felt dry.

Jorge took a breath. "It's for the safety of us all. Now go."

Outside, the truck honked again. Jenny and Eduard rushed out. Sitting in the back of the truck, they watched the winery slowly disappear. Jenny snuggled into Eduard's arm and wondered whether this was it, the end of the suffering; whether from now on things would start looking up.

<<<<To be continued>>>>

Thank you for purchasing my book. I hope you have enjoyed the story. If so (or even if not), please leave an honest review on Amazon.

Reviews and social proof are the new currency that help independent authors get established and sell more books.

Appetite for more stories? Stories out and novels around the corner:

**Peak Democracy**

Book one of the Peak Democracy series, published October 2017

In a world where data is power, one man must choose between corporate success and the fight for freedom...

August Remules is a rising star in the mega-conglomerate that houses nearly all of the world's data. While his years in IT have taught him not to ask too many questions, a fateful interview could take him all the way to the top of the corporate ladder... or send his family crashing down.

Niklas Soderstrom has worked with August for years, but he has far less trust in a system rigged for those at the top. When his friend ventures into the heart of the corporate jungle, Niklas realizes his influence on the data that drives society could turn the tide in a growing resistance...

August's new position of power seems too good to be true, but it also puts him at odds with Niklas and the people he loves the most. August and Niklas have no choice but to summon their courage to save their friends, their family, and the system that keeps civilization alive...

Peak Democracy is the first book in a fast-paced near-future dystopian trilogy. If you like corporate drama, nuanced characters, and future worlds crafted from current socio-political issues, then you'll love G.D. Leon's eye-opening trilogy.

This book can be found on Amazon as eBook or paperback

### Unleashed
Book three of the *Peak Democracy* series

Torn between revenge and survival, one man has the power to save civilization...

Niklas has left the divided United States far behind. In the aftermath of the data purge that brought the world to its knees, he's found peace running a Patagonian hostel with the woman of his dreams. It's almost enough to make him forget he's a wanted man...

When rising powers begin revamping the fragile data system, Niklas learns the powers-that-be haven't forgotten his role in the data catastrophe. And they'll hunt down everyone Niklas loves to make him pay...

Niklas must team up with the growing rebellion to unleash a cyber weapon only he can yield. To safeguard the peace he left behind, Niklas must plunge headlong into war...

Unleashed is the final novel in the Peak Democracy series, a trilogy of chillingly-real dystopian tales. If you like fully-imagined future realities, complex characters, and rebellions against all odds, then you'll love the thrilling conclusion to G.D. Leon's thought-provoking series.

Release date is set for February 2018. Intrigued? Sign up to my mailing list at http://www.gd-leon.com/readers-group-pd for more updates and to know when it's ready for pre-order.

### The Frigorifico
*Literary Fiction*, published August 2016

A dying town. A family on the rocks. Can Ruben break the cycle of destruction before he loses it all?

Ruben and the entire town of Santa Rita, Argentina depend on the Frigorifico, a major factory and the town's main source of work. When the factory closes down, Ruben must make a choice: hope for a reopening or start over somewhere else. After deciding to move, Ruben must do so without any of his family or loved ones. As he makes a new life for himself in Buenos Aires, he watches the situation in Santa Rita deteriorate.

The most disturbing part is that his brother, Frede, is immersed in the violence that continues to spread. And as a result, everyone Ruben loves has drifted into harm's way. When tragedy strikes, despite his best efforts, Ruben must come to terms with the past, the present, and what will become of the future.

The Frigorifico is a work of literary fiction for the 99%. If you like powerful storytelling, real characters, and literature that peels back the curtain of today's society, then you'll love G.D. Leon's chilling look back into a bygone era.

This book can be found as eBook on Amazon, Apple iBooks and Kobo or as paperback on Amazon.

## AUTHOR'S NOTE

While the story is pure fiction, the background is based on real    places.    Please    find    the    visual    inspirations    at
http://www.pinterest.com/gd_leon

### Fairview, Montana

I have to be honest. I've never been to Fairview, Montana. I
looked at pictures of the town, but that's not the Fairview I imagined for this story. When thinking about the corporate headquarters of The Holding I had cities like Brasilia or Canberra in mind—
just more corporate places. I somehow had the feeling that while
planned capitals follow a logic of distributed power, a planned
corporate city would need to have an epicenter of power; hence
the 75-floor building with the oversized office on top.

### Apache-Sitgreaves National Forest, Arizona

Forests can be dark and dense, almost menacing. I've been in
such forests and every movement or sound is daunting and un-
canny, like the rainforest in 'Heart of Darkness'. The Apache-
Sitgreaves National Forest is different: light and bright. The
ground covered with needles of the ponderosa pines is soft like a
carpet. It's a sharp contrast to the barren landscape east of it and

if you come out of this direction, the forest seems like a miracle—almost enchanted.


### Cuzco, Peru

Cuzco is a divided city—at least that's how it appeared to me: a mix of a tourist hub and a local epicenter. On every corner you see backpackers, offers for backpackers, or locals minding their business that you will never understand. Maybe, if you spend time there you would. I had friends that stayed for a while and with time they explained to me that you would find your way around. However they also said that you will always be passing through in their eyes—never one of them.

Cuzco has also a different face, a colorful and mystic one. Large boulders are stapled on each other, building a wall or a house. Looking at them, you know they were built before they had machinery for it; you wonder how they did it. Cuzco is an old city—older than most cities on the continent and it tells it on every corner. At night, it is dived in the orange light of the street lanterns and the reddish stone intensifies the color.

It's been a while since I backpacked through the region, but a few glimpses of memories stuck till today. Like the wheeking of dozens of guinea pigs when I entered a staple of a small farm in the sacred valley of the Incas or the owner who poured out the first gulp of his corn-beer on the ground—the first gulp is always for Pacha Mama: mother earth. Also unforgotten is the moment when my friend and I ordered coffee in a small restaurant outside town. We got two empty mugs with a small jug of coffee—barely enough for one. Assuming it is for one and we'd get the other one separately, my friend poured the coffee and took a gulp: he almost jumped up and you could see the caffeine surge in his eyes and it took him a couple of minutes to calm his heartbeat down. A little later the waitress brought another jug with hot water. It turned out that the small jug was concentrated coffee which we were supposed to thin down with hot water. Her eyes were priceless when she realized that she had drunk the concentrate and I bet she recognized which of the two of us drank it.

### Uyuni, Bolivia, and the way to the Chilean Border

A dusty street, a couple of houses left and right. Uyuni is not beautiful. People are nice, but the town seems to be the end of the world. When you arrive, you already know when you will be leaving again, but you don't expect the beauty that lies behind Uyuni, where the salt desert starts and your trip takes you through a wonderland. The desert is like a flat ski slope, but in the early morning hours it turns into a mirror of dawn and you completely lose the horizon. It is almost a Ganzfeld experience.

From the salt flat, the usual journey takes you past the red lake and the green lake, both colored in a way that appears magic: The water is clear when you look up close, but red or green when you look from a distance. In between you go over a pass that is 16,000 feet above sea level, but it doesn't seem like it. Around you, everything goes further up.

One last thought about that altitude—I was pretty athletic back then, but when I had to run half a mile to not miss a bus, I was out of breath for at least a quarter of an hour. Strange feeling: to breathe and still not get enough air.

### The Winery, Argentina

I've never been to the Argentinean wine region, but I always wanted to. Lucky for me the internet has enough information and pictures to, so I decided to take the Estancia Colomé as my setting for the winery—although it is actually located in Salta and not in Mendoza.

### El Cafayate, Argentina

El Cafayate is a hick town in a state that claims to have more sheep than men, but its location is unique. Situated on the shore of Lago Argentino you have a marvelous view and it is a perfect starting point for excursions to the Perito Moreno glacier and other trips or hikes in the Southern Andes region.

I spent a couple of days there to visit Perito Moreno and was deeply impressed. The glacier grows slowly across the lake and pushes against the rock on the other side—cutting one arm of the lake off. Without drainage, the water level grows on the cut-off side of the lake until the pressure gets too big and the water crashes through the glacier. I've not witnessed a breakthrough, but a 10 feet scar with no vegetation around the cut-off arm is testimony for the heightened water levels.

However, what I witnessed was the breaking off a humongous piece. We did a boat trip to the glacier tongue. It moaned and groaned until you see it breaking off. For the blink of an eye the there is no sound until the piece crashes with an ear-battering noise on the water, followed by the surge you can still feel even though you are two hundred feet away.

## ACKNOWLEDGEMENTS

Thanks to everybody who made this book possible—the professionals helping me to polish my words and create the beautiful look and feel: Clare Diston (edit and proofread), Simon Avery (cover design), Bryan Cohen (sales description).

I don't want to miss the chance (again) to thank all the people who help other authors by showing the way, including all trial and error: Joanna Penn with her Creative Penn podcast as well as Jim Kuckral and Bryan Cohen with their Sell More Books Show.

Also, I want to thank my friends who sedulously share my posts and my enthusiasm, help me with getting the book out into the world.

Last but not least, I want to thank my wife for her invaluable support that allows me to write.

## ABOUT G.D. LEON

G.D. Leon is a novelist with roots in the German language.

Gilbert David Leon's journey brought him from Zurich, where he grew up, to the greater New York area, where he lives with his beautiful wife. Stations on his journey included Berlin and Buenos Aires, leaving impressions that remain until today. Even though it has been more than a decade since he left Buenos Aires, he still enjoys drinking mate, playing Truco and listening to Argentinian music, from tango to folk music.

He has a bachelor's in Business Administration from the University of Applied Science, Zurich, a master's degree in MIS/IT from the University of Wales, and a master's in Business Administration from the Robert H. Smith School of Business at the University of Maryland, College Park.

Outside writing, sports and reading have been given spots on Gilbert's agenda, and he loves to travel the US and the world. Other hobbies include old books and book sales. He can spend hours hunting treasures, and usually he ends up with one or two boxes of used books.

Connect with Gilbert online:

(e) gd(at)gd-leon.com

(w) www.gd-leon.com

(f) http://www.facebook.com/gilbertdavidleon

(p) www.pinterest.com/gd_leon

## <u>NOTES</u>